A Rebellious House

A Rebellious House

A Novel

Barbara M. Dickinson

Brunswick

Library of Congress Cataloging-in-Publication Data

Dickinson, Barbara M., 1933–
A rebellious house : a novel / by Barbara M. Dickinson.-- 1st ed.
p. c.m.
ISBN 1-55618-165-5 (hardcover : alk. paper)
I. Title.
PS3554.I3238R4 1997
813'. 54--dc21 97–23505
CIP

First Edition

Published in the United States of America

by

Brunswick Publishing Corporation

1386 Lawrenceville Plank Road
Lawrenceville, Virginia 23868
1-800-336-7154

Son of man, thou dwellest in the midst of a rebellious house,
which have eyes to see,
and see not;
they have ears to hear,
and hear not:
for they **are** *a rebellious house.*

EZEKIEL, 12:2

For my mother, whithout whom there would never have been a Rose.

~~~
~~~

Acknowledgments

No book is written without help. I am especially grateful to my mother, who always believed in my abilities; to my husband, Billy, ever-patient and supportive; and to each of my five children, who shared with me their wit and wisdom. There are countless friends who encouraged me. I cannot name you all, but you know you are remembered in my heart of hearts. To Lynn Eckman, Teresa, and Alan, I give profound thanks for your sharp eyes and wise counsel.

A *Rebellious House* took a long time to build, brick by brick. With the help of the people I have just named, it was a labor of love.

~~~
~~~

Wynfield Farms and its residents exist, alas,
only in the heart and mind of the author.

WYNFIELD FARMS

. . . since 1872

Wynfield Farms is located in the Shenandoah Valley of Virginia between the cities of Roanoke and Lexington. The mansion, built in 1872 by railroad magnate Samuel Thomas Wynfield, replicates St. Edmund Hall, Oxford University, where Mr. Wynfield, an ardent Anglophile, received his Doctorate in Humanities. Three generations of Wynfields have enjoyed the house and its surrounding 450 acres of formal gardens, natural woodlands and lakes. The Nottingham Corporation purchased Wynfield Farms six years ago for the purpose of redefining retirement living and major modifications were made at that time. All of the expansion has been completed with respect for the previous owners and consideration for the future residents' needs.

Wynfield Farms is committed to providing superb security and programs of highest quality for older citizens. This full-service community includes a chapel, bank, library, recreation areas (a nine hole golf course is within the grounds), greenhouse, bus service, and managed health care facilities. Living units are available in studio and one or two bedroom apartments, each with kitchenette and spacious storage.

Wynfield Farms' Dining Room, painstakingly restored to its 19th century grandeur, has bird's eye maple flooring, said to have been hewn from trees felled on the grounds. The room also boasts a mantel designed by Mr. Wynfield and carved to his specifications from Carrara marble. Present day cuisine caters to the discerning palate.

Wynfield Farms—where the emphasis is always on individual freedom and comfort and the lifestyle is synonymous with good taste and elegance. The gracious ambiance of Mr. Samuel T. Wynfield's original estate endures.

Wynfield Farms—the perfect place to reside and retire.

~~~

WYNFIELD FARMS as described in invitational brochure.
~~~

Wynfield News Bulletin, March 25

A WYNFIELD WELCOME

Welcome to Wynfield Farms!

Mrs. T. B. R. McNess moved to Wynfield Farms on March 3. She and her Scottish terrier, "Quintus Maximus," live in Apartment 208. Mrs. McNess has moved here from Roanoke. She lists her interests as her three children and six grandchildren, walking, reading, writing, painting, and Max.

We are glad that she has become a part of our little family.

Welcome to Wynfield Farms!

A. Elvina Moss, Resident Manager

~~~
~~~

1

"Emma Bovary was a fool!"

"Not as big a fool as Charles! He was, as my grandchildren say, 'a wimp'!"

"True enough."

"Why did Flaubert so despise the middle class? Was it the hypocrisy that riled him?"

"And what about his attitude toward adultery? I doubt that he was above reproach in his own life."

"Let's get back to Emma. I don't agree that she was a complete fool. More of a hopeless romantic than a fool. Believed that things would surely get better as time went along. And that there were many finer things to be had in the good life ahead."

"Just as we all felt when we moved to Wynfield Farms," sighed one of the eight women sitting on either side of one of the long oak tables in Wynfield Farms' Library.

The morning sun streamed through the mullioned panes of the room's tall windows, and broad shafts of warm October light poured over the heads of the noisy, chattering group. Tiny dust motes filtered in the beam and mingled with the occasional wiry white hairs that escaped from the matrons' heads. *Footnotes*, the literary club at Wynfield Farms, was in session.

"Ladies, Ladies! I think we've dissected *Madam Bovary* quite far enough," cried Rose McNess, attempting to quell the escalating voices. "Unless you want to discuss Flaubert's attitude regarding adultery a bit longer. Where in the world did Lib go today? We need her expertise on this tome."

"You have to admit it was a spicy discussion, Rose," spoke Eleanor Whittington. "As for Lib, I bet that her grief finally caught up with her."

"You're exactly right, Vinnie." Susan Warfield spoke so softly that everyone immediately hushed and leaned forward. "Lib never missed a beat when Ed died; turned up here to work every day without fail. That has to wear thin after a while. But don't worry about Lib. She'll meditate a bit then return full of vim and vinegar."

"With a book already chosen for next month. You're absolutely right, Susan. I'm glad I was able to fill in for her today, though I am a very poor substitute when it comes to the classics," Rose admitted with candor.

"You were wonderful, Rose," chorused the group almost as one.

"I loved rereading this old favorite," said Madelyn Kinsey, speaking so enthusiastically that the tiny cluster of whiskers huddled in a fold of her dimpled chin quivered vigorously. "I can't wait to call my daughter; she thinks all I do is play bridge or watch the soaps, that I'm the typical one-dimensional mother; no thoughts outside hearth and home. Wait 'til I tell her all about *Footnotes*' literary menu!" Suddenly self-conscious after her long outburst, the pudgy, white-haired Mrs. Kinsey readjusted her lime-green cardigan and stiffened her shoulders against the back of the hard chair.

"If we have dispensed with Emma and Charles and all the *Footnotes*' formalities, then I, for one, shall wheel back to my apartment for a rest. This delicious talk of adultery and illicit liaisons has worn me out!" With a wave of her ever present lavender-scented handkerchief Eleanor Whittington smiled, turned, and wheeled deftly from the library.

"Such a gracious lady," murmured one of the remaining.

"A true Southerner," added another.

"And always cheerful and smiling," chimed Rose.

"More than can be said of Miss Elvina Moss," whispered Louise Montgomery. "Let me tell you her latest caper!"

"Ladies, Ladies!" protested Rose genially. "Please don't let me get involved in one of your intriguing discussions about Miss Moss. I must rescue Max and get him out for his walk. Come to think of it, I need a good stretch too; these hard chairs have put my bottom to sleep. Even with our stimulating discussion! Thank you all for coming today! I'll see you at dinner!"

Rose waved to the six women who sat rooted around the table and dashed from the room. She smiled to herself, thinking that the group had just devoured hapless Emma Bovary as appetizer; the main course was Miss Moss.

~~~

Rose and Max made it as far as the stairwell door leading to the Reception Hall when they were stopped by The Voice.

"Welcome to Wynfield Farms! Welcome to Wynfield Farms!"

Always twice! She thinks we're all deaf. Why, oh, why, always twice?

Rose flattened herself against the wall and tightened Max's leash so that the terrier had no choice but to sit on her feet. She hoped fervently that the bulky Chinoiserie screen she so despised would hide them both.

"Welcome to Wynfield Farms! The perfect place to reside and retire!"

Rose shuddered. She straightened her thin shoulders and pushed her glasses up on the bridge of her nose. She pressed further against the pale yellow wall. Even Max was stilled by The Voice. Rose was trapped.

Her day, until this incarceration by the Chinese landscape, had been spinning along as effortlessly as a ball of yarn unwinding on polished parquet. A walk with Max at six, quick breakfast for the both of them, brief stint of typing, mixing batter for "Ranger" cookies, more typing, *FOOTNOTES*, and now . . . a halt to
~~~

everything. She knew that if she fell into Miss Moss's clutches and had to meet the new resident—no matter who he or she happened to be—that this would cancel any remaining plans. Not that Rose had too many plans: she had too many projects. All boiling along like sixty.

Rose, at seventy-two years of age, moved with the sprint and spirit of a marathon runner. Short, but not small; wiry, but not tough; pert, not petite: Rose McNess hurtled through life with a fierce and focused energy that often left her children and peers shaking their heads. Her one serious deficiency was that she lacked a modicum of patience. And now she tapped her feet impatiently as she studied a column of Chinese water-bearers trudging up a six-inch mountain sprouting masses of chrysanthemums.

Crash! Boom! Boom! Boom! Cr-boom! Noises erupted all around her.

Max's ears became sharp black tents as his body tensed. The clatter of heavy objects being dumped or thrown resonated throughout the high-ceilinged room.

Rose grasped the leash even more tightly. Max tucked his tail between his legs and shivered.

"Oh, my poor, poor Vincent! He's loose! Poor baby! This will not do . . . " A rich, throaty contralto with no defined accent floated above the cacophony that gradually, finally, subsided.

"*Weel not dew* . . . " repeated Rose. *Deep South flattened by Midwest. Alabama? Georgia? Certainly not from around here . . . and who—or what—is Vincent?*

A gentle bubbling bottomless brook of a giggle now broke the stillness.

Kate! Thank heavens she's at the desk!

The giggling continued, now almost suffocated by the scuffling and gasps and shouts of "Oh damn!" that were punctuating what was obviously a foot chase of sorts.

And then, "Damn! I've got the little sucker!"

What is it, Max? What have they got?

"Thank you, sir, thank you," sang the contralto. "Vincent, you are a bad boy! This is not the entrance we were supposed to make into our new home. But it wasn't your fault and we are here . . . at last!"

"Do not worry about your bird, my dear. I am sure he will survive; feathered creatures usually do."

Aha! So Vincent is a bird, Max!

The Voice boomed at its most imperious: "Miss Alexander will take care of the taxi. And you, sir, will observe the speed limit as you exit these grounds. Which should be promptly. Do not fail, Miss Alexander, to get his license number. And the name of the company."

The timbre of her voice left no doubt that the driver of the taxi, the miscreant who had allowed Vincent to escape, would slip away like melting butter.

Miss Elvina Moss now directed her full boom to Kate Alexander who had suppressed her attack of the giggles and resumed her role as Receptionist/Coordinator for Wynfield Farms. For two years Kate had minimized the effect of Miss Moss's severity and obdurate directives. Every man at Wynfield had a crush on the lithe redhead; every woman longed to adopt her as a daughter.

"The manner of that man's driving is deplorable. I hesitate to think of the damage to our driveway," continued Miss Moss.

Driveway? What about the passenger? thought Rose.

"We shall have you settled in no time, my dear. I trust that you had a good trip, other than this incompetent man? Come . . . a cup of tea would be most comforting for both of us. Just step into my office, please . . . "

Rose tilted her head and peered to the left around the Chinoiserie camouflage. She saw that Miss Moss was now directing her attention and her lowered octaves to an apparition standing before her. The back of a flawlessly coiffured head topped a cape with multi-flowing folds the color of faded violets. Rose had an instant image of the arbor in the backyard of her childhood home with its canopy of weighty purple wisteria swaying in the summer heat. The memory was so acute that she half-expected to hear the buzz of bees and to smell the cloying perfume of the plump clusters.

Rose held her breath, silently willing Max to do the same.

Miss Moss ushered the newcomer into her office at the rear of the hall. When Rose heard the reassuring *whoosh* of the closing door she ventured forth from her refuge.

"Come on, Max," she whispered. "You begged for this excitement. Let's get on with our walk. I still have cookies to bake!"

Kate, smiling as she looked up from the telephone, greeted the pair with a wink and a wave.

Kate is calling Romero for help. Probably Ernest, too. They're going to need more than a dolly to haul all that luggage to its destination. Which apartment could she be getting?

Rose pondered this while gazing around the once tranquil lobby. Four large cases stood at angles on the vast Oriental carpet. An oversized cigar-shaped case of vivid green canvas, rested on the floor to the right of Kate's desk.

That, Max, has got to be Vincent.

The puffing driver, not yet released, was unloading an array of hat boxes. He considered the placement of each container, as if his choice of location might somehow salvage his reputation and his good name. Defeated by the magnitude of his task, he finally deposited the boxes one-on-one upon the larger cases, building colorful, crazy towers such as a toddler would erect. The outcome of his labors was rakish rather than haphazard.

Rose surveyed the scene. *She won't be wearing a lot of hats around Wynfield. Nice luggage, however. Expensive. Well-traveled. Where is she going to live? Thank heavens all this scampering around didn't knock over Jocey's flowers! Given five more minutes of freedom, Vincent probably would have made a nest in them!*

An antique copper urn on the drum table in the center of the Reception Hall held a brilliant array of autumnal offerings: yellow and bronze spider mums, fall asters and sedum, lacy artemisia and Japanese anemones. Tall slender spikes of the red leaf sumac reached toward the high ceiling. Rose knew that Jocey had worked long and hard to install the arrangement early this morning. *What a pity it would have been if this new arrival had ruined it!*

Max's plaintive grunting bullied Rose's daydreams away. The

pair stepped briskly through heavy, mahogany double doors propped open for the driver's convenience. Max bounded down the three wide stone steps and strained at the leash. He continued to pull ahead as they passed the ancient sundial and followed the worn brick walk that meandered through the front lawn until it met the West Parking Pavilion.

From here it was possible to view the impressive entrance to Wynfield Farms. Soldierly rows of Lombardy poplars, planted over a century before by patriarch Wynfield, fortified both sides of the quarter-mile driveway. From the circular turn at the main door the drive returned arrow-straight to culminate at a pair of massive gates of intricately fabricated wrought-iron grill work topped by the Wynfield crest. Imposing stone columns anchored the gates at the border of the state road.

Rose hesitated for a moment and took in the sweep of the rigid row of poplars. *It's either your beginning, Max, when you pass through those gates, or your ending. Life's choice: rest and conform or rise and rebel.*

Rose turned back to look at her home for the past seven months. Wynfield Farms—that had been Mr. Wynfield's pride and passion—was part medieval, part peculiarly English Gothic: an architectural sprawl. *Curious jumble of a house. Certainly the Oxford look he was after. The builders preserved the antiquity and charm when they added our modern plumbing and elevators. Yes, Max, the Wynfield estate rests here comfortably, precisely as a house should do. All right, Sir Max, I'm ready to walk now!*

Out of the corner of her eye Rose spied a figure near the gates. *Must be the Keynes-Livingston woman, Max, collecting her lichen. Who else in this place wears a pith helmet? Good boy, Max, keep moving. I won't even wave; no more distractions.*

Rose stepped gingerly onto the pebbly surface of the parking area, crossed to the far side, and then just as cautiously stepped onto the grassy area known as Montremont Gardens. She stooped to unsnap Max's lead and the little dog raced away. He snuffled out squirrels and flushed three ground sparrows before scampering across the narrow foot bridge to vanish from Rose's sight.

A scattering of horse chestnuts lay beside the path and Rose picked up one of the giant, oversized nuts. She looked up, shielding her eyes from the sun. *Ah! There's the tree; another week and there will be a bushel down.* She fingered the brown and bronze buckeye. It was cool and smooth as marble in her palm. *What's the old saying? Rub a buckeye and it'll bring you good luck? I'll rub hard*! She laughed aloud, remembering some thirty-five years ago when eight-year-old Paul, her second son, had collected dozens of the nuts and secreted them in his dresser drawer. Some days later when she was putting away socks, Rose had opened the drawer to discover a squirming, wiggling mass of tiny worms that had emerged in the warmth and darkness. So ended Paul's collecting buckeyes. *Ummm. Nature's perfect sculpture in the palm of my hand.*

Rose paused as she approached the bridge. Upon reaching it she usually allowed herself another pause to watch the trickle of water trace through the gardens as it began its descent to the lake below. She rested both elbows on the wooden railings and looked toward the hill that was her goal.

It is a mystery to me why old Mr. Wynfield, an avowed Anglophile, built a copy of Monet's bridge, gave his garden a French name, and raised water lilies and carp in a catfish-size lake smack in the middle of his English country estate.

Rose resumed walking in the direction of the bench on her favorite ridge.

Since her arrival at Wynfield she had come to think of this stone bench as *her* bench. She had come here almost every day, often with Max but occasionally alone. The silence and serenity, the view, were incomparable. *This is*, she willingly admitted, *my restorative. It is tonic for the soul, my secret power . . . to pull me through some of life's crowded moments. It has helped me accept, finally, that choice, not chance, brought me here to Wynfield.*

I've always heard that three moves are as good as a fire. Well, this was my third and my last. I emptied the house and I'm free! I still have what is important: good health, some good mind, family and Max.

I am a perennial: I endure. Ha! Maybe I should tell the children to put that on my tombstone: "Rose McNess—She Endured." No, that makes it sound as if I were merely existing here. This is where I wake up, where I go to bed, where I take what life brings to my doorstep. Such as this view! Snail-like, I have shed my old home and chosen Wynfield as my destination.

Rose paused again and looked into the distance. She never tired of the muted panorama of the Blue Ridge Mountains silhouetted against the curving expanse of the sky. The constantly changing blues, mauves, umbers were clear even from here. Today she looked with her artist's eye. *A perfect collage. The mountain ranges are ragged strips of colored paper torn out and pasted against a cerulean sky. I remember taking a second grade art class out to the playground and showing them this very thing. Then having them troop back inside to make their first collage. I should try that myself . . .*

Rose experienced a heightened awareness of all her senses each time she looked at nature's grand exhibition. Bird songs were sharper. Earthy smells of fall flooded her nostrils: musty leaves, still damp from the morning's dew, wisps of wood smoke carried on the whiffle of a breeze, the tang of apples. *Mmmmm, definitely apples.* She sniffed the air again. *Someone must be gathering the last of the windfalls in the orchard.*

She stood and drank in the view fanning out from the base of the hill. She felt giddy and hugged herself with the sheer delight of the vista. The colors were late this season, but shards of brilliant yellows and reds and oranges pushed through the boughs of lush evergreens with dazzling clarity. Carefully selected and planted decades earlier by the prescient and prudent Mr. Wynfield, this planned forest of oak, poplar, maple, mountain ash, fir and Virginia pine had flourished, growing tall and straight. They formed a backdrop for the natural body of water that rippled in the slight wind.

This is by far the best view on the estate and I thank you for it, Mr. Wynfield.

Rose came here with her head often full of questions and thoughts about her new surroundings. Nearly eighty seniors lived in the roomy Wynfield mansion. Of this number about one half were married couples. The remaining were a diverse group of widows and widowers, spinsters and one or two bachelors. *All under the eye of Miss Elvina Moss, of course. What is this latest gossip? Bet the* FOOTNOTES *are still sitting there chatting! Curious how one makes new friends in a new situation . . . similar interests bring people together but it takes tolerance and good humor to cement the mix. Everyone here seems united on one thing: their opinion of Miss Moss. Practically a quiet rebellion. Well, I'm one of the fortunate ones. Roanoke and Hollins are less than an hour down the road and I do have a few ties left there. When I feel I have to get away, I can go.*

On her more recent ramblings, Rose had taken her notebook along in order to jot down ideas for the weekly Wynfield newsletter.

What possessed me to volunteer to revamp that newsletter? Well, it was dreadful. Incredibly boring. People actually read it now, and not just for the dinner menus. And I am proud of the new name: Wynsong. That marvelous little bistro in Provence. What was the name of the town it was in? Minerve? Yes, that's it: Minerve. Buried in the mountains of Provence. I remember crusty duck baked in red wine and honey, and a view that never ended! I'm probably the only person in ten states privy to knowing the significance of the name, Wynsong. Not that it matters. Oh, my goodness! Who did I promise to interview this morning? I remember writing it down . . . but where did I put the slip of paper? My mind is leaving me! I dropped everything tearing out of the apartment. I'll blame it on the new arrival and the noise. Can't worry about it now. Too beautiful a morning for worries. I'll finish the cookies when I get back and take whoever it is a dozen or so as a peace offering.

Rose climbed the last few yards toward her bench and admitted to herself that her knees felt wobbly. *Funny, I don't recall being one bit tired when I hiked the English dales a few years back. And this is exactly like Simon's Seat. That wasn't even a strenuous climb. Of course, I was younger then. I'll be perfectly content to sit and wait for Max. That minx; he probably hopes I've forgotten him.*

Shifting her focus from the Wynfield forest at her feet, the Yorkshire dales in her memory, and the cavernous valleys of Provence that she could imagine, Rose stood on the ridge she so loved. She was startled to find that she was not alone this morning. *Her* bench held an occupant.

~~~

~~~

WYNSONG

E C H O E S

You must plough with such oxen as you have.
English proverb

On a day long ago Mr. Samuel T. Wynfield looked over the Blue Ridge Mountains past unplowed fields and lush forests and envisioned his dream house. His house, our home. And he may have called to his men as he exhorted them to work:

You must plough with such oxen as you have.

That was as appropriate then as it is now. You, dear readers, are stuck with one who shall persevere and plough her way through the forthcoming issues of *Wynsong* (formerly known as the *Wynfield News Bulletin*.) In the weeks ahead I hope to interview and spotlight every resident through written profiles. (Don't worry: I will not ask for your date of birth, your AARP number or Medicare files!) As a newcomer I am anxious to get to know you and your interests. It will be fascinating for me to learn something about you and to attempt to convey that to your neighbors. If you have a poem, a story, a recipe you'd like to share, please do! I am starting off by sharing one of my poems. (Did you ever feel the way the poem describes when you told *your* house 'goodnight'?) I am also introducing the Wynfield staff in my first series of interviews.

When your knees ache, when your glasses aren't strong enough, when everyone around speaks so low it is impossible to hear, just remember:

You must plough with such oxen as you have.

Rose McNess.

CLOSING THE HOUSE

Soft velvet dark drapes its star-sequined cape
over gables and gambrels and gutters.
A quilt of quiet wraps the neighborhood
in monochrome counterpane camouflage.
No barking dogs, no shutters touch.
The world is still . . . and yet

Inside my house I begin solemn rites
of putting my dominion down to sleep.
Feed the fish, turn off den light. Is it safe
to let the gray cat sleep upstairs this once?
No sirens shriek, no blaring horns.
The world is still . . . and yet

The apple log in the fireplace burns bright,
gasps, crumples in on itself. The blaze leaps
then sleeps as strong screen suffocates the light
that was unselfish friend throughout the day.
No skirt of fire, no cinder fright.
The world is still . . . and yet

I scrutinize. Lamps to quench, blinds to close.
Is that a fresh scar on the table top?
Did I water the tatty fern today?
Will the old couch make it another year?
No outside beam spotlights the drive.
The world is still . . . and yet

I, reluctant, tiptoe up deep, steep stairs,
each foot placed on stale boards that mutely
speak.
Why does this nightly closure seem so dear?
Have two become one inside aging husks?
No shard of light, no ticking clock.
The world is still.

Rose McNess

ECHOES

A. Elvina Moss

"Welcome to Wynfield Farms!"

If those four words have reached your ears, you've been officially greeted by MISS ELVINA MOSS. Miss Moss is the Resident Manager of Wynfield Farms, a position she has held for five years. She not only knows every inch of Wynfield, but she has inspected and passed judgment on it. Miss Moss is a master planner with an interest in details ranging from paint colors to Persian carpets.

Before her move to Virginia, she was Director of Human Resources at a Quaker residence in Newtown Square, Pennsylvania.

Miss Moss's married brother and his family live in Oregon.

Elvina Moss's knowledge of Virginia lore in general, and Wynfield, in particular, is encyclopedic. You will find an answer to every question when you chat with our efficient Resident Manager, Miss A. Elvina Moss.

Rose McNess.

~~~
~~~

2

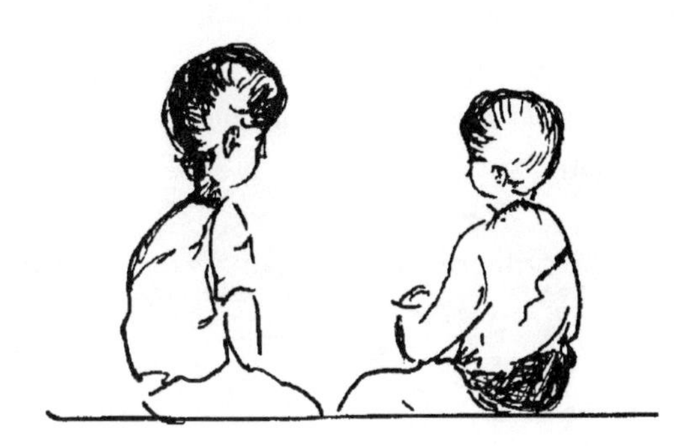

"Why Lib! Lib Meecham! What a surprise to find you here!"

The occupant of the bench, a thin woman with a silky cap of short, curly white hair and a pale, pretty face, turned at the sound of Rose's voice.

"Hello, Rose," she said, starting to rise, "I know this is your bench. I didn't mean to intrude. But I simply had to get out today. I felt as if I were suffocating in my apartment. And the view is so lovely from this spot." She spoke softly, hesitantly.

"You most certainly are *not* intruding, Lib," replied Rose adamantly. "I know that cooped up feeling! And although I do regard this bench as my own, I have been known to share. May I join you? My old knees are about to give out."

"Oh, please, join me," Lib responded with more than a little relief as she scooted to the end of the stone seat.

"We missed you at *FOOTNOTES* this morning, Lib. I filled in as best I could but I'm a poor substitute. I fear Emma Bovary was slighted . . . "

Lib was aghast. "I completely forgot! I never even thought about the Library or the book club or *anything* but myself. Can you forgive me?"

"Forgive you? About time you thought about yourself! Nothing to forgive! You might want to recap Bovary at next month's meeting. We kept going off in tangents about her adulterous ways and Charles's weaknesses and all sorts of various thoughts. But *you* know that group! Far better than I, actually."

Lib chuckled. "I'm sure for most of them this was a naughty piece of literature. And I'm glad! How was Susan Warfield? Did she come?"

"First one," replied Rose. "She's one of your biggest fans, Lib. I think you've reawakened her love of literature. I suspect Susan is a very smart cookie; she's always got a book tucked under her arm. And not for show, either; she reads every opportunity she gets."

"Susan is a love. And Louise? Did she make it?"

"Indeed she did. I had to leave just as Louise was about to impart some delicious morsel about Miss Moss. I really didn't have time to stay and get involved. Knowing that group, they are still sitting in the library talking their heads off. And I am curious; any idea what it could be, Lib?"

The tidbit about Miss Elvina Moss had been nagging at Rose. She posed the question to Lib without really thinking that her quiet, bookish friend would have a clue to the mystery.

Lib surprised her. "I think I do, Rose. Something odd is going on at Wynfield."

"Besides us?" burst out Rose, laughing heartily.

"Between Miss Moss and the Wynfield Board," continued Lib evenly. "Louise Montgomery and I were shelving books last week when two of the Board members came into the Library for a talk. They didn't see us in the back but we couldn't help overhearing some of their conversation. They were arguing fiercely. Both men looked angry and they kept pounding the table for emphasis. They made some effort to keep quiet but their voices rose and fell several times."

"And?" Rose had no intention of letting Lib stop at this stage of her recollection.

"All we heard were the words 'birthright' and 'life estate.' And 'Moss,' of course. Louise and I practically stopped breathing. We couldn't get any closer and that's all we heard. When the two men left we almost collapsed. It worries me. And I hope Louise won't tattle; we really don't know anything. It was such a bizarre incident and we don't know the context of the conversation . . . " Lib's words drifted off as if she were pondering anew the implications, if any, of the incident.

"Oh, my goodness, Lib," Rose said, pausing to breathe in deeply the fine fall air. "This could mean nothing, or *everything*. It could explain the grip Miss Moss has on her job. Do you suppose she might be a twig on the Wynfield family tree? I don't even want to speculate further. Let's pray Louise didn't blab. I doubt if she told everything. She's one who likes to drop subtle hints like a trail of bread crumbs. Maybe she left the gals little teasers. Let's keep quiet ourselves, Lib, and listen. The termagant Moss obviously has some hold on the Board. Thanks for confiding, Lib; hereafter my lips are sealed!"

"Agreed, Rose. Look at those mountains! Don't they seem close today? Reaching out and friendly." Lib seemed to share Rose's unspoken relief at the change of subject.

"Friendly. Precisely how I would describe them, Lib. All of Wynfield behind and the whole world ahead. I recharge my batteries each time I come up here. When I reach this bench I just think."

"You are an inspiration, Rose," spoke Lib. "I mean that, an inspiration."

"Inspiration! Pshaw! You're the one doing the inspiring, Lib. How long has it been since your husband died? And you haven't missed one day in the library since that time? You've turned your scars into stars!"

"Until today! Why, Rose, I never knew you noticed. Ed's been gone almost two months. I spoke to Kate right after his death, to tell her to save my library days. I can't imagine what I'd do without my work."

"Wynfield is mighty fortunate to have your talents, Lib. There are others here who would just closet themselves. You are channeling your energy and grief into accomplishing good."

"I was either going to go to pieces, or continue being active in something that had mattered to both of us. So I chose the latter. You know, Ed always hoped that he'd go just the way he did. He was gone in a few minutes and I will be forever grateful that he didn't suffer. But you know, Rose, it will take me some time to believe he isn't here. When I return to the apartment in the afternoons I burst in with so much to tell him, I completely forget that he is not there to listen!"

Lib talked rapidly, her hazel eyes directed at Rose.

"Do you find that you talk to yourself, Lib?" Rose asked laughingly. "I know that I did it all the time after each of my husbands died."

Lib nodded. "Oh, yes. At least you have Max to listen to you. But I'm finding others are supportive. Many here at Wynfield have gone through the loss of a mate, including you. Twice! I cannot imagine the pain, Rose. I'm glad Ed and I came here when we did and I have no home to break up now. That makes it a little easier."

"It never gets easier," said Rose. "Time just takes the edge off our grieving. Time and hope. Hope is the core of everything I believe in. It keeps me centered. It is my faith, the engine that runs this old heap. Oh dear, I'm not putting this very well, am I?"

"Very well. Without hope, I couldn't have let Ed go. Father Charlie's homily at Ed's memorial service captured it so well. The homily was so full of hope and cheer."

"And brief," remembered Rose. "Ed would have liked that, wouldn't he?"

"Absolutely. He was a man of few words. Brevity was his middle name. And now look at me; have I rambled on too long?"

"We both have," teased Rose. "I'm glad we've had this conversation. But I must get Max, if he is still in this part of the country. Max! Max! Come to me right *now*!"

Max's instincts had led him in pursuit of squirrels and chipmunks to the far corner of Montremont's boundaries. Deer scat had enticed him to follow the perimeter of the lake, and he was on the far side, sniffing eagerly, when Rose called.

"Max! I want you *now*!"

It was the emphasis on the "now" that brought the terrier

scampering happily until he collapsed, tongue lolling sideways, at Rose's feet.

"Good boy, Max. You've had your run for the day. Now make your manners with Lib and then we'll go back and get you a treat."

Lib Meecham reached down to fondle Max's ears as the terrier settled into an instant nap.

"Have you been out here long, Lib?" inquired Rose.

"Since breakfast, or a little after. I needed some of your 'recharging.' I bet you came up here to plan your next column and I've talked your ear off. You've done wonders with that pitiful newsletter, Rose. 'Echoes' is wonderful. And your poetry! You enjoy writing; it comes through."

"You're kind, Lib. I'm no reporter but I'm enjoying the challenge. I do like to keep one step ahead of Miss Moss. Find out the facts about the residents before we hear her surmises. But the reason I asked about your walk is the new arrival. I guess you missed all the hoopla in the Reception Hall. Max and I thought an army had marched into Wynfield."

"My gracious; I can just hear Miss Moss and her boom."

"Quite!" snapped Rose. "And you can picture the scenario: gray lady ushered into the hushed inner sanctum . . . "

"Gray lady?" queried Lib. "Resident ghost?"

"If so, substantial resident ghost. Ample proportions. All in gray, or sort of gray-violet. She goes into office, is properly impressed with glowing fire, gleaming andirons, antique Sarouk on the floor. Offered coffee or tea. 'Tea? Of course we have Darjeeling. Or Earl Grey . . . ' Obligatory small talk. Contract discussed, pen at the ready for signing. All short and simple. I can't believe that seven months ago I was the new arrival doing the same thing!"

"Nor I, Rose. Seems to me that you've always been a part of Wynfield. You keep everyone *up* with your good humor. Don't you ever feel down, or out of energy?"

"Of course! But I am determined not to be a crabby old woman. I've known a few of those. My bad days are the ones I try to keep private."

"Well, you do a grand job of keeping a low profile on your off days. Mmmmm. New resident. Did you hear which apartment?"

"No. She could be my new neighbor; the apartment across from me is still vacant, you know. Are you ready to return? We'll beard the lioness in her den, so to speak."

Rose snapped Max's leash and the threesome leisurely retraced the path back to the main doorway. When they reached Wynfield's portico Rose saw that Romero was polishing the brass on the heavy doors. His stepladder and bucket of cloths barred any possible entrance so Rose, Lib and Max stood silently and watched the sinewy man rub the fixtures with furious energy. When he finally turned, his wide mouth curved into a smile.

"Mees McNess! Mees Meecham! So sorry I stand in your way. I move my things right queek . . . "

"No hurry, Romero," called Rose. She was fond of all the Wynfield staff but reserved a generous portion of her affection for this hard-working immigrant from El Salvador. Rose had been impressed from the first with Romero's energy and genial nature. He attacked every assignment enthusiastically as if it were exactly what he'd been hoping to do at that very moment.

Rose and Lib looked at each other.

"You ask him," whispered Lib.

"I shall," replied Rose. "Romero, did you get the new resident moved in?"

Romero bowed. Then he pulled himself to attention and proudly began his announcement, clearly relishing the opportunity to impart news.

"You will like thees new lady, Mees McNess. She go right upstairs beside you. Two-oh-nine. A real lady. You theenk she like books, Mees Meecham? You get to know her too?"

"I'm sure I will, Romero," said Lib. "And if you both will excuse me, I'm going to see after my books right now. I've been gone a long time. Thanks, Rose." With a smile she was through the door.

Rose felt her heart flutter. Its tempo had picked up a beat at Romero's words.

"Thanks for the news, Romero. I'll keep an eye out for her. Your family well?"

Romero beamed. Holding up two fingers he said, "Twins!"

"Twins? When . . . or are they here already?"

"No, no!" Romero exclaimed. "Estella, she theenks *marzo* . . . Romero theenk *abril*."

"Well, for goodness sakes! I hope you get it sorted out!" enthused Rose, skirting the ladder, the bucket and the attendant sponges and leading Max into the Reception Hall.

~~~

Rose fairly dragged the now-weary Max across the hall. They had just reached the door to the stairwell (Rose's Rule: Never ride the elevator if you can still climb.) when they heard a loud and urgent whisper: "Rose! Rose!"

Max and his mistress came to a halt.

"It is Rose, isn't it? Do I have it right? Rose like the flower?"

Rose turned to acknowledge the source of the whispers.

Mary Rector, more than slightly disheveled, was sitting on one of the Chippendale settees that flanked the imposing doors of the Reception Hall.

As a matter of fact, she was here when Max and I left for our walk. And yesterday, too. Poor soul; does nothing but wait, day after day.

"Why, Mary Rector. Good morning! Yes, I'm Rose. Not the fairest flower but the only Rose! What in the world are you up to today?" With deliberate sincerity Rose addressed the troubled woman now standing before her.

"Rose! We have a new person, just this morning. I was sitting right here and the bus never came. Where can it be? I'm going to the village but it hasn't come yet and if it doesn't come I'll miss lunch and . . . "

Rose interrupted Mary's worried litany.

"Tell me about her, Mary The new resident. What is she like?"

"Ohhhh . . . Rose, she's a movie star! Has so many suitcases. It took the men three trips to carry her suitcases upstairs. Miss . . . Miss . . . "
~~~

"Miss Moss? The official Wynfield greeter . . . "

"That's right," murmured Mary. "Seems like I can't remember many names any more. 'Cept yours. I've known you since that first day." She fiddled nervously with the limp belt around her plain cotton house dress.

That yellow cardigan of Mary's is more hole than sweater. Plump she may be but Mary will freeze as the days grow colder.

"What about Miss Moss, Mary? What was it you were about to tell me?" Rose spoke to Mary with the careful attentiveness one used with small children.

"Miss Moss didn't speak to me, but the lady did! And smiled! Then she looked at me and winked when Miss Moss took her into the room there. Do you think she knows where Suzanne is? Should I go talk with the police? Would the lady go with me?"

"I wouldn't do that just yet, Mary. The lady is new here at Wynfield. I doubt if she even came from anywhere near Winchester. Tell you what, Mary. I'll go meet her and find out all about her. Then I'll tell you everything. How does that sound?"

"Will you ask her about Suzanne? Please?" Mary looked pleadingly at Rose McNess. Her eyes were two windows of tears in a house full of sorrow. Her mouth quivered as Rose patted the plump hands, and began to extricate herself.

"I promise, Mary. Perhaps we shall both have a new friend."

Mary, satisfied at the word "promise," returned to the settee and slumped back to wait for the Wynfield bus.

~~~

"OK, Mr. Max. No elevator today and you know it. If you can chase around the lake and back, you can certainly climb the steps to the second floor."

"Are you addressing me, Madame?"

Rose jumped, almost stepping on Max. Rolling along noiselessly in his wheelchair, Major William Featherstone had given Rose a jolt with his stentorian tone.

"Major Featherstone! I . . . I'm sorry. I didn't see you come in. Of course I'm not addressing you. Just chastising Max. No offense, I hope."
~~~

The Major, impeccable in tweed Norfolk jacket and yellow worsted shirt and paisley ascot, looked at Rose and snorted.

"I wish I *could* climb those steps!" He stroked the ends of his generous silver mustache.

With his brisk manner, he seemed the stereotype of a career military officer. Rose noted that his tan trousers were so sharply creased one could suffer a cut from brushing up against them. Brown military boots, his pride and joy as he had once explained to Rose, gleamed. As she looked at them Rose could hear their *snap*! as the Major marched down a parade field. She was on the verge of commenting on his natty attire when he spoke.

"Great animals, these terriers. Roosevelt had the pick of the lot, at least as far as the public was concerned. Are you old enough to remember Fala?"

"Major! I certainly do. You and I share about the same number of years."

"Indeed," he barked. "Say, I understand we have a new neighbor up on Two. Met her?"

"Not yet. Have you?" Rose peered into her empty mailbox and turned back to speak to the Major. "Max and I were heading out this morning as she made her grand entrance. Miss Moss was rolling out the red carpet. Romero told me that he had moved her up on Two. I thought perhaps you had met her in the hallway. Now I'll be able to step across to borrow a cup of sugar."

"Or pop over for a martini!" roared the Major. "Myself, I can't wait!"

They both laughed as the courtly gentleman began to wheel away. Rose uprooted Max from his prone position and started once more for the stairs.

"Oh, say, Rose," the Major called, "have you seen Mrs. Whittington today?"

"Vinnie? My favorite pink lady? Not since *Footnotes* this morning. Last seen, she was rolling back to her place for a rest."

"Ah, yes. She does love pink. So becoming to her complexion. She may be waiting for me now. We discussed a stroll for the afternoon. Rather, a *roll*. Sorry, didn't mean to detain you further."

"I'll tell her to hustle on down if I see her, Major," sang Rose.

Her mind whirled over this last exchange as she and Max climbed the twenty-two steps to the second floor corridor.

Major Featherstone and Vinnie Whittington! Two old war horses just made for each other. Certainly are the same age and stage . . . but then aren't we all? I'm an incurable romantic . . . maybe it was the Flaubert!

I am excited about my new neighbor. I hope I like her . . . I hope she likes me! Suppose she has allergies and can't abide Max? Or what if Max and I are allergic to that bird? Better than a cat across the way, perhaps . . .

Rose turned the knob silently and let Max precede her into Apartment 208. She was not yet prepared to meet or greet the new neighbor.

Rose reached out and squared the trash basket in front of her apartment door and thought once more how civilized this custom was, much more so than a curt "**DO NOT DISTURB**" sign. Then she returned to Max and unsnapped his leash.

"Max," she confided, "you and I are going to have to put our best feet forward. We *may* have a new best friend."

~~~

~~~

E C H O E S

THE WYNFIELD STAFF

You see these friendly folks every day--but do you know the story behind the face?

~~~

FAYE GILLESPIE, Dining Room Hostess, sees that we each get our favorite seat at every meal and a glass of wine if we so desire. Faye is definitely the driving force in our Dining Room. She started to work at Wynfield when the doors opened and has performed her work professionally, cheerfully and energetically since the first day. Faye has that rare gift of being able to see the whole scene at once, and runs the Dining Room with grace and ease. (Or, at least, she makes it look easy!)

Faye is the mother of three teenage sons. Tony, her eldest, picks her up in the evening and occasionally may be persuaded to help the Wait Staff. He is as polite and efficient as his mother.

Faye, we thank you for all that you do for us.

Rose McNess.

~~~

MONIQUE LEGARD and JEAN BELEN, Wait Staff, are exchange students from Lyon, France. This is their second year at both the local high school and at Wynfield Farms. With their charm and sophistication, they are indeed gifts to us. Both girls had worked in large restaurants in Lyon and wanted to continue practicing their skills in the States. Monique and Jean are seventeen years old, devotees of country music, American television shows and blue jeans. If you've been anxious to practice your French, stop Monique or Jean and have a *Bon Jour!* and a conversation.

R. McNess.

~~~
~~~

THE GOLDFISH

The Goldfish swims in its translucent cube
with suspicious strokes and transitory glee.
This ephemeral existence is doomed:
a wisp of gauze tied to an ascending kite

R. McNess.

~~~
~~~

3

Afternoon tea in the Music Room was an honored tradition at Wynfield Farms. Sunlight streamed through the wide French doors that were opened in all but inclement weather onto an adjacent paved quadrangle. Sunday afternoon concerts were held here throughout the summer, and residents sometimes provided music for other occasions. The interior was spacious and airy with excellent acoustics and a superior grand piano. The room was cheerful and wore an aura of English manor house charm for which Mr. Wynfield's estate was noted. The Music Room was altogether a delightful setting for an hour much cherished by every resident at Wynfield.

Promptly at four o'clock in the afternoon, with the exception of Saturday, two of the kitchen staff rolled laden trolleys into the room and dispensed cups of steaming tea and plates of both egg salad and cucumber sandwiches and a variety of sweets. Voices that tended to deafen and swell dropped one or two octaves automatically. Infusions of bracing tea, served in the Wynfield Wedgwood, and heaps of shortbread petticoats fortified the timid. Conversations flowed. Civility prevailed.

Betty Gehrmann, an accomplished musician, was just

concluding a movement from a Mozart divertimento when Rose entered the room. Rose did not join the tea ritual often, but today after the morning's intimations of mystery, she felt need for the lift that only a cup of the freshly brewed stimulant provided. Rose believed, as did a majority of Anglophiles, that a good "cuppa" cured all ills and put iron in one's backbone. *A cup of tea with new friends will do me far more good than a solitary nap at my typewriter.*

"Milk, please, Monique, and no sugar. Thank you. Rather, *merci*." They both smiled. Rose enjoyed the two ruddy-cheeked teenagers.

And now to find a seat. Rose looked around the room. She adjusted her glasses. Friendly faces but few empty chairs. The Jenkins were deep in conversation with the Wilsons. Lucille Hopgood, her crooked body almost parallel with the floor, was shuffling her aluminum walker toward a gathering of three ladies seated in the corner. Jean was following with her tea plate, stacked, Rose observed, with sandwiches and sweets. Miss Hopgood got good value for her money. *And it wouldn't surprise me if that frugal little lady tucked a few goodies in her pockets as she leaves here,* Rose thought. Mr. and Mrs. Stone gestured animatedly to the Cunninghams. *Probably recounting their trip to Alaska last spring. No, thank you, I really do not want to hear that again.*

The one conspicuously empty chair was the one next to Miss Moss. In profile Miss Moss was a pinstripe, bent and folded into the seat of a hard Windsor chair near the open French doors. She was staring intently at a squirrel that was worrying an acorn across the stone patio. Nothing in her appearance indicated she was enjoying the afternoon's interlude. A full cup of tea, its milky surface skimmed and cold, sat untouched on the floor by her chair.

Well, here goes. It's not my idea of relaxing but I guess I should do it. I cannot harbor these feelings about Miss Moss indefinitely. I'll smother her with kindness and see what happens. Perhaps I can coax her out of her shell.

"May I join you, Miss Moss?" Rose asked brightly.

"Oh, . . . why . . . oh, yes, certainly Mrs. McNess. I am just leaving. Take my chair."

"Oh, no. This is fine. I'll pull this one up and we can chat. Lovely afternoon, isn't it?"

"Indeed. Tomorrow is supposed to be raw. Rain."

"Isn't the tea table bountiful today?" continued Rose.

"Kitchen should stop the cucumber sandwiches. The cucumbers are past their prime. California vegetables. No taste."

My, oh, my, thought Rose. *Does this woman see the worst in everything?*

"Have you been to England, Mrs. McNess?"

"I have. I've been fortunate, Miss Moss. I've been to the British Isles many times. In fact, I believe I could happily live there forever if it weren't for my family here. I'd miss them too much."

"Yes. Mmmm. Family. I do think tea time is one of Mr. Wynfield's finest imports. So refined. Genteel. Yes, *genteel*."

Rose listened intently. *She has an aversion to any reference to family. "Family" out; "genteel" in. Strange duck.*

"Oh, I agree. And one of the best things tea time does is stop everything for an hour or so. A real pause in the day. We tend to become too busy and too ingrown." Rose intended to follow this with "I know you stay so busy, Miss Moss . . . " but suddenly her companion stiffened like a tent pole, transfixed by the view through the doors. Rose followed her line of vision.

The Music Room commanded an unobstructed survey of the long driveway leading to Wynfield's front door. Miss Moss and Rose watched as a Sheriff's car from the Botetourt County Sheriff's Department slowly inched through the line of poplars, circled in front of the portico and came to a stop. A tall, burly officer in a wide-brimmed hat and brown uniform emerged and opened the rear door of the vehicle. A chubby policewoman climbed awkwardly out, encumbered by the prisoner handcuffed to her right wrist.

Miss Moss and Rose gasped in unison: "Mary Rector!"

Wedgwood teacups rattled in their saucers and spoons clattered to the floor. Shocked voices cried "Oh, no!" and "Not our Mary!" Monique and Jean, wearing stunned expressions, left their serving stations and hurried to see for themselves.

"I want everyone to remain in this room. You have seen

nothing. I shall handle this matter. Did you hear me? Remain in this room. Please." Miss Moss fairly barked her directives in a voice full of venom.

"Mary is my friend and I am coming with you, Miss Moss," Rose declared.

In her haste to reach the Reception Hall, Miss Moss either did not hear Rose or did not choose to hear her. They both reached the area as the two officers, Mary in tow, were entering. Kate Alexander, her face the color of *blanc mange*, stood bewildered at her desk.

"Officers, what is the meaning of this? Why do you have one of our residents in handcuffs like a common criminal? Surely if she is a missing person . . . "

"Are you Miz McNeece?" drawled the burly man, wide-brimmed hat glued to his head.

"I am Miss A. Elvina Moss, Resident Manager of Wynfield Farms. I am in charge here."

"Well, uh, you see, this little lady here says she wants to talk to Miz McNeece. And only her."

Rose stepped forward. "I am Mrs. McNess and Mary is my friend. Oh, Mary, wh . . . ?"

"I shall handle this, Mrs. McNess," Miss Moss stated emphatically, breaking in before Rose had a chance to speak to her silent friend. "Where did you find her, officer?"

"Well, uh, Miz Moss, this here is no runaway and no missin' person. This little lady just tried to rob the bank in Fincastle. We need to talk. Or call a lawyer."

Rose was thunderstruck. She spoke to Mary for the first time.

"Mary, it's Rose. Would you like to tell me what happened?" she asked gently.

Plump-as-a-pudding Mary Rector was more untidy than ever. Tendrils of damp hair stuck to her moist forehead while the rest strayed in all directions, resembling a wind-tossed bird's nest. Bits of tissue, leaves and small twigs were clinging to the oily strands. Something purple had dribbled down Mary's chin and her eyes were red from crying. A button had escaped from the tight bodice of her house dress and the limp yellow cardigan sliding precariously off one shoulder had also served as Mary's handkerchief.

"This hurts, Rose," she said, nodding at the handcuffs. Rose saw red welts where the tight metal circles immobilized her plump wrists.

"I just wanted to visit my money and they wouldn't let me, so I wrote it down and they still wouldn't let me in. Then I got mad, real mad, and the lady behind the glass started to look at me funny so I had to hide. And they came after me and caught me . . . and Rose, can you get them to take these off? They hurt so much . . . "

"Officer, I would be happy to be responsible for this woman. If there is a question . . . "

"You are overstepping your privileges as a private citizen, Mrs. McNess," Miss Moss shouted with such vehemence that even the two deputies were taken aback. "This is my jurisdiction and I shall handle it. Officers, will you please bring Mary into my office? This shall be discussed in private."

Miss Moss stood aside as she ushered the trio into her inner sanctum. For the second time in one day Rose heard the closing *whoosh* of the office door.

White with anger, Rose wheeled around to Kate. Through clenched teeth she muttered, "Inhumane!"

Kate's blue eyes were brimming with tears and she, too, shook with indignant rage. "Our Mary, rob a bank? It's laughable! Pitiful. Can't they see that?"

"I am more upset over Miss Moss's reaction than I am about Mary. That woman! Oh, Kate, she is impossible. No heart, no sympathy, no feelings. Compassion? She's never heard the word, much less felt any for her fellow man."

"What in the world do you think happened, Mrs. McNess?" asked Kate, sitting down at last and wiping tears with her crumpled handkerchief.

"I think I know exactly what happened. Mary is always talking about 'visiting her money.' I think she likes the idea of having something in the bank, whether it's five dollars or fifty. She likes to check on it. She rode the bus into town early this afternoon and hopped off in Fincastle. Then she went to one of the banks. When they wouldn't let her 'visit,' as she puts it, she must have written some sort of note and handed it to the teller. If the teller didn't recognize Mary—probably never saw her before—she may have panicked and called the police. A perfectly logical reaction if you think your bank is about to be robbed. Even by a harmless little old lady in a tattered sweater.

"And poor Mary. She got scared and scurried out the door. Remember, she said she hid from them. So here she is now in handcuffs. And the saddest part of the whole sad tale is not that Mary has very little money, but what little she has is right here at Wynfield. In our Wynfield bank. She's confused again; had Suzanne on her mind, and wanted to collect her money in order to search for her. She is *ruining* the Perfect Wynfield Image, Miss Moss believes. That's bothering Miss Moss more than Mary's suffering."

"You are absolutely right, Mrs. McNess. And I think you are the only person here who truly takes time to understand Mary. Most of the other residents seem to, well, avoid her. Mary's no genius but she is harmless. And such a sweetie. Tell you what, why don't I get Faye to fix a supper tray for her? On the quiet, of course. Would you be able to take it up?"

"Kate, you are so smart. Wise beyond your years. A wonderful idea! Not only will I take it up, I'll go ask Faye this very moment. You stay here at your post and wait for them to come out. And insist on escorting Mary to her apartment; surely they'll let her stay here. Miss Moss has been embarrassed enough for one day; she would never let Mary be taken off to the county jail. But she won't let me get near Mary again; I might usurp the Moss authority!"

"Fair enough," said Kate. "See you upstairs as soon as Mary is allowed to leave."

Rose bounded off to the Dining Room. *From Wedgwood tea cups to handcuffs in one afternoon*!

~~~

~~~

E C H O E S

Romero Quintero

To paraphrase Shakespeare, "Romero, Romero, wherefore art thou?"

How many times a day (or night) do we each call upon Romero for some sort of help? Wynfield Farms' genial man-of-all-work is a gem! He is literally the "man around the house" for all of us. Neither the simplest task nor the biggest move is too complicated for Romero.

A native of El Salvador, Romero came to the United States six years ago and has been at Wynfield for the past three. He has been diligent in attending ESL (English as a Second Language) classes and is rapidly becoming fluent in his new tongue.

Romero lives nearby with wife Estella (a talented seamstress) and his four children who range in age from six months to eleven years.

Romero, with his ever-present smile, makes hard work look easy. It is a pleasure to be acquainted with someone who takes such obvious pride in his work. We wish you and your family all good fortune in your adopted country, Romero!

~~~
~~~

4

The new resident of Apartment 209 was tired.

Eloise Johnson—known as Ellie since kindergarten—sat down wearily on the floor among piles of luggage.

"Whew!" she exclaimed. "What a trip!" She glanced at the gold watch on her left wrist and saw that it was after one o'clock.

I'm worn out . . . and famished. On the go since five. Completely forgot to calculate the time change. Seems like I left Denver three weeks ago . . . .

She fumbled in her copious leather purse until she extracted a compressed and dented foil packet. *Thank God for friends like Elizabeth, her sandwiches have lasted all the way across country. I'll call her first thing when I get my phone.*

Ellie Johnson then pushed the largest suitcase away from her head and stretched out full length on the floor of her new living room. With her left foot she managed to jiggle the square cosmetic case a few inches closer so she could use it for a foot rest. She kicked off Ferragamo sling-backs and maneuvered both stockinged feet onto the case.

"Ah, heaven!" she cried, finishing the pimento cheese sandwich and greedily licking her fingers. "A cup of coffee would be perfect right now. But that can wait. Oh, my, how good it feels to stretch out . . . . "

Yawning, Ellie looked around the spacious and newly-painted room.

What did the brochure say the dimensions were? 18' by 24'? Seems larger from this angle. Studio was the way to go; certainly don't need more space. I don't intend to cook and I certainly don't expect overnight guests. Besides, old sourpuss mentioned guest rooms here when we talked this morning . . . Was it just this morning? I'm exhausted! No use unpacking . . . I'll get to that when my furniture arrives. Not going anyplace . . . anymore. Wish I had one more of Elizabeth's sandwiches; I'd hole up here until I got settled . . . Lovely crown molding in this room; wonder if all the studios are this nice? Window is generous. I love the light. Have to get sheers up, though; valance doesn't give much privacy. Not that I need much; nothing but woods out there! I'll call Roger. He'll know just the effect I need.

"Vincent, you stay asleep over there, y'hear?"

With final thoughts of her decorator and her bird, Ellie Johnson drifted into a sleep that her body cried for. The thick wool carpet cradled her ample form as softly as a cushion of eiderdown.

Ellie dreamed. She was home in Alabama and sleeping in her walnut spool bed with the deep feather mattress and layers of eyelet-edged cotton sheets and comforters. She dreamed of the time she was quarantined with German measles and forced to stay in a darkened room for three weeks that for a ten-year-old stretched endlessly into black nothingness. She had scratched at the ugly red spots with the eyelet and Mommy got mad. Ellie was deep into these dreams when a soft knocking penetrated her subconscious.

She woke slowly, heavily, with the hazy disorientation of the very tired. *Oh my God, where am I? Alabama? Denver?* Finally it dawned on her: Virginia. She was finally here. Wynfield Farms, Virginia. *Yes, Virginia!*

"Coming! I'm coming," she managed to croak as she kicked at the vanity case and eased herself up painfully from the floor.

Where in the world is the door? How did it get so dark? Did I sleep . . . ?

The soft knocking had stopped, then resumed, directing Ellie by its cadence to the closed door. She pulled the door open to find a slim, short woman standing in the hall.

"I know this is presumptuous of me . . . but I'm your cross-the-hall neighbor, Rose McNess, and I wonder if you would care to join me for a martini? It's that time, you know!"

A drowsy, bleary-eyed Ellie blinked in disbelief. But even in her disbelief, she managed to take in the appealing and unexpected array that the neighbor held up for her inspection: a silver tray bearing two Waterford tumblers filled with a clear, icy liquid, a short crystal pitcher half full of the same liquid, and a saucer of cheese wafers centered with fat pecans.

"My dear, you are a sight for sore eyes! I must have slept for hours. Do come in; I'm Ellie Johnson, and it's now 4:30 Denver time and . . . "

"Don't say a word! I was told that you had traveled a great distance today. May I shut the door? Good . . . or would you prefer to come across to my place? I didn't realize that you had no chairs or anything yet . . . " The woman looked around the dark, bare room. She balanced the tray carefully as she stepped over the cases.

"Oh, no," said Ellie, "if you don't mind sitting here on the floor. I don't think I'm capable of crossing the hall. Let me switch on the bathroom light; that should give us enough light in here. I can't wait to get to that martini!"

She crossed to the bathroom and turned on the fluorescent lighting. The soft glow enclosed the two women in a dim sphere of warmth.

Ellie took one of the short frosted tumblers from her new neighbor who was smiling at her warmly.

"To Ellie Johnson," the woman said. "New neighbor and, I hope, new friend. Welcome!" Her smile was genuine.

Ellie raised her own glass in salute. "And to . . . I'm sorry, I didn't catch your name . . . "

"Rose. Rose McNess. Just Rose to my friends. Miss Moss didn't tell you all about me?"

The two sat down, slowly, backs against the wall, legs stretched out in front. Rose placed the silver tray on the rug between them.

Ellie shut her eyes and sipped sparingly of her drink. She picked up a cheese wafer and began, "Not at all! Not a peep about any of the residents here. That dreadful woman. Cold as ice. I needed sympathy when we finally arrived, not a lecture on her antiques. The cab driver missed two turns, Vincent got loose in the lobby and she shouted at me as I came in. I'll get over her but . . . "

Rose nodded. "Miss Moss can be somewhat loud," she commented.

Ellie laughed. She was relieved the morning was over, and glad that this new friend had appeared.

"Rose McNess, amidst the detritus of my life you are a star! How in the world did you even suspect that a martini would pick me up like nothing else? I'm overcome and loving it!"

"Actually," Rose began cautiously, "I took a chance. Martinis are a part of my private rebellion against aging. I guess I hoped so much that you would be the type who'd enjoy the occasional martini that I just convinced myself you would. Its a celebratory drink! There are not many here who share my view about martinis, though. Oh, they're not prudes, don't let me give that impression. Just more sherry-in-the-evening type. Besides, I needed a martini after this afternoon." Rose did not elaborate.

Ellie Johnson, late of Denver, now of Virginia, looked at her visitor. They tipped their glasses to each other once more, smiled and sipped.

What a breath of fresh air, Ellie thought. *About my age—perhaps seventy, seventy-one? A bit thin; probably always has been, the lucky duck. Doesn't seem to be ailing like so many I keep hearing about.*

The two women stretched their backs and Ellie sighed loudly. "Rose, you're a mind reader to think I'd enjoy a martini.

Tell me about yourself, please. I mean it: life story. And if I doze off in the middle, just remember it's the drink not the drone!"

"Ah, if I started telling you about myself we'd be here all night. I'll let my story unfold gradually. I'll just tell you that I am twice widowed, have three children, all grown, of course, and only one living near enough to keep tabs on me. And Max. I have a Scottie that I love more than life."

Rose kept her promise and stopped at this point.

"Lucky you," confided Ellie, rolling her eyes. "I have neither chick nor child. Just Vincent, my canary over there." She gestured vaguely in the direction of the green "cigar" resting in the corner.

"Love dogs, though. I'm a widow also. Married late, widowed early. Oh, my husband had children by his first marriage, but they have their own lives and their own families and certainly don't need to take care of me. Not that I'd want them to try."

"Miss Moss said you had come here from Denver. I am absolutely bursting with curiosity. Why Virginia? Why Wynfield Farms?"

"Oh, my dear," gushed Ellie, "Wynfield Farms has a fantastic reputation and rating. I made a thorough study of retirement areas all up and down East *and* West coasts. This place ranks as one of the top ones. 'Intergenerational programming.' Whatever that means. And then my mind was made up before I started. You see, Duke, my late husband, was VMI. He came to the Institute at age seventeen, spent four years there, and never got over it."

"So many of them don't," Rose interjected wryly.

Ellie laughed, her guffaw filling the room. "I agree! People used to tease Duke about VMI everywhere we lived. He simply worshipped the place." Her voice dropped and she became pensive, recalling Duke and the happy times they had shared.

"What do you think Duke would have said about VMI's admitting women?"

"Duke loved Virginia Military Institute so much that I think he would have considered that policy as a sign of the changing times after 150-plus years of history and tradition. I don't think he'd object to a few women there. Besides, he was quite fond of the opposite sex."

"We'll drive up some afternoon. I haven't been to Lexington in weeks. Usually head south, to Roanoke, from habit. I'm sorry, I interrupted you. Tell me more about your moving to Virginia, Ellie."

"We had returned to VMI every year of our marriage. I fell in love with the entire area. We visited in all the seasons and each time was more memorable than the last. When Duke died, I stayed on in Denver for two years. But I kept thinking about our good times in this part of the country. Three months ago I picked up the phone and called Wynfield for information. After looking at the brochure I decided it was time to move. Put the house on the market, gave Duke's children everything they could cart away, sold what I could, and here I am."

Rose raised her glass.

"To Ellie," she said. "You are one gutsy lady! Duke would be proud of you."

"Thank you, Rose. I was fortunate. One love, one marriage, one man. But, God, what a man! Duke was special. And I'm not all that 'gutsy.' It didn't take much courage to move. But tell me more about Wynfield. I know what the brochure says, but what's it like living here? *Really*?"

"Ellie, as they say about Harrods, 'you can be married or buried here.' In other words, practically from womb to tomb."

Ellie guffawed again. "But what about . . . adjusting to this kind of life. When you know that this is your *final* move before being carted away by the knacker man . . . how do you adjust?"

Rose straightened, pushing her shoulders against the wall before answering.

"Ellie, I don't look at this phase of my life as one I have to *adjust* to. I just live! You know, I'm sure, from all your research on retirement homes, aggregate community living—don't you just love that term?—that our generation is living *at least* twenty years longer than our grandparents did. Well, right or wrong, I count that twenty-year bonus as money in the bank. *My* bank! I intend to get more hours out of every day and more days out of every year. All twenty of them!"

"And this life-style—I mean Wynfield Farms—has everything you need to fill those extra hours and days?"

"Ellie, when I first moved to Wynfield I resented being displaced. I was angry at Annie, my daughter, for instigating the move. Angry at everything; I felt uprooted. When Spring came and I began to walk the grounds I started to feel more at peace with myself. I began to hope that the next day was going to be better. And it was. I hoped I would sleep soundly and wake up the next day. I did! I hoped I would rejoin the flow of life with some of the interesting people I had met here. And I did. I replaced despair with hope. Which is pretty much what life is all about. *That* is how I regained enough of my old sass and spirit to elect myself Tour Leader. Secretly, of course. Would never do for that to get out!"

"Pardon?" quizzed Ellie, wide awake and fascinated by Rose's peroration.

"Sorry. Another part of my private philosophy. I view Wynfield Farms as one great big tour group. Everyone here is riding through life on the same bus. Did you and Duke ever go on any organized tours in your travels?"

"Just once," answered Ellie. "A real mixed bag of folks."

"Exactly!" cried Rose. "We are a mixed bag! You remember what characters there are on a tour: some fun, some boring, some that nothing suits no matter what it is, some romantics, some realists. Personalities do not change. The bored have been bored all their lives, the cranky have always been curmudgeons, the perpetually tardy have forever been tardy. The ones that enjoy life are the *doers* and the *givers*. They want to be part of everything and hope they miss nothing. That is how I look at life at Wynfield. One big tour, and I, secretly, am the Director. I look ahead with hope. I am having *fun*. I go my own way, and projects and people keep popping up. So that, my friend, is the how and why I have filled my black hole. And I manage to stay so busy that I don't even have time to consider anything as serious as—what was your word?—'adjustment.'"

"Rose, Rose. I don't know what to say. If I could become one-tenth the resident you are . . . Top off my drink, will you my dear?"

"With pleasure. That's it. One large martini only. As my mother used to say, 'a good deed in a naughty world.'"

The two women sipped in silence. Ellie felt buoyed by the cool slide of gin and the immediate bonding of two like spirits. Rose spoke first.

"You know, I think often it is harder on children than parents, this kind of move. Take Annie, my one daughter, middle child. She wants so badly for me to be happy. She misses my funny old house more than I do but she wouldn't admit it."

"Is Annie married?" Ellie inquired.

"Oh, yes," answered Rose. "To a successful lawyer in Roanoke. Great children. Interesting thing about daughters. They get along with their mothers like cats most of their lives. Then at a certain point they become the parent and the parent becomes child. A real role reversal. Even if I were not happy I would pretend to be. For Annie's sake. But each day, when I start my tour, I find I don't even have to pretend. Am I silly or what? Silly . . . or senile?"

Rose looked at Ellie with these last questions, a frown knitting together her blue eyes.

"Rose, you're wonderful. You have found the secret of survival. May I join your tour? Only please, a *cruise ship*, not a bus!"

Both women erupted in laughter.

Ellie, giggling, continued, "I mean it Rose, you are the proverbial Rock of Gibraltar. And that is NOT the martini talking either!"

"Ellie, you're kind. I am just being neighborly. The South is famous for that, you know. But we've got to think about dinner. The evening seating runs from five to seven and good heavens! It's already a quarter 'til right now!"

"Six or seven?"

"Seven. You do feel hungry, don't you?"

"Not really. My timetable is so mixed up. I have a comforter in one of these bags and my travel pillow. I think a hot bath and a good night's sleep would do me a lot more good than a meal I wouldn't appreciate. Incidentally, is the food good? As good as that slick brochure says it is?"

Rose nodded emphatically. "Better. The chef is fabulous, the servers are all young and the Dining Room manager, Faye, is a mover and a shaker. It really is four star cuisine most of the time. Reminds me of *Pensione Bellduccia* in Florence."

"The *Bellduccia* and Madame Ponzini?"

"None other. Is there any other pension in Firenze? I knew we were kindred souls, Ellie. What good taste we have!"

Congratulating each other on their choice of Florentine lodging, Rose and Ellie clambered up from their places on the floor. Rose collected her glasses, picked up the few crumbs that had spilled onto the carpet and walked to the door.

"We seldom lock doors here at Wynfield. Maybe that's silly but we all feel safe. We each have an innate trust and respect for one another."

"Rose, the way I'm going to sleep tonight, the devil himself couldn't rouse me. He could come in and rob me blind and I wouldn't lose anything but a dozen wigs and a few sweaters."

"Wigs?" Rose repeated, turning from the door and looking at Ellie in surprise.

"Wigs," giggled Ellie. "I'm bald as a billiard. You didn't think I came halfway across the country and arrived looking like I'd stepped out of a salon, did you? Now, Rose!"

"Well," stammered Rose, "the first thing I noticed was your perfect hair. *Beautifully coiffured*, I believe, were my thoughts."

"Thanks, love. I had a radical mastectomy last year and the chemo and radiation did away with everything but my eyelashes. I still don't even have peach fuzz. Probably never will. Do I look too wiggy? I have wigs for every day of the week. Practically every hour."

"No one will know unless you tell them. I promise."

"Oh, I don't mind people knowing; I just don't advertise my illness. Or my wellness. I got a clean bill of health before I left Denver. No checkups for a year. No hair but I have something else!"

"What's that, Ellie?"

Ellie leaned forward and held Rose's gaze with the intensity of her expression. "Inner strength. Having cancer gave me an edge of courage that I never had before or ever expected to have. It makes me feel stronger than someone who has never had to go through this awful experience. Life may not have given me twenty extra years, but it gave me a second chance. And I mean to use it. I repeat: I'm glad I'm on your tour, Rose."

"Oh, Ellie, so am I," Rose cried. The two women impulsively hugged each other.

"Thank you, Rose. You have brought me everything I could possibly desire: food for my body *and* for my spirit. Good night, Rose McNess. I'll sleep like a baby!"

"Good night, Ellie. I'll check on you in the morning. Sleep well!"

~~~

Rose closed Ellie's door and crossed to her own apartment. *I told Max I thought we might have a new friend.* She placed the tray on the kitchen counter and gave the terrier his milk bone before hurrying to reach the dining room before seven.

Tomorrow night will be time enough to launch Ellie Johnson!

~~~

ECHOES

Albert Corning Coatsworth Warrington

If you hear the strains of the "Whiffenpoof Song" wafting from Apartment 240, chances are that ALBERT WARRINGTON is at home. Wynfield Farms' Number One Yalie is a former tenor of that distinguished university's singing group and owns all of their recordings.

Albert was born in Boston but after undergraduate studies and Yale Law School, he decided that Connecticut was his true home and settled in the community of Old Lyme. A busy legal career, world travel and various civic boards consumed Albert's working life. He never married but enjoyed his brother's large family. One niece lives in Lexington and is a frequent visitor to Wynfield Farms.

Albert was attracted to Wynfield because of its location in our beautiful Shenandoah Valley. He is an avid bird watcher and one has to rise early in the morning to catch Albert Warrington as he begins his morning hikes.

Rose McNess.

(I am dedicating the following poem to you, Albert.)

MOURNING DOVES

The mourning doves have just returned.
Pine boughs dip and sway with the weight
of their fragile bones as the dank earth below
grows white with their midden.

Where did they go, my grave gray pair?
Did they hold evensong or mass
beneath angled eaves of a forgotten chapel?
Or was it time past due?

Return. They whisper, nod and speak
sibilant tones by cellar door.
It is said they mate for life, this winged pair;
mortals can merely hope.

Rose McNess.

5

Albert Corning Coatsworth Warrington stood before his six-drawer Hepplewhite chest and inspected the brasses. Every pull was burnished, smooth and lustrous, the color of North Carolina sourwood honey. Each pull handle rested in correct position, downward against the inlaid maple shield.

His attention now fixed on the hand-turned Hepplewhite shaving stand. Albert was a tall man, an inch over six feet, so he had to stoop, hunching narrow shoulders forward, in order to see his face. The face that was reflected in the slightly rippled, yellowing oval antique glass gave him much pleasure to view. His face. Mr. Warrington's egg-shaped physiognomy matched the shape of the mirror with the precision of the final piece of an intricate jigsaw puzzle. Hair the hue and texture of damp barn-straw framed a visage that remained unlined, pink in color and full of cheek. Pale eyebrows sprouted as unruly hedgerows from the breadth of his unusually wide forehead to acknowledge the opalescent blue eyes beneath.

These marble-like orbs gazed at the world with obvious intelligence and not just a small hint of superiority. They were also prone, of late, to brim with unexpected tears. These Niagara strength deluges were immediately labeled 'sinusitis' and swiftly stifled with a monogrammed linen handkerchief hastily withdrawn from the bearer's breast pocket.

An aquiline nose ("the true Coatsworth nose, Dearest," his mother had always insisted) led to a generously wide mouth with lips that were thin. Too thin, he mused, coaxing this mouth into a semi-smile.

Albert Warrington wore a perpetually passive expression, neither pleased nor displeased, neither glum nor cheerful. Merely satisfied. When he did smile, rarely in public, it was authentic. The prospects of the morning, unfolding in his mind, pleased him. His smile stretched into an arc, revealing perfect teeth. He was exceedingly and justifiably proud of this asset.

He paused in his morning assessment.

Did he need a haircut? Mr. Warrington had his hair cut once a month without fail to ensure that its length did not inch toward his collar and indicate a certain seediness. A side-wise glance assured him that the present fullness of his thin hair was due to the morning shampoo and not to a spurt of rapid hair growth.

Albert Warrington collected the loose change from the silver porringer (Old English script, "ACCW," on the much dented bowl identified it as his own) and dropped the coins into the left pocket of his gray flannel Brooks Brothers trousers. He aligned the monogrammed Sheffield plate Gentleman's Set at right angles to the shaving stand.

He directed his gaze to the vial from the pharmacy. He unscrewed the child-proof cap and removed his Betagan.

One drop in the left eye, hold, block with tissue, count slowly to ten. Repeat process for right eye. A small inconvenience of time and effort but it halted the possible advance of dreaded glaucoma. This daily procedure was his one concession to aging.

He opened the closet door to the right of his chest. On the back of the door hung his collection of ties, eighty-seven, all but five of them from Brooks Brothers in New York City. Purchased there, not ordered. The five defectors were from Liberty of London. Gifts.

Albert Warrington had his ties arranged as neatly and masterfully as he had his life. The ties hung on a unique handmade rack (from the hand of a master craftsman) of ingenious design (Mr. Warrington's own). One gentle push at the beginning of a row repositioned all the ties to a military-correct upright stance. Each row was color coded vertically and horizontally according to the predominate primary color, starting with cool and advancing to warm. The visual effect was stunning, a canvas worthy of the Impressionists. He occasionally thought it a great pity that no eyes, save his own, had ever viewed this display.

This morning he selected a blue, with citron, European-style stripe. The tie would contrast quietly with his blue Oxford cloth shirt. He returned to his shaving stand, stooped, and deftly tied a regulation Windsor knot. The larger knot emphasized the narrowness of his button-down collar.

He removed his second best navy blazer from the valet stand, scrutinized it for particles of lint and slipped into it with the practiced ease of one who has repeated the practice for more than sixty-five years.

Albert Warrington then picked up the scuffed but handsome brief case resting on the faded toile of one of the Hepplewhite open arm chairs flanking his front door. He checked; yes, the case was locked. He looked around, once more admiring the subdued elegance of his apartment. Then he silently opened his door and stepped into the hallway.

Door key? His door was the only one in the complex that locked automatically upon closure. Double locks.

Feeling the key among the jangle of coins in his left trouser pocket he exhaled deeply, thrust his firm chin slightly upward, and strode briskly down the maroon-medallioned carpet toward the stairs.

Upon reaching the first floor and the Reception Hall he hesitated as he passed the Receptionist.

Pleasant young woman, that. Attractive, efficient. I like that.

"Good morning, Miss Alexander."

"Why, good morning to you, Mr. Warrington," responded

the blushing Kate. "You are up and out early this morning! Looks as if you have a very important meeting in the city."

I like the way she blushes. Delightful. "Appearances can be deceiving, Miss Alexander," he replied seriously.

Smiling his half-smile, Albert Warrington continued walking, and passed through the heavy front doors and out into the cool October morning.

~~~

From the window of Apartment 208 Rose McNess watched Albert Warrington move briskly across the walk and down the drive. She noted that his long legs moved purposely and that there was little wasted motion in his lean body.

Certainly dapper for a man of his age. Must be closer to mid-seventy than late sixties. Where is he going at this hour? It's only seven o'clock. Breakfast meeting? Bank business? Nothing's open yet. Still . . . he has his briefcase with him . . .

At that instant a loud knock on her door, followed by Max's strident bark, banished Rose's interest in her fellow resident. Rose moved quickly and opened the door to find Ellie Johnson.

"Ellie! Come in, come in! Did you sleep at all? Aren't you a sight this morning!" Rose, startled at her visitor's early appearance, blurted out her greeting involuntarily. Then she began to giggle, and to giggle so much she had to pull Ellie into the apartment without a word because she was convulsed with laughter.

Ellie had wrapped her head with a bulky, multicolored batik turban that encompassed all but her ears. Large copper hoops dangled from each of these. She wore a voluminous, gaudy, black, orange and yellow caftan that gave her the appearance of a brightly wrapped bag of Halloween candy.

"Isn't this hilarious?" asked Ellie. "My best chums in Denver presented it to me before I left. Said if I wore this to breakfast I'd surely shake up the Old Folks Home. Like it, love?" She raised her arms and did a quick pirouette around Rose's living area. Max scurried for his cave behind the dust ruffle on Rose's bed.

"Ellie, you are priceless," cried Rose, collapsing weakly into her wing chair. "Tell me you were a Palm Reader in your former life. Read my lines, Madame Ellie!"
~~~

"No, my dear, 'tis only the disguise. But I must have some caffeine in the morning. I slept straight through and I'm slept out. I simply have to have some coffee before I am able to function. May I bum a cup?"

"Surely, Ellie, but come over here to the window first," directed Rose. She steered her neighbor toward the spot where she herself had been standing minutes before.

"Look! Look at that, Ellie. It's barely 7:15. Where is that man going?"

"What man, Rose?"

"Look, over there, by the cedars, just before the gates. It's Albert Warrington."

"Is he a resident of Wynfield?"

"Absolutely. And a real mystery. Trotting off at this hour, dressed in his Ivy League outfit. Four times in two weeks he has done this." Rose stopped. With a rush of insight she realized she was involving the new resident in events and petty gossip about which she had no knowledge whatsoever. Or interest. This was all the more puzzling because she herself did not understand the intrigue of Albert Warrington's whereabouts or why she was the least bit concerned.

"I'm sorry, Ellie," she confessed. "Forgive me? I feel like the town snoop. A real Nosy Parker. I am up early every morning and I love to look out my window and watch the sun come peeping through the trees and see the birds skittering about. I can't help but see Albert Warrington go striding through the gates and I can't help but wonder where he is going. But I didn't mean to involve you in the mystery. Now, let's have that coffee."

"So I didn't wake you?"

"Heavens, no. Max and I are early risers, but there is another who beats us. I have secretly dubbed him The Virginia Creeper; he walks up and down the hallway two or three times before I even get out the door. Max and I are out for our walk around 6:30. Max has had his breakfast and now I am ready for mine." Hearing the words "walk" and "breakfast," Max reappeared.

"Hello, Max. I've heard about you." Ellie knelt to ruffle Max's coat and then abruptly withdrew her hand.

"I forgot. Max is a Scottie. They are rather aloof, aren't they?"

"They are and he is," Rose retorted. "He'll come around soon enough. And love you. But in his own time and on his own terms. He has great dignity when it comes to showing affection. Come, sit down. I'm tickled to have company this morning. Black, I hope?"

"Any other way?"

The two women sat in silence and sipped Rose's strong black coffee and shared the last of the banana nut loaf that had been warming in the toaster oven. The mingled smells of fresh coffee and spicy bread wreathed the tiny dining alcove with delicious aromas. Both Rose and Ellie savored this unexpected pocket of quiet friendship. Each recognized a thread of communication growing between them. Neither woman spoke for fear of breaking the precious moment. There were muffled sounds of the building waking up: a delivery truck arriving and departing, shouts from kitchen help, birds trilling from the trees.

Ellie spoke: "I could never live without birds around me."

"You'll see and hear plenty here. Funny, you don't strike me as the bird watcher type."

"Only from a golf cart. I just enjoy hearing the birds singing. They add so much life to a place. Can you imagine living in a condo twenty-six floors above ground where you could never hear a chirp?"

"I have to admit, I cannot. One of the pleasures of Wynfield Farms is being in the country, or relative country. We're isolated here, yet the city is thirty minutes away. Buses run every hour, and of course, many of us still drive. I do. If there is something special going on in Roanoke, I just hop in my old Nova. I still have a fair number of friends living in the city and my daughter, of course. I enjoy catching up now and then. But you know, recently I feel more and more as if this is my real home."

"And do the buses run to Lexington, too?"

"Oh, yes, and of course Miss Moss encourages everyone to ride the bus. It really is safer at our age, though I'd never tell her that. I prefer my independence, and I have that behind the wheel of my little car."

"I'll get you to show me where they post the bus schedules, Rose, after I get settled. But now, tell me about some of our neighbors. Are there lots more eccentrics like that fellow who just walked through the gates and the old gal in the lobby yesterday?"

"Miss Moss?"

"No, no. After a good night's sleep I don't categorize her as an eccentric. Just a sourpuss; too smart for mere management and not qualified for the Board. No, I mean the pathetic creature by the front door."

"You mean Mary Rector. She told me she saw you when you arrived. Even described you as a movie star. Her story will break your heart. Mary's only daughter disappeared at a shopping mall over twenty years ago and Mary's still convinced she is coming back. Apparently Suzanne, the daughter, told Mary to be looking at china while she had her wedding dress fitted. When closing time came and Suzanne had not returned, Mary couldn't believe it. Suzanne had never even arrived at the fitting room. Mary lost it, right then. I think I would have done the same thing."

"Oh, for goodness sakes! I believe I remember reading about an incident like that in some paper. An AP report. How tragic. Think it could have been the same pair?"

"Has to be," said Rose. "In Winchester, up the valley. Mary's husband wasn't well at the time and he died about eight years ago. The son brought Mary here. Just dumped her with a handful of possessions. Mary's intelligence is fine; she just lives in her own little dream world. Talks about Suzanne and the Barbie doll collection the girl had. Then waits for the bus. Goes wherever the bus goes. Yesterday Mary took the bus into town to visit her money. Only the bank in Fincastle didn't quite see it that way. It wasn't Mary's bank and the teller thought it was a holdup. The Sheriff brought her back here in his car. Miss Moss nearly expired. I felt so sorry for Mary. There but for the grace of God go I! But I didn't mean to go on and on about the poor soul . . . "

"I'm fascinated. Any others as interesting as Mary? How about our neighbors up here on second floor?"

"Several quirky personalities for sure! You'll see the whole lot at dinner tonight. I'd say the average age at Wynfield is around seventy. And two-thirds of the group are really sharp. Of course, still waters run deep; we could have an ax murderer among us and I wouldn't know it. Not yet! Just bear in mind, Ellie, that everyone has a story."

"I'm looking forward to hearing every one. Who lives behind the door with the posies?"

"Miss PuffenBARGER. And do be sure and say BARGER, not burger."

"Gracious! I hope she has a first name."

"Almost as much of a mouthful: Henrietta. But it was Miss Puffenbarger seven months ago when I moved in next door to her, and it is still Miss Puffenbarger to this day. A retired schoolteacher. Extremely quiet. Keeps to her room. I've never been invited inside. Keeps to herself, requires no company. I respect that. Neither Miss Puffenbarger nor I mind being by ourselves. That is the one thing we have in common, I suppose."

"I'll take note of that, Rose, never fear. I don't want to get thrown off your tour!"

"Not a chance. We are going to enjoy each other; I feel it. And you have some terrific neighbors on the other side of you. Vinnie Whittington is next door and beyond her, Major Featherstone. Now there is a character!"

"Does everyone decorate their doors?"

"Some do, not all. My door is bare. I find that the fresh flowers in the Reception Hall and the arrangements on every floor are quite enough. Jocey does that; she's the horticulturist. A decidedly elegant touch, don't you agree?"

"Oh, yes," sighed Ellie. "I'd better go write these names down or I'll forget before I cross the hall. And I don't want to wear out my welcome. Have to clean up a bit and then I'll begin unpacking. At least I'll have my closets arranged. I have to say, Rose, that you certainly travel light." Ellie was making a frank appraisal of Rose's apartment, an activity in which she had been engaged since entering.

Rose McNess lived with a minimum of furnishings.

"Annie calls my apartment 'early Spartan.' I prefer to call it 'uncluttered.' I gave up my things when I moved to Wynfield Farms: my collections, my antiques, most of my books. No regrets. I am comfortable in my surroundings: one bed, four chairs, two small rugs, desk, a few paintings and my kitchen. And family photos, of course. I do enjoy sorting through recipes and cooking now and then. You look upon a satisfied woman, Ellie. One devoid of baggage."

Ellie sighed again. "I'm envious. I pared down tremendously, or so I thought. Now that I see how well situated you are with so little, I wish I had insisted on Duke's children hauling off even more. No use worrying about what you can't change, is it? I'll be happy to see my furniture when it arrives. If I don't have room for everything . . . well, I'll cross that bridge when I come to it."

"That's the spirit, Ellie."

"I'm gone, Rose. Thanks so much for breakfast. I promise you won't have to feed me every day. I'm beginning to get acclimated to your Virginia climate. Almost feel energized once more. See you later!"

With a jaunty wave Ellie was out the door, leaving behind her the heady scent of a flowery perfume and a smile on Rose McNess's face.

Ah, Max, how satisfying to have a genuine, uncomplicated female friend! Who cares where Albert Warrington was going!

~~~

~~~

E C H O E S

Elizabeth Anderton Meecham

ELIZABETH MEECHAM's favorite corner of Wynfield is—no surprise—the Library! She may be found there most of the time. Lucky for us! Lib, as she prefers to be called, has loved books all her life, "ever since I was crawling." Surely that can't be too long ago. Lib has crammed a lot of learning and living into her lifetime.

Born in Minnesota, she migrated south to Illinois for university study (University of Illinois, '22) and then east to Columbia University (MLS, '25). While in New York she met and married her late husband, Edward. The Meecham family (two sons and a daughter) lived in Rochester for many years before moving to Bristol, Virginia, where Ed retired. Lib reports that she got to know the libraries of both cities well. In addition to volunteering in her children's schools, she managed to find time for regular work at the public libraries.

This talented lady sews, works needlepoint, and plays bridge under duress. And she reads. Her favorite books? "English mysteries, classics, and anything by Edith Wharton."

Lib is currently putting all her considerable energies into updating Wynfield's fine library facilities. "I'll get us automated yet!" she vows.

And knowing Lib, I'm sure she will.

R. McNess.

~~~
~~~

6

Wynfield Farms' Dining Room was redolent with the pleasures of gracious living, past and present. It was a room that held the promise of cheerful hospitality to everyone passing through its massive Brazilian mahogany doors, now resting in stately majesty against the textured buttery plaster walls of the hallway. These portals were opened daily at seven for breakfast, 12 o'clock for luncheon, and at five in the evening. Sunday dining at Wynfield was less formal, the hours being seven in the morning until three in the afternoon, with pick-up snacks offered as light supper. Holiday meals proved exception to all schedules.

The Dining Room was the one room of the entire estate that had been left intact. It was described thus in the glossy brochure mailed in response to every serious inquiry and presented to interested guests. Miss Moss's standing orders were that visitors were to be ushered *post haste* from Reception Hall to Dining Room to ensure that they might gaze upon the crown jewel of Wynfield Farms. Anyone seeing this room, either by casual glance or careful examination, could not help being impressed with the atmosphere of sustained refinement emanating from within.

At eight minutes before seven in the evening Rose McNess escorted her new neighbor to her first real meal at Wynfield. In comparison to many residents, they were late. Many evenings found a small gathering outside the doors long before the doors opened. Faye Gillespie, a fair, sensible martinet listed in the Wynfield brochure as Dining Room Hostess, ceremoniously unlocked the latches punctually at five to a crowd that had been patiently waiting for her to do just that. Faye long ago realized that it was not merely the excellent cuisine of Wynfield that occasioned this rush to meals; rather, above all else, the seniors cherished the honored ritual of eating and socializing.

Ellie Johnson stopped at the entrance, mouth agape. "Oh, Rose, how beautiful!" Her eyes swept over the scene. "I feel as if I had been whisked away to a movie set, or at least to one of those huge castles in England. Do we have time for me to linger a second?" Ellie plainly had no intention of hurrying in to dine.

Tall casement windows lined the ivory walls of the room. These were adorned with simple fabric swags that softened the cross hatching of the mullioned panes without barring welcome outside light. Three brass nine-branch Flemish chandeliers, now electrified and suspended from the ceiling by maroon velvet cords, filled the octagonal room with subtle light. The glow spilled upon linen cloths and pooled on wreaths of Wynfield ivy and fresh seasonal flowers encircling slender tapers in hurricane chimneys. These anchored each of the 24 tables that appeared to be at full capacity. The scene sparkled as candlelight danced across fine crystal, heavy silver and the contented, happy faces of the diners.

"What do you think of the mantel, Ellie?" asked Rose.

"I'm just getting to that," she replied. "This room is . . . so lovely. Did you say it was the ballroom in the original estate?"

"Correct. The Samuel Wynfields had four daughters so they must have married them off by throwing great balls and entertaining all the eligible bachelors in the county. It must have worked as all four married."

"What a fireplace! That opening is positively yawning at me;

has to be six feet across if it's an inch. And the mantel! Did I read, or did you tell me, that the great man himself designed it?"

"You did your homework, Ellie. Miss Moss will enlist you as tour guide! Isn't it magnificent? You're right, it is his design. He put a simpler, Adams mantel in the South Lounge. Virginia pine, I believe. And this, of course, is Carrara marble; Louis XVI/ Adams. I am convinced that Mrs. Wynfield was responsible for the French flavor in the estate. I keep meaning to research this. See the *putti*, those little angels, that are carved on the cross bar? Rumor has it that they are the five Wynfield children, plus one little outsider. Adds a bit of spice, true or not!"

One little outsider . . . there's another item I think I'll research. Rose mulled over the smiling *putti* as she encouraged Ellie to move along.

"We'd better find a table, Ellie, and then you can admire at your leisure. And I'll tell you about St. Agnes in the tapestry."

"Tapestry? I'm still gaping at those cherubs. I could swear they are watching me."

"Every resident thinks they resemble his or her grandchild! The high relief is so detailed and is sculpted so finely that they seem freestanding in this light, don't they?" Chiaroscuro, that fickle play of light and shade, gave the frieze of *putti* such dimension that the cherubs did indeed seem to be skipping merrily among their garlands of fruits and flowers, grinning mischievously in their freedom.

Faye stopped them, saying, "Mrs. McNess, I think your friend Mrs. Meecham is saving you two places."

"Oh, thank you, Faye. I'll do introductions later. Yes, I see Lib now. This way, Ellie."

Lib's table was in the far alcove and she indeed was waving the pair on. Rose nodded and steered Ellie past Major Featherstone's wheelchair. She dodged a walker that stood mutely by a table, keeping her right hand on Ellie's elbow in a firm vise. She knew that if she paused for even the briefest "Hello!" she'd never reach Lib.

"Well, we did make it!" triumphed Rose. "Sorry we're disrupting the first course with our tardiness. I am grateful to you, Lib, for saving us a place."

"You are right on time, Rose," responded Lib graciously. "I'm just happy we had two extra places for you and . . . "

"Lib Meecham. Arthur Everett. I want you to meet our newest resident and my new neighbor, Mrs. Eloise Johnson. Ellie."

"*Salve! Quomodo vales?* Or, if you prefer the English version, greetings and how do you do?" Arthur Everett had risen at his place and bowed his tall, fine-spun frame slightly as he presented his hand to Ellie. In carefully modulated tones he continued, "Am I correct in assuming that you are the new arrival from Denver?"

"The new arrival from Denver! Listen to that! News travels fast in Wynfield. How did you know?"

"Welcome, Ellie," laughed Lib Meecham. "We don't get too many citizens from Denver, as you might imagine. Your arrival here is big news. Why, I bet Rose has already started her column on you. And to answer your original question, Kate at the front desk alerted Arthur and me this morning. Did she say you were in 209?"

"That's right. Rose and I are neighbors. Do you think I am in good hands?"

They all laughed at this and turned to Rose, who, at this remark, was blushing. She could feel the creep of color warming her cheeks.

"Rose, you didn't tell me you were the 'Village Voice.' What's this about a column?"

"*Facta non verba*; literally, deeds not words," volunteered Arthur Everett. Then he expanded. "Rose is our resident writer. She is the founder, publisher, columnist, you-name-it of our in-house paper. *Wynsong*. And a damn fine job she does. As we say in the Mother Tongue, "*Orator fit, poeta nascitur.*"

"What did you say that time, Arthur?" asked Lib.

"Literally, an orator is made, a poet is born. Rose is Wynfield's resident poet."

The four enjoyed another laugh and then Rose sat back to observe Ellie as she chatted, perfunctorily at first and then more animatedly, with Lib and Arthur. Ellie had slipped into an obviously expensive navy knit dress that flattered her ample curves. Her blond hair, tonight more ash blond than gray, fell in loose waves around her face. Rose did not need to look around to realize that every pair of eyes in the room was focused on Ellie. But they reacted the same way to every new resident.

Plates of steaming consommé were placed before each of them. The clank-clank of spoons silenced conversation for some minutes. All at the table were suddenly struck with pangs of hunger.

"I think this evening calls for wine, don't you, ladies?" proffered Arthur, glancing first at Lib, then Rose, and finally, Ellie, who was clearly enjoying her role as featured guest.

"Wine?" repeated Ellie. "Why, Arthur, how special. I would enjoy that. Rose, you neglected to tell me about such an amenity. I never thought about that here."

"And why not wine? This is our home. I suspect that many of us enjoyed the pleasure of wine with our meals before we moved to Wynfield. I see no reason to stop simply because of a change of venue. What is it they say? "A day without wine is like a day without sunshine." Arthur was reveling in his status as host as much as Ellie hers as guest.

"I can't boast," he continued, "that the Wynfield Farms' cellars rank among the finest on the East coast, but I can state with some certainty that they shelter some quite acceptable potables. Especially the house Cabernet Sauvignon. May I assume everyone will drink the red?" Arthur watched as the three women nodded vigorously as he summoned Faye to place his order.

"I mentioned that we did eat well, Ellie. I'll take you by the office in the morning and show you the meal preference slips we fill out in advance. That way there are no surprises. Tonight you'll get the standard: roast beef." Having said this, Rose remembered her first evening meal at Wynfield. Before she had a chance to reconstruct the occasion in her mind, the exact meal was placed before her and the others at the table.

Faye arrived with the carafe of Sauvignon and smiled as she

was introduced to Ellie. Arthur Everett sipped deeply, then bowed his assent, and Faye filled glasses all around.

Pouring the wine, *Faye stole a glance at the new resident. Now this one's a real looker! I'll wager she'll liven up the second floor. A real match for Miz McNess.*

The beef was excellent ("English cut, I'm glad to say," pronounced Arthur); the potato croquettes crusty on the outside and melting on the inside; the tiny peas, lackluster in content and color. Hot rolls were passed. "Wynfield's bread is always delicious," contributed Lib.

"I must admit," confessed Ellie, pausing to pat her mouth with the generous linen napkin, "that the meal measures up to this magnificent room. I do not think the picture in the brochure does it justice. Or is it because I was ravenous tonight?"

Her three companions smiled serenely, even smugly, not unlike proud parents whose children have just been praised.

The remainder of the meal passed in a pleasant, constant hum of effortless conversation. Rose watched Ellie become equally attentive to Lib, then Arthur. She listened as her friend parried their questions about her former life and her decision to come East. Ellie chatted with the confidence of someone who had always met life head on, no matter what the circumstances.

Arthur is being positively debonair tonight, mused Rose. *He does enjoy the ladies! And a chance to spout his Latin. He is a consummate gentleman; knows how to make one feel downright girlish.*

Arthur's voice broke into her thoughts.

"More wine, ladies? Last of the carafe, I'm afraid. Here, a jot for each of us. In vino veritas! Who knows what secrets shall unfold? Thank you, Faye; no more this evening."

He smiled at Faye who had adroitly served their table and three others. The foursome continued their unhurried pleasure in parfaits and Sanka and quiet talk.

Lib Meecham was more articulate and expansive than Rose had ever known her to be. *Our visit on the ridge is paying dividends,* Rose concluded. Lib's delicate face was softer in the low lighting and she wore a deep blue blouse with ruffles at the neck.

It was clear from her explanation to Ellie that she was familiar with virtually every book in the Wynfield Library. Rose listened as Lib invited Ellie to join her for the next meeting of *FOOTNOTES*.

"It's Rose's doing; she began our literary group and then insisted I take over, under the guise that I knew more about current literary trends. Say you'll come, Ellie."

"Well, it is something to think about," said Ellie.

"Tell her what good times we have, Rose!"

"Oh, we do, indeed. Doesn't matter if you have read the book or not. Discussion even gets a bit raucous at times."

Arthur Everett *tsked-tsked* at this tidbit. "My dear Ellie, beware or you shall find yourself in the clutches of the Bloomsbury brigands of Wynfield."

Ellie considered this last remark before both Lib and Arthur began plying her with inquiries about the new airport in Denver. No one noticed the handsome woman standing beside the table until a cultured voice interrupted their talk.

"Cards tonight, Arthur?" questioned the striking reed of a woman in an understated, silk shirtwaist dress. Steel gray hair escaped in wisps from the bun pinned haphazardly at the nape of her neck. The single strand of pearls at her throat was the only evidence of excess visible on her person. The pearls were so large and so perfectly matched they gave the immediate impression that the wearer had been born with them. Rose felt convinced of this, and convinced that the pearls were never, ever, removed.

Right hand resting firmly on Arthur's left shoulder, the woman again asked, "Cards tonight, Arthur?"

"Ah, my dear Mrs. Keynes-Livingston, the card shark of Wynfield," cried Arthur, struggling to rise at his place with the woman's hand still gripping his shoulder. "But of course! First, here is someone you must meet. Mrs. Eloise Johnson, may I present Mrs. Keynes-Livingston?"

Mrs. Keynes-Livingston released Arthur's shoulder and extended long, tapering fingers to Ellie.

"How do you do? Welcome to Wynfield Farms, Mrs. Johnson."

"Ellie, please. Thank you. I am very happy to be here."

Rose watched this not-so-chance encounter between the patrician Mrs. Keynes-Livingston and Ellie. *She's been eyeing Ellie all evening. Just waiting for an opportunity to saunter over for an introduction. Why does that woman make me feel unsettled? Is it her height?*

"Will that be all, ladies and gentleman?" broke in Faye. She was clearing away remaining dessert plates. "More Sanka, Mr. Everett? Cup looks like it has a hole in it."

Arthur Everett chuckled and shook his head, enjoying their standing joke.

"No, but thanks for everything, Faye," said Rose, speaking for the group.

"Well, I'll run along then," continued Faye. "Waitress will finish; don't hurry. I have a meal going up, so, if you'll excuse me, I'll take it while it's hot."

Rose, Lib, Arthur and Mrs. Keynes-Livingston exchanged solemn looks.

"Second floor, Faye?" ventured Rose.

"Yep. I'm off," replied Faye.

Still wearing a rather somber expression Rose stood and looked over at Lib. "Thank you for saving places, Lib. A lovely dinner with good friends. Arthur, the wine was the perfect complement. And now, if you will excuse me, I am heading upstairs. I know Max is wondering about his walk. Ellie, are you ready, or do you feel like lingering?"

I will at least give her an "out," thought Rose.

"I most certainly am ready. Suddenly I'm exhausted. Yesterday's miles are catching up with me. Thank you all for such a pleasant dinner. Lib, Arthur, Mrs. Keynes-Livingston. Good night!"

Ellie smiled at each of them in turn as she repeated their names.

Rose stood aside to let her friend precede her through the double doors, noting that there were few other residents remaining in the Dining Room. She walked beside Ellie down the corridor.

"Rose," whispered Ellie, "I am not deaf and blind. Why did

everyone at our table suddenly look worried and lose their tongues when Faye announced she was carrying a meal upstairs? Is that a no-no?"

"It's not that it isn't allowed," replied Rose. "Rather, just not done. If you are too sick for meals, then you should be in the Nursery. That's what we call the Health Care Unit. And it's not a bad spot, a mini-hospital right here. This meal business has happened too many times though, in the past few weeks. We are puzzled by it. Actually, I think we are all rather envious: 'meals on wheels.' Another of Wynfield's little mysteries, Ellie."

"But not one we have to solve tonight, is it? I am exhausted, but what an exhilarating evening! Such lovely people. Good food, good wine, good company. Who could ask for more?"

Tonight's dinner has been Ellie's first triumph. I never doubted that it would be otherwise. Must follow up on that extra putti on the mantel face. I have the strangest premonition about that. Better watch it; my friends will start calling me the House Snoop. And just who is it on Two that requires "meals on wheels"?

~~~

~~~

E C H O E S

Mary Elizabeth Greenway Rector

MARY RECTOR holds the distinction of being Wynfield Farms' first resident! She moved here five years ago from her home near Winchester. Widowed, Mary has one grown son who lives in Pennsylvania.

Mary was a part of Wynfield Farms' beginnings. She remembers many meals when she was the only guest in our now-crowded dining room. "And the food was delicious, right from the start!" says Mary.

Mary has a large Barbie collection and is always on the lookout for additions to her dolls and their wardrobes. Mary also enjoys Wynfield's many outings and bus trips.

When you spot a rosy lady waiting for the bus, stop and greet Mary Rector!

Rose McNess.

~~~
~~~

7

Bzzz . . . Bzzz . . . Bzzz.

Rose turned onto her right side and reached across to silence the buzzing alarm of the clock radio that occupied most of the bedside table. She searched the glowing numerals: 6:01. *Should I get up? Max hasn't budged.* She propped herself on one elbow and looked at the black Scottie, a curved apostrophe on his tartan bed. The corner posts of her bed were barely visible in the feeble light. Solid posts. Dependable posts. They reminded Rose of the prayer her children used to recite at bedtime. How did it go? *Something about ". . . Matthew, Mark, Luke and John, bless the bed I lie on . . . four angels 'round my head; one to watch, one to pray, two to bear my soul away . . ." Wonder if that frightened the children when they were small? Goodness, that was a long time ago.*

Another dark morning. The nights are definitely growing longer. Why, it's dawn but looks as if it were four in the morning. Perhaps this eastern exposure isn't telling me all I should know about today's weather. For a half-second Rose pondered her choice of location. She knew she had not wanted the western side with rooms hot in mid afternoon and the glare so intense the curtains would have to be pulled every day at three. And the apartments facing north were all two-bedroom suites; she didn't require more space.

No, this is exactly right. As if confirming the wisdom of her choice she stretched luxuriously and snuggled once more under the soothing warmth of the electric blanket.

As a matter of fact, Rose said, half-aloud, *why do I keep that clock set for six? I have absolutely no reason to get up this early. Am I getting crazy in my old age? No, you old fool,* she answered herself, *you are merely a creature of habit. Matthew always got up early and so did I. "Hate to waste the morning, Rose," he would say. "Best time of the day for thinking."*

A smile came to Rose's face as she thought of Matthew, her second husband.

Best time of the day for snuggling, too, she remembered. Ah, Matthew! What would you think of my moving to Wynfield?

Rose was now fully awake. She drew the second goose down pillow close, doubling it under the one cradling her head. Pulling the blanket taut she could tuck it around her shoulders. Thus propped against the broad headboard and snug in a blue cocoon of electronic coziness, Rose McNess considered the prospects of her life.

If only a cup of coffee would mysteriously appear! I would do some serious thinking. Matthew didn't even require coffee. He got up, dressed, went straight to the kitchen and fixed his cereal and toast. Brought me my coffee before I was out of bed. Such a kind man! Rose smiled again at her memories.

She stretched once more in the double bed, silently offering her daily thanksgiving for a small body that had, so far, not betrayed her by breaking down in crucial hip, knee or shoulder joints. *After 70, Lord, we all start crumbling. Just like the sign on the highways: Road Work Ahead.*

Rose simultaneously thanked the Almighty and said a prayer for her less fortunate friends. *Please watch over Mrs. Hopgood and that skittish walker of hers and keep an eye on Mary. And don't let me break a hip on that patch of uneven pathway by the lake.*

She considered her bed. *Thank heavens I didn't let Annie persuade me to trade this old bed for one of those efficiency numbers. What did she call them? "High rise with trundle." I don't want anyone sleeping up here with me. That is precisely why there are guest rooms downstairs and motels in the village. And I do not mind one bit if my large bed makes the alcove crowded. I'm the one who changes the sheets. I've slept in this bed too many years to give it up now. Forty-plus years, two lovely husbands. Yes, I am a creature of habit.*

Rose smiled again, a deeply satisfied smile.

After I'm dead they can burn this bed if they choose. Of course, it matches the bureau I gave to Rob and Judy. Well, that will be up to them. I've been fair about dividing the furniture . . . or else all three were good liars. They've been grateful for things I've tried to do for them along the years. They know gifts I've given have been from my heart. I am a fortunate woman to have three good children.

Thinking of her offspring, all married, all presumedly happy, all preoccupied with the care and feeding of their own children, Rose again offered her thanks to the Almighty.

"Thank you, Father, for I know I am blessed among women," she spoke softly in the stillness. Since her first husband Tom's death, forty-five years ago, Rose had accepted God as an intimate friend. Whispering the simplest offerings, as now, Rose felt as though she had slipped her hand into God's and had been answered with a comforting squeeze. Her faith in His response was rock-solid. She had never confided her beliefs to anyone, not even Annie. This belief, that God was there for her personally, as an intimate and listening friend, was far too private to verbalize.

What started me on this? Thinking about the children? Oh . . . I was reminding myself again how fortunate I was to have caring children. Poor Ellie—"neither chick nor child" as she expressed it. Just Vincent. Named for Van Gogh, I wonder?

Why has Ellie's arrival perked me up so much? My adrenaline is positively working overtime. What did she ask the other night: was I happy here? Maybe I am just realizing that I am really and truly happy and content here. That could cause my heart to flutter a bit faster. At the pinnacle of my life I have reached a momentous self-realization. Even though I think I've always been a fairly happy person, I do believe I have become even happier since moving to Wynfield. I have a purpose here, if only to smile each morning. And I have Ellie to thank for making me step back and see that. I guess it takes longer to spot the truth as one grows older. Just as it takes longer to do everything else.

Brrr. Older! Merely thinking that word caused Rose to shiver. She glanced at the clock.

Seven-fifteen! I have been woolgathering one hour and fifteen minutes! No wonder I spend my days in a perpetual rush trying to grab the minutes that flew away.

Guilt swiftly propelled Rose from the warm bed. Switching off the blanket controls she watched Max stretch and sit up sleepily. Rose padded into the bathroom to attend to her morning ministrations. Completing these she grabbed her flannel robe hanging on the back of the bathroom door and entered her minuscule kitchen.

"OK, old friend," Rose greeted Max, "one minute. Let me put the coffee on first."

She had just poured water into the coffee maker when the piercing ring of the telephone shattered the silence.

"Seven-fifteen? Who would call this early? One of the children?" With a mother's intuition about early morning or late night calls, Rose hurried to snatch the phone.

"Good morning, Rose McNess here."

"Mother! It's Anne." The ebullient voice leaped into the room.

"Oh, Annie! How good to hear your voice, even at this early hour."

"I didn't wake you, did I, Mother?" asked Anne, the latter more a statement than question. "You are always up with the birds." Anne Brewster hated her mother's use of the diminutive form of her name but somehow could never summon the courage, or right moment, to correct her.

"Of course I'm up," Rose protested. "I must admit that I am

just up, however, and I have to walk Max before he pops. So what is going on with you?"

"Something fantastic!" Anne's voice rose with excitement. "Tom is coming home in three days!"

The news of Anne's son, Rose's oldest grandchild, sent a shiver of pleasure along Rose's spine and caused goose pimples to prick the sleeves of her flannel wrapper. *Coming home safely! Oh, thank you, Father!* Rose hugged the receiver to her chest and looked at the ceiling in silent prayer.

"Mother, did you hear me?"

"Yes, darling, of course I heard you. I'm too excited to talk. And thankful. When did you hear?"

"He called last night from London. Has a flight the day after tomorrow, Heathrow to JFK. He'll stop in Princeton for a few days and get home soon after that."

"London? How did he get from Tokyo to London, or wherever he started?"

"Mother, you know as much about it as I do. All I do know is that he is on his way home. And I am so thankful."

"I know you are, dear. And wild with excitement; I can hear it in your voice. You know how I feel about your Tom. I can't wait to see him, but I'll practice my patience. He has lots more important things to do than visit his old granny in the retirement home."

"Now, Mother . . . " came the patronizing voice of a wounded daughter. Anne heard this last statement as a cry of self-pity.

"Now, Annie, listen to me. I am not feeling sorry for myself. Sorry if it came out that way. I am just being realistic when I say that Tom will have plenty to do after two years abroad than rush right over to Wynfield. I shall practice my patience, gladly."

This seemed to mollify Anne.

"You know how he feels about you, Mother. Just don't expect him immediately. But I knew you'd want the latest bulletin on his whereabouts."

"I'd be furious if you had not called. Thank you, dear. Anything else going on?"

"Not really. How about you? Tour business still in operation?"

"Of course. Better every day and I have a new member."

"Who's that?" asked Anne.

"Who's what?" countered Rose.

"Mother, your new passenger. You said you had a new tour member."

"Sorry, darling. My mind was wandering. I'm watching Max at the door and thinking about Tom and trying to talk to you. What I meant was that two days ago a lovely person from Denver arrived here at Wynfield Farms. She is delightful and happens to have moved into 209, right across the hall. And just happens to share my fondness for martinis."

"Mother! Splendid! You sound positively smitten with her. Does she make martinis as well as Matt did? What's her name? How did she get to Virginia from Colorado?" Anne was as curious as Rose had been.

"Eloise Johnson. Ellie. But I really have to go, darling. I wish you could see poor Max. He is sitting pitifully by the door. And I have a busy day ahead. Aren't you glad to hear me say that?"

"I'll let you run. I've got to get moving myself. I've never worried about your running out of projects. I just worry about your running. I'm so afraid you'll slip and fall. Please be careful! And Mother, you'd better write to your sons. I had a call from Rob *and* Paul wondering how you were getting along. Even a postcard would do . . . "

"I need to do that. Thanks for reminding me. And I will be careful, dear. Thanks so much for letting me in on the good news. It means more than you know. Always special to have something to look forward to! Love you!"

"Love you, Mother."

Their farewell ritual completed, Rose replaced the receiver on the ridiculously slim instrument resting on the lamp table and continued to sit for a moment in her one comfortable chair, the worn wing chair by the window. She looked to the northeast. The sun was barely discernible over the blue Virginia mountains. It gave faint assurance that the October day was going to hold much light or warmth.

Max had settled down in his 'rug position' by the door and seemed resigned to wait.

Rose's thoughts were filled with news of her grandson. She was unabashedly fond of Tom. But, she reflected, she had shown the utmost discretion about her feelings around the other five grandchildren and their parents. They all seemed to think her pride in Tom was due mostly to the fact that, of the six grandchildren, he was the only one to follow his grandfather's path to Princeton. Rose allowed them to think that.

What they did not realize was that Tom was so like his grandfather in so many ways he could not help but endear himself to Rose. He kept Rose in touch with his generation. What's more, he seemed to value Rose's opinions and asked for her ideas on relationships and career possibilities. Rose secretly thought Tom got along better with her than he did with his own mother. And his letters from Japan these two years! Their arrival had been the high point in Rose's day. Annie's excitement was contagious; Rose hugged herself in anticipation of Tom's return.

"Poor Max! I've made you wait, haven't I?" crooned Rose as she quickly struggled up from the depths of her chair. "I won't even dress," she said, pulling on worn moccasins and her heavy raincoat hanging on the hook in the hall. She snapped on Max's leash and opened the door for both of them. Rose knew that the likelihood of meeting many early morning walkers at Wynfield was slim to nonexistent. Besides, after hearing Annie's happy news she felt she could outdistance the best of them.

~~~

At 8:20 Rose and Max hurried back through the side doors of the Wynfield Reception Hall, returning eagerly to the warmth of the room after their brisk hike. It was chilly for October. The grass and leaves had been wet with dew that would not burn off until midmorning. Faint but welcoming aromas of coffee and sage-laced sausage now assaulted Rose's nostrils and made her hungrier than she had thought possible. She wavered a moment.
~~~

Sausage and fried apples? One of my favorites. For a brief instant she regretted her decision not to eat breakfast in the Dining Room. Max, panting at his morning's exertions, dragged himself wearily to the desk and stretched full-length at Rose's feet as she stopped to speak to Kate Alexander.

"Good morning, Kate," sang out Rose.

"Good morning to you, Mrs. McNess," returned Kate. "And good morning to you, Mr. Max," she added, leaning over and scratching Max behind his ears. "All right to give him a treat, Mrs. McNess?"

"Just a half, Kate; neither of us has had breakfast. And Max doesn't need to add one more ounce. But a half-biscuit to be social; he would love that."

Both women watched as the recumbent Max sprang to life with the mention and presentation of a treat and then collapsed with it on the rug.

"You don't eat breakfast in the Dining Room, Mrs. McNess?"

"No, Kate, never have. Breakfast is so simple, really, I prefer it on my own. But then I may view things a bit differently from others."

"Each to his own," offered a smiling Kate.

She really is a lovely young woman, concluded Rose. *Wonderful red hair. About twenty-three, twenty-four years old?*

"Kate, what's the latest on Mary? Has the bank dropped charges?"

"I think so, Mrs. McNess. Miss Moss and the lawyer zoomed off yesterday afternoon to meet with the bank officials. At least they didn't cart Mary off to jail. I think Miss Moss wishes they could. I'm sorry, that was extremely unprofessional of me . . ."

"You are forgiven, Kate. I think you and I are allies in our thinking. But best to be silent allies. I'll go and see Mary today."

"Oh, would you? And when you go, could you . . ." Kate hesitated, her face clouding with lines of distress.

"What is it, Kate?"

"Well, there's another problem. Another *Mary* problem.

She's been . . . peeing in everyone's apartment. And here!" The young woman pointed to two large towel-covered areas on the rug behind her desk.

"Kate!" Rose cried. "I don't believe it. On second thought, I do believe it. It is Mary's cry for attention. Pour soul! Yes, I'll go to see her today, this morning if I can."

"And Mrs. McNess," Kate went on, smiling now, "those panty liners? I'm sure the store sells them. Could you take a box of those up to her and sort of, well, insist that she try them."

"Of course, Kate. Leave it to me. Sorry to rush but these delicious smells are making me weak in the knees. Now don't you worry about Mary; I'll see her today!"

With a good-by Rose and Max exited up the stairs to the second floor. Rose was so preoccupied with how Mary's latest capers must be giving Miss Moss apoplexy that she almost bumped into a lean, sallow man making his way down. She paused mid-stairs to allow him to pass.

"Good morning, Mr. Jenkins. Bob, isn't it?"

Mr. Jenkins was stepping cautiously down the steps, his face in anguished concentration. His mouth was moving as if he were calculating the precise distance between risers and treads. *He looks,* Rose mused, *like a predatory bird ready to pounce on a grub.*

"Good morning to you, Rose McNess. And Bob it is. Don't tell me you've been outside?"

"Yes, indeed! Max and I have at least three walks a day, four if I can manage. This early morning one is his favorite." Rose was tempted to add, "and you should try it . . . ," thinking that the bracing air would put some color in Bob Jenkins' pallid cheeks.

"You are brave, Rose. Me, I never walk outside. My feet never touch the ground."

"But . . . why not?" asked Rose, shocked at this admission. *Why, he's the one I've been secretly calling The Virginia creeper!*

"Reducing my hazards. I do not trust natural surfaces. Nothing is absolutely even. Too many bumps and ridges. Person could trip over a pebble and wham! Plaster for eight months. Or longer. No sirree, just call me 'the Prowler.' I log about three miles a day through the hallways. Not counting the stairs. That's what I am doing this morning, measuring the mileage of the stairs. Walk outside? Never. Reduce your hazards, Rose, reduce your hazards!"

With that exchange they both continued their respective ways, Mr. Jenkins to the foot of the steps and Rose and Max up to Apartment 208.

We learn something new every day, Max! I bet he taught algebra or calculus where nothing was left to chance. Maybe he's a hopeless romantic under that pale skin but he still stalks like a bird. He's correct about the terrain, but what a pessimistic philosophy in this beautiful countryside. "Reduce your hazards"; that might just be the watchword for each of us! There are all sorts of hazards out there.

Rose, opening the apartment door, caught sight of a white envelope resting on the Delft blue carpet.

Bother! What is this? Too big for an invitation; looks more like a summons.

Closing the door, Rose pulled off her raincoat and picked up the envelope. "Occupant, Apartment 208." *That's me,* she thought wryly.

A maize sheet of paper fluttered out as Rose opened the envelope. Rose retrieved this and read:

RESIDENTS' MEETING
10:30 A.M. FRIDAY, OCTOBER 22
SOUTH LOUNGE
Please be prompt! NO PETS.
Miss A. Elvina Moss,
Resident Manager

What, Rose asked herself, *could be so important that a meeting has to be held with a mere two hours' notice? Emergency? Quarantine? Evacuation? Ah, we travel better with a full stomach, don't we, Max?*

Rose hurried to fix Max his usual Senior Canine breakfast

and then indulged herself with a soft-scrambled egg, croissant, and her first cup of coffee of the day.

The best laid plans . . . ah, me. I'll start my column on Jana after I get dressed. And I must write the boys. Guess I have to go to this meeting, and Ellie certainly should. Bother! It simply kills the morning. But go I shall, reducing my hazards! I like that: Reduce your hazards! A battle cry for the AARP!

~~~

~~~

WYNSONG

WHISPERS

Do you realize you are living in the footsteps of one of America's greatest citizens?

Thomas Jefferson!

Not only was our third President born a mere one hundred miles away, near Charlottesville, but he admired and owned one of the Seven Natural Wonders of the World that looms just twenty miles away: Natural Bridge. Majestic Monticello, his dream home, sits high atop a "little mountain" outside Charlottesville, and his sunny summer home, Poplar Forest, is near Lynchburg. Each is but a day trip from Wynfield Farms. Indeed, the energetic Mr. Jefferson literally covered the state with his explorations and acquisitions.

But historian I don't pretend to be, and what I wanted to share with you today was another aspect of Jefferson's personality.

He was an optimist. He regarded the glass as half-full, not half-empty. Jefferson forged ahead with seemingly impossible ideas, as monumental as the Lewis and Clark expedition or as minute as one that appears trivial in comparison: what varietal grape to plant in the Monticello vineyard? He was, in truth, a dreamer.

I share with you one of my favorite Jeffersonian quotations:

"Friendship is precious, not only in shade,
but in the sunshine of life . . .
and, thanks to a benevolent arrangement of things,
the better part of life is sunshine."

Thomas Jefferson,
October, 1786

As the fall days grow shorter, let's keep the sunshine in our lives.

R.McN.

~~~
~~~

SUNDAY MORNING

Leave the shuttered windows.
Gray light feebly knocks for entrance,
   blurring the still cocoon of the bedroom.
Wake the sleeping dog.
He stretches, yawns, feigns a sneeze
   then lurches on unsteady legs down darkened
stairs.
Start the fecund coffee maker.
It will simmer, steam and fill our addiction
   as aromas tease impatient cravings.
Rescue the paper.
That turgid orange lozenge floats on dripping steps
   while we forestall news of deaths and debts.
Climb back in bed with me.
This is what Sunday mornings were meant to be.

~~~

Rose McNess
~~~

8

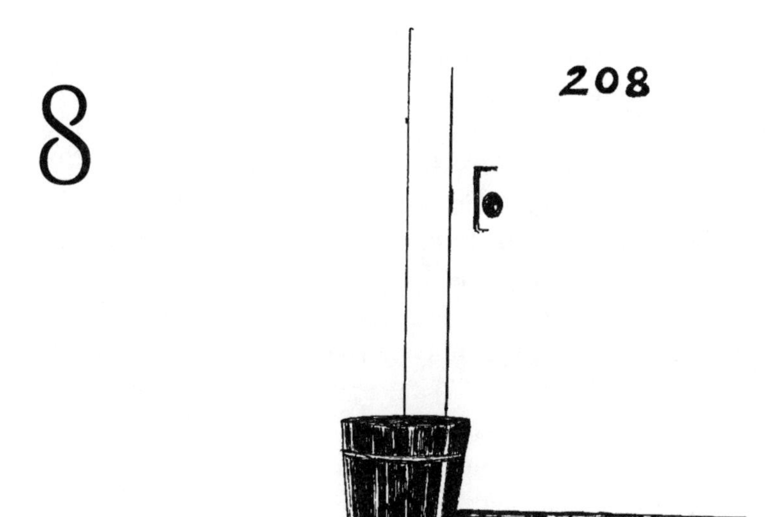

Rose positioned her office trash basket squarely in front of the portal and shut the door with such force that it rattled.

"There. If my neighbors don't know by this time what the dustbin by the door means, I'm here to tell them. Bother Miss Moss, anyway. Letters to write, Mary to tend to, Jana's profile to finish. And now a meeting in two hours. It better be important. Maybe, Max, I 'll be able to finish this 'Echoes' before the meeting starts."

Rose sat down at her desk and rolled the paper in her ancient Smith-Corona electric typewriter and shoved her glasses up the bridge of her nose.

Now Jana's a real lulu! Rose picked her way slowly over keys that occasionally stuck and tabulators that constantly balked. *Fascinating life she has led. Hope this doesn't make her sound too zany. Wish we could persuade her to sing. A native of the Czech Republic who speaks fluent French, Italian and German and calls her dog something French and now lives in Virginia. "The Queen of Prague": that should be the title of this profile!*

Rose typed and recalled her first impression of Jana Zdorek.

At first, Rose had thought she was merely eccentric, an older woman striving to disguise her age with layers of eclectic clothing and habits to match. But after observing her in the Library, the Dining Room and at various residents' gatherings, Rose had changed her mind. She concluded that Jana was a true original. Just like an authentic curio or valued antique, Jana was to be prized for her rarity. Her mind was razor sharp and she displayed a keen intellect. She listened eagerly to her companions and asked thoughtful, insightful questions. Remarkably, for Jana was well into her eighties, she wore no hearing aid, no dentures, and no bifocals. And walked sans cane or crutch. Jana was, no doubt about it, an aristocrat. Rose hoped that she had conveyed this fact ever so discreetly in her profile.

Madame Zdorek had invited Rose to her apartment for the interview. The apartment was the largest of the two-bedroom suites on the west wing. Not for Madame Zdorek a small studio! This elegant woman had filled her home with *objets d'art*, books, pillows, swags of brilliant fabric, and, huge pots of grasses and flowers that she had gathered in wanderings over the Wynfield grounds. All of this was packed into her apartment along with a piano, a collection of classical recordings and the trappings that belonged to her constant companion, an apricot poodle named Mille Fleurs. Jana had confided to Rose the name meant the plant, hydrangea, "thousand flowers," and her pet was more precious to her than ten thousand flowers. She addressed the dog in French: Fleur.

Rose pulled the page from the machine and glanced at the clock. It was 9:21. *What in the world could be so important that we all have to meet this morning? Surely Miss Moss would not humiliate Mary Rector in front of the entire group. It would never do to miss the meeting, I suppose. Have to set a good example for Ellie. I'll collect her in a moment. What do I wear, Max?*

Rose reached into the spacious closet and chose navy slacks. From the neat row of six hangers bearing six starched blouses she chose a navy and tan tattersall checked blouse with long sleeves. She looped a red scarf under the collar and knotted it in front. On this she fastened the gold Scottie pin that Tom had bought her in Princeton. She brushed her short, more gray-than-brown hair until it crackled, then gave it a quick *poof* of hair spray. Looking into her bathroom mirror for the first time that morning she carefully applied a soft shade of red lipstick and swiped at her nose with a thin powder puff. *I don't want to be one of those old dames in fire engine red lipstick. Well, Rose, how do I look? Not so bad for an over-the-hill senior,* she answered herself. *Even a senior with lines as deep as the Dixie Caverns etched on her face.* Rose tucked her shirt under the waistband of her slacks. *They still fit! A minor miracle after all these good meals. Must be my walking; better keep at it. I'd a whole lot rather be a prune than a balloon!*

Rose was still purring like a tabby cat over the news of Tom's imminent return. She grinned, thinking of him. She thought about her new neighbor and continued to grin. *And I finished the piece on Jana . . . I feel positively giddy with good will. Nothing is going to undermine my mood today: not Miss Moss, not pseudo-bank robberies, not poor Mary.*

Knock-Knock. The noise startled and annoyed her until she heard "Rose? Are you there? It's me, Ellie."

Rose hurried to admit her friend. "Ellie! You beat me to it, come on in."

"Is it trash day, Rose?" Ellie asked, pointing to the trash basket.

"No, it's neither trash nor cleaning day, Ellie. I should have explained. I think all my other neighbors know about it by now. When my trash basket sits outside my door it means do not disturb. It's a tradition I borrowed from Cambridge University many years ago. I just like the civility of it."

"I'm so sorry. I burst in on you. I'll leave right now. . . ."

"No, no, I'm all through typing. Finis! Don't apologize; you had no way of knowing what it meant. Here, I'll bring it in now. I was just coming over to collect you for the meeting. Glad to see you up and dressed. Sleep well last night?" Rose recalled vividly her own first sleepless nights at Wynfield.

"Thank you, dear," came the chortling, throaty voice. "I slept like the dead. Whoops! Guess that's not a good analogy, but I did sleep well, thanks. Best night yet. The cot they brought up to me felt like a feather bed. First thing I heard were footsteps back and forth in the hallway. Your 'Virginia Creeper,' I suppose?"

"I'm sure of it," confirmed Rose. "Only he calls himself 'the Prowler'; I met him on the stairs this morning. Bob Jenkins, a rather pale, pedantic sort of a fellow. A harmless prowler, I assure you. Ellie, have you had any breakfast?"

"As a matter of fact, I have. Matron Moss saw to that when she sent Romero to fetch the cot. He brought me juice and muffins and a cup of cool instant coffee. But at least it was coffee. And he also brought me a notice of this morning's meeting. What is this about, Rose?"

"Ellie, I'll be perfectly honest; I have no idea! To meet you? That's a good reason but I don't believe it's the only reason. Could be a warning: Do Not Visit Your Money and Do Not Rob Banks! Miss Moss is always calling meetings but never at this hour and never on such short notice. We are not going to miss it."

"I wouldn't dream of it. Vincent will pout, naturally. I've been meaning to ask you, Rose, do many other residents have pets?"

"Quite a few," replied Rose. "You'll meet our zoo eventually. Several cats, maybe six dogs, one or two other birds. And Father Charlie has the one parrot, the gray sort that lives positively forever. Speaking of our feathered friends, have you had Vincent very long?"

"Duke gave him to me as a joke on our third anniversary. So I'm hooked, sentimentally. Actually, I've grown quite fond of the little yellow devil. He's uncomplaining, doesn't eat much and is good company. I need something to take care of. But today's meeting is not about pets, is it?"

"Good heavens, no. Even Miss Rolling Stone wouldn't toss out someone's ancient cat if it howled too loud."

"Miss Rolling Stone? Pardon?"

"Oops. That slipped out, Ellie. 'Miss Rolling Stone' is my private appellation for A. Elvina Moss. You know . . . 'A rolling stone gathers no moss.' Not to be repeated outside these doors."

"My lips are sealed."

"Ellie, you should know that Miss Moss sees everything, hears everything, senses things before they happen here at Wynfield. Call her prescient, if you will. I know that Faye would never tattle about bringing meals up to Miss Puffenbarger, if that's who has been getting them. But old Rolling Stone could have sniffed it out. The impropriety of it would offend the old gal. I bet that is it! Emergency meeting because of two or three 'meals on wheels.' "

"Could Miss Puffenbarger be seriously ill?"

"Possibly. Too sick to go down for meals and too afraid to go to the Nursery. And too proud to ask any one of us for assistance. I told you, she is virtually a recluse, an extremely private individual."

"Aren't most of us?"

"To a point," responded Rose. "But here at Wynfield one has to socialize to some extent. It's a simple matter of survival for us seniors. Miss Puffenbarger seldom leaves her apartment. I mean, rarely. And if she does, one day she may greet you with a smile and the next, pass you by as if she had never seen you before. And it's not just me; I've seen her do the same thing to Major Featherstone and Vinnie. A singular lady. But if anyone can bring her out, Ellie, I think it's going to be you. We'd best be on our way, don't you agree?"

"You have an exalted opinion of me, Rose; I'm eager to meet our mutual neighbor. I'm ready; do I look presentable?"

"Perfect, Ellie, just as lovely as last night. You'll be glad you wore slacks; it's fairly casual here. Common sense sort of dressing. Evening and special events are the only time we get really dolled up. That's a heavenly shade of mauve you're wearing; good looking!"

Rose picked up the neatly folded copy for *Wynsong* and placed it in the depths of her Coach purse. She double-checked to verify that both stove and coffee maker were turned off (they were) and reached into the Maggie Walker shortbread box (long ago converted into a repository for Max's treats) and took out a milk bone for Max.

"Sorry, old man, but you are excluded this morning. Here's a treat; you've been a good fellow. Mother will be back soon. Ready, Ellie?"

The two friends bounced through the door of Apartment 208.

"All right, Rose, I'm in your hands. Lead on! Let the adventure begin!"

~~~

~~~

WHISPERS

Bon Bons (More or Less)

(A recipe learned at my mother's apron strings. So many of you have asked me for this recipe that I am happy to share it.)

1 pound box confectioner's sugar
1/2 to 1 pound REAL butter
1 Tablespoon vanilla flavoring
1/2 Tablespoon almond flavoring

Mix well with your hands, then knead, pinch off and roll into small balls. Refrigerate. Melt 1/2 stick paraffin with 1 bar semi-sweet chocolate. I use an empty mandarin orange can for this mixture. It is perfect dipping height and fits neatly in a pan of boiling water.

Dip hardened balls into chocolate mixture. Cool on wax paper. Sometimes I decorate with a pecan. Makes about 6 dozen if you don't eat too many along the way. These are delightful Christmas goodies and so easy to make. (Calories don't count at holiday time!)

Rose and Max

~~~
~~~

9

Rose linked her arm through Ellie's as they strolled down the corridor.

"This will be a good opportunity for you to meet many of the other residents, Ellie. I'm afraid I've been selfish with your time. You'll see that not everyone is as opinionated or outspoken as I am."

"If they are all as nice as our table mates last evening I could not ask for more. Everyone looks so *young* here, Rose. Perhaps it's a Martini Secret. Shall I ask if anyone makes a martini as well as you do?" teased her friend.

The women laughed and continued down the stairs and into the Reception Hall. A group had assembled near Kate Alexander's desk and was chatting noisily, oblivious to the rapidly approaching meeting time.

"Wonderful!" cried Rose. "I'll introduce you to some friends right now. My favorites! Bob, Bob Lesley! And Major Featherstone! Just a minute, please!"

The amiable group turned and smiled spontaneously as they all greeted Rose and the attractive blond newcomer in the mauve pants-suit.

"Everyone—since we are pressed for time—I want you to meet my new neighbor, Ellie Johnson. She's moved into Number 209 and I want you to be nice to her!"

"We shall shower her with attention, Rose, and warn her to beware of your energetic outbursts," roared the distinguished occupant of the wheelchair.

"Ellie, this is the character I told you about: Major Featherstone."

"Light as a feather, heavy as a stone . . . that's me! And I would like you to meet Eleanor Whittington. We're all up there on Two beside you and Rose."

"So nice to meet you both," replied Ellie. She stared for an instant at the pink-and-white matron with sapphire blue eyes also seated in a wheelchair. *What a pretty face,* thought Ellie. *Hardly a wrinkle! Yet—that white hair, a few lines in her neck. Why, she must be eighty if she's a day! A true Southern belle, just as Rose described.*

"And this, Ellie, is Bob Lesley. Always good to have a doctor in the house, though he swears he doesn't make house calls anymore."

"So nice to meet you, Ellie. I know your former home; we must talk about Denver soon." Robert Preston Lesley was short and compact. His head appeared too big in proportion to his wide, solid body. This was due in part to a bush of wiry, white hair that sprouted erratically all over his skull. Ruddy cheeks and merry blue eyes did nothing to dispel the image of a slightly naughty, off-course angel. His handshake, Ellie noted, was firm. It conveyed confidence and strength. *In fact,* Ellie smiled, *Bob Lesley's entire demeanor makes me feel good. I bet he was a marvelous doctor before he retired.*

"Ahem," declared Kate Alexander, clearing her throat. "I hate to break this up but I think you'd better head for the Lounge. You know how Miss Moss can be . . . "

"Say no more, Kate," whispered Bob Lesley. "You never even saw us." And he shepherded the small procession on to the meeting.

The tall walnut case clock that stood opposite the entrance

doors to the South Lounge chimed the half-hour. Romero and Ernest finished unloading the last of the folding chairs they had placed with precision on the worn Kirman. Five or six Wynfield residents had arrived early and had selected the comfortable lounge chairs dotting the perimeter of the paneled room. They were absorbed in their morning newspapers. Mr. and Mrs. McKeever were jointly working a crossword puzzle.

High backed, well-used leather wing chairs and plump club chairs, their chintz slipcovers long faded to a brick-red sameness, were pushed against the walls. Usually these seats were scattered around randomly, and welcomed visitors for five minutes or five hours. Three game tables with waiting boards of backgammon and cribbage normally had participants poised and waiting to play.

Floor-to-ceiling shelves were stuffed with books on subjects from the African veldt to fly-fishing in Montana. Alternating with the volumes were glass cases of local wildlife—voles, a red fox, raccoons, rabbits, birds—that Mr. Wynfield had preserved in a state of mummified surprise.

Tall, old-fashioned brass floor lamps stood ready to shed circles of light on all but the far corners. With two Stubbs oils over the mantle and a collection of well-framed Audubon prints tastefully grouped on the walls, it was a room remarkable only for its atmosphere of inviting comfort.

Which is what Miss A. Elvina Moss had counted on when she scheduled a Residents' Meeting with scant notice. Heretofore, meetings had been announced at least three days in advance, with postings on all bulletin boards and "tents" on each table in the Dining Room. But this matter—rather, matters—had come up too suddenly for that. Plus, there was that other bothersome detail.

Miss Moss paced nervously in front of the fireplace. She consulted her watch and restacked the papers she placed and replaced on the sturdy Jacobean table she would use as a lectern. She peered at the doors and wondered what was keeping the residents.

Finally! Mrs. McNess and Mrs. Johnson. And here comes the Meecham woman. Ten-thirty-four. I'll wait five more minutes.

The retired Episcopal minister, Father Caldwell, eased his comfortable body onto a front-row chair. He casually crossed one khaki-clad leg over the other, bent to pull up a slumping navy sock that was inching into his scuffed left loafer and reached into his back pocket for a portion of the *Times* travel section.

"Now don't you worry, Miss Moss. Everyone will get here," he called out reassuringly. He knew instinctively from his brief association with Miss Moss that she was agitated. The meager crowd was the cause of her nervous pacing. Father Caldwell had known a few Senior Wardens with Miss Moss's attributes.

"Thank you, Father Charles." Miss Moss was the only person at Wynfield Farms who insisted on calling him "Charles." He had been "Father Charlie" since his first parish, and that was over forty-five years ago.

"You will give us a little prayer, won't you, Father? Or benediction; yes, something at the end of the meeting?" Her sallow face was almost twisted with the crushing realization that Father Charles had every right to *refuse* her request.

"Happy to, Miss Moss. You know I'm always delighted to serve." Father Charlie smiled at the angular, not-wholly unattractive woman in navy pin-striped suit who was peering at him through thick, horn-rimmed bifocals. *She is thin as a pin,* he observed. *Turned sideways she'd be a margin.* His beatific smile usually put even the most anxious supplicant's mind at ease. This morning it beamed toward a void.

"Thank you, Father. Now, if everyone would just assemble . . ."

Scraping of chairs and bursts of laughter caused Father Charlie to turn and look toward the rear of the room. *Ah! Here we come,* he thought. *Nothing but a meal gets folks out on time. Just like my old flocks, meandering in of their own accord.*

"Mind if I join you, Father?" asked Major Featherstone, deftly rolling his chair beside the rector's place. "I always liked the front pew myself!"

"Please, roll on in. I vowed that once I joined life on the *other* side of the pulpit I'd sit in the front row whenever I had the chance. Never could understand congregations filling up the back. Afraid of the preacher, perhaps. Enough room, Major?"

The Lounge was becoming crowded. The couples on Two-West came in together. Miss Hopgood teetered in, her walker adorned with a swirl of vibrant peacock-blue ribbons. Lib Meecham switched chairs and slid into the end seat on the second row. She leaned over and tapped Father Charlie's shoulder.

"Stop by the Library this afternoon if you get a chance. I have a new Inspector Morse you'll enjoy."

The last stragglers took their seats.

"Ladies and gentlemen," Miss Moss intoned. For someone who had been a ragged clutch of nerves moments before, the appearance of a full house boosted her self-assurance and gave her voice the liquidity of warm maple syrup.

"I regret very much that this meeting was called on such short notice, but circumstances dictate action. We have *much* business to discuss this morning and I shall get right to it.

"First things first. Flu and pneumonia shots. Health Care is advising that everyone have these shots if you have not already had them. Nurse has scheduled two extra doctors for this afternoon and tomorrow morning. Three to five today, nine until eleven tomorrow. In the Clinic. I know with the balmy weather we have been experiencing that *Old Man Winter* seems far away. But believe me, it is not. It is *later than you think*. Need I say more?" Her imperative voice took over and soared.

"Where do we go, Miss Mmmmmm . . . ?" Mary Rector's reedy and querulous whine carried from somewhere in the Lounge.

"The *Clinic*, Mary. And do go, please. I happen to know that you have not, as of today, availed yourself of the precautionary shots."

Rose leaned across Ellie and the three ladies ahead of her, and nudged Mary's sagging shoulder.

"Mary! I'll take you! Don't worry!"

Mary turned, her face alight with relief.

"To reiterate: today, three to five; tomorrow, nine to eleven. Flu shots in the Clinic." The voice climbed to a higher altitude.

"And now, folks . . . ," she paused, as if she were measuring the effect her pause had had on the audience, "I have news that should be of interest to each and every one of you."

Rose, frowning, felt her antennae shoot up at Miss Moss's use of the term "folks." *This woman does not exercise good judgment. We are not a troop of overage campers.*

"I know you are just holding your breath with excitement and anticipation at what I am about to say."

Oh, for heaven's sakes, growled Rose under her breath, *get on with it, please!* She looked around; the expression on everyone's face told her the entire audience harbored the same impatience.

"We have been chosen," articulated Miss Moss, plucking each word as if it were a rare pearl being pried from its oyster, "as THE residential retirement venue for the Winter issue of *Virginia Venues* magazine."

The assembled crowd was silent. One or two murmured, "Never heard of it," or "So what?"

Miss Moss was nonplused by this nonchalance. "This means that we have been selected as the very finest residential retirement facility in all of Virginia. Of course, we know this to be true but the recognition will let our light shine brighter and cast a much wider glow! The Editor and I have been in constant consultation for the past three weeks. You may see photographers around here as early as tomorrow morning. They want to 'shoot us' as we are. Tres naturellement."

This last phrase came out "trez naturemint"; mastery of the French language was not among Miss Moss's accomplishments.

Poor Miss Moss! Her few French phrases just don't roll off her tongue, thought Rose. *How in the world did she get this position? Why in the world would a person with her personality want it, dealing with people like me, like us, every day?*

The Resident Manager went on, her voice shrill with excitement as she detailed the magazine's plans for the winter issue. Exterior shots, interior shots. The staff of "VV" (as Miss Moss now began calling the publication) would cover all aspects of life at Wynfield Farms. Even a few of the residents' apartments. Mention of the latter caused some heads to turn and a number of hands to be raised.

"I will not pause for questions now, due to time constraint. I can assure you that your permission will be requested before any photographer shoots you, or your home."

She loves that word "shoot," mumbled Rose.

"Next item on the agenda. It has been suggested that we hold a Fall Festival: a genuine celebration. And since we have not had Dance Night in three weeks perhaps it would combine dancing and music. Mrs. Keynes-Livingston has graciously consented to chair this event. Mrs. Keynes-Livingston, would you like to make any announcements at this time?" Miss Moss stepped back, relinquishing her role to that unflappable lady.

Mrs. Keynes-Livingston was attired in her everyday uniform: pith helmet with chin strap; long-sleeved khaki shirt; narrow khaki skirt; tan, cotton lisle knee stockings and thick-soled ankle-high hiking boots. And pearls. She considered this her working outfit when she gathered lichen and numerous other botanical species throughout the Wynfield grounds. Obviously, Miss Moss's call for the morning assembly had disrupted her daily routine.

"Ellie, do you remember her from last night? She's the one who snared Arthur for cards."

"Surely, but what is that crazy get-up, Rose?" Ellie replied, *sotto voce*.

Rose chuckled softly. "That's her everyday attire, *including* the pearl choker, of course. She busies herself with nature. Don't know what has come over her to chair a festival!"

"Nothing to report," responded Mrs. Keynes-Livingston. "I shall be contacting various members individually regarding their contributions to the *Fete*. Just circle November 19 on your calendars." She spoke in well-modulated tones obviously practiced on Junior Leagues and Garden Clubs.

"Thank you, Mrs. Keynes-Livingston. I know that this will be a gala occasion. Aren't we looking forward to it, folks?"

"Folks" again! Looking forward to it like junket running down our throats, thought Rose.

Miss Moss now resumed her ramrod, tent-pole position with stern countenance to match.

"I have, as the young say, good news and bad news. First the good. We have a new resident from Colorado. May I present Mrs. Eloise Johnson, lately of Denver, to all of you?" She gestured dramatically with her left hand, indicating Ellie should stand.

"I just know that each of us will want to get to know Mrs. Johnson and in the days to come, extend to her a warm Virginia welcome. A real Wynfield welcome."

Ellie half-rose at her seat, smiled at the turning heads, waved quietly and then quickly sat back down.

"Now the bad news. It has come to my, ahem, attention that one or two of you have been ordering *room service* for your evening meals. *This* simply is not permitted. If you are unable to come to our lovely Dining Room for the evening serving, then your special needs must be met in the Health Care unit. I regret that I must speak about this, but it is adding additional burdens on our exceptional wait staff. I repeat: carry-out service is NOT permitted. I KNOW that I shall not have to mention this again."

Miss Moss paused portentously. She leveled her gaze at the silent, stunned audience as if fully expecting a specific monster to rise up and confess to so foul a deed.

Rose and Ellie exchanged conspiratorial glances. Rose looked around surreptitiously, hoping to see Miss Puffenbarger. She was nowhere to be seen.

"There. I believe that I have covered everything. Let me run down this list once more: flu shots, "VV," Fall Festival, Mrs. Johnson, meals." Miss Moss was talking to herself, checking off notations and rapidly losing steam and assurance. "Thank you for coming on such short notification. I did not want anyone bumping into a photographer in the morning and wondering what was happening. Nor did I wish to observe further transgressions in the food department. Father Caldwell, a word before we dismiss?"

Father Charlie stood at his place. In a languid Southern voice he invoked pleasant platitudes of benediction for the crowd. A few echoed his "Amen" before rising and heading for the exit.

~~~

~~~

E C H O E S

The Reverend Charles Andrew Caldwell

"FATHER CHARLIE," as he prefers to be called, apologizes in advance for his pet's bad manners. "Caesar," the gray parrot, is both forward and impertinent, and hops on shoulders without provocation or warning. No matter! An hour of Father Charlie's good humor more than compensates for Caesar's persistent ear-nibbling!

Charles Caldwell was born in Richmond and studied at Washington and Lee University and attended Virginia Episcopal Seminary in Alexandria. He has served churches all over the South. Except for his thirty months on Munda during WWII (where he was a Navy Chaplain) he says he has loved every one of his assigned parishes. Father Charlie no longer preaches on a regular basis but he does officiate occasionally at services in the Wynfield Chapel.

A widower for ten years, Father Charlie taught himself to cook, and now cooking ranks as one of his favorite hobbies, up there beside golf, Gilbert and Sullivan, travel and teaching Caesar how to recite verses by Poe. *Bon appetit,* Father Charlie!

R. McN.

10

The denizens of Wynfield were rapidly leaving the South Lounge, many of them shaking their heads in consternation. Flu shots, festivities, even the invasion by the magazine were to be tolerated, but a reprimand about ordering meals. Indeed! The general consensus was that this time Miss A. Elvina Moss had overplayed her hand.

Major Featherstone patted Father Charlie's arm. "Thanks, Father. We know not what we doest or whither we goest, except for you!" He stroked his mustache, spun his chair with finesse and wheeled toward the door and Vinnie Whittington before Father Charlie could think of a rejoinder.

Arthur Everett passed the popular priest, whispering "*Cave adsum*!" followed by a solemn wink, then, just as quietly, "*Vale*!"

Rose saw that Madame Zdorek was also making her exit but decided this was not the time to introduce Ellie. She watched the erect figure adjust her normally animated steps to the rocking, lurching gait of Miss Hopgood. The two women were heading for their noontime meal in the Dining Room. Rose knew for a fact that one or the other was always first in the serving line at 11:55.

"Father Charlie!" Rose hailed her friend with a wave. "I want you to meet my new neighbor, *our* new neighbor. Ellie Johnson, Father Charlie Caldwell, retired, but still in good grace with the Almighty and all of us. And one of the nicest men in Wynfield."

Father Charlie accepted Rose's greetings with one of his beneficent smiles and extended his hand to Ellie's well-manicured one.

"A genuine pleasure to welcome you to Wynfield and Virginia, Mrs. Johnson."

"Please, Father, it's Ellie," a blushing Mrs. Johnson answered. "I am delighted to be here and happy to see a man of the cloth so beloved by his fellow residents."

"Well, I am retired, you understand. Perhaps they wouldn't like me if I were the acting priest. I have a reputation as a terrible preacher."

"I don't care a fig about your reputation. What's more, I don't believe it could be terrible. I maintain it is comforting to have a man of the cloth among us . . . elderly folk."

The three laughed at Ellie's gently mocking tone and drifted toward the doors of the Lounge.

"Father Charlie, tell Ellie about meeting Eleanor Roosevelt," entreated Rose.

"Eleanor Roosevelt!" repeated Ellie.

"Ah, yes," replied the pastor with self-deprecation. "It was my one brush with fame."

"But when was this?" pressed Ellie, eagerly catching the whiff of a good yarn.

"Go on, Father Charlie; Ellie's a new audience. And you know I don't mind hearing it again."

The threesome had stopped near the doorway, and Father Charlie leaned on one of the chintz-covered club chairs for a podium.

"It is not significant, Ellie, but you know a preacher never misses a chance to speak his piece. And since Rose has resurrected my old war story, I don't mind reminiscing."

"Please do, Father," spoke Ellie with sincerity. "I happen to believe that reminiscing is one of age's greatest rewards. Mind you, I happen to know which war you're referring to, and what Eleanor Roosevelt did during that war. The story, please."

"Ah, my dear," replied the pastor, by this time relaxing against the back of the chair and slipping comfortably into his role of storyteller, "thank you. As Navy Chaplain during the war I served two and a half years on the island of Munda, in the South Pacific. Not the garden spot of that part of the world. But the natives were friendly and the youngsters I was ministering to were young, gung-ho, typical American boys. I did everything from helping construct the Chapel and preaching, to assisting the payroll clerk and umpiring baseball games."

"But never on Sunday," inserted Rose.

"Right. While I was acting as umpire in one game I lunged forward to avoid getting hit by someone's line drive, lost my footing, and fell, hard, on my right arm. Broke it in two places." Here Father Charlie paused, unbuttoned his cuff and pushed shirt and sweater up past his right elbow.

"And?" persisted Ellie.

"Well, the doctor on Munda did the best he could, but the darn thing got infected and before I knew it, I was on a MedVac plane to Guadalcanal. They operated and found out the infection was in a chipped elbow joint. Put me in the hospital for six weeks."

"Six weeks!"

"Correct. Remember, sulfa was just about the only wonder drug available then. But after four weeks I was feeling fine so I enjoyed my R & R. I did some counseling with the wounded, that sort of thing, lots of reading and sleeping. Until Eleanor appeared."

"And she found out that you were a fraud just taking up bed space!" exclaimed Ellie.

"Not exactly. She just made me feel so damn guilty that I couldn't get out of the hospital fast enough! She came into that ward all dressed up in one of those perky WAVE uniforms with the silly hat perched on her head and stopped by every bed, talking, listening, making notes of each man's address. Sort of everybody's grandmother, you know. And some of those cases weren't easy to look at: burns, amputations, quadriplegics. But that lady never wavered. By the time she got to my bed I didn't know whether to pretend I was asleep, or to just lie about my injury. After all, I was the only man there who had not been wounded in combat. But she never asked me the how question. Said she understood that I'd been such a support to my fellow patients, that I was always cheerful and unselfish with my time, and I never complained, et cetera, et cetera. And all this without a note! She had been briefed, that's for sure, but she remembered, and made each visit a personal, caring one. I tell you, once Eleanor left that ward I called the head nurse and told her I was ready to return to the war zone. I was back in Munda in two days! And that, dear Ellie, is my fifteen minutes of fame; rather, brushing shoulders with the famous. I tell you, she taught me humility in more ways than one. End of story."

"Father Charlie, that was fascinating," said Ellie. "I remember when Mrs. Roosevelt made that trip to the Pacific. She was quite a gal. I feel as if I had been right there with you."

"As do I, Father Charlie," called Henrietta Puffenbarger. "I have been hanging on your every word."

"Well, maybe I should pass the collection plate," laughed the genial pastor.

They all laughed at this remark and resumed their exit from the now-empty Lounge when Miss Puffenbarger added, "I want to meet Mrs. Johnson, Rose. I have been waiting patiently."

"During my sermon!" called Father Charlie as he bowed slightly.

"Certainly, Miss Puffenbarger," chirped Rose. "I'm sorry, we second floor folks have got to stick together. Ellie, come over here a minute. Meet 212; sorry, Miss Henrietta Puffenbarger."

I could almost vow that Miss Puffenbarger was not in this room when Miss Moss made her speech about the meals, Rose thought. *I bet she came in after the meeting ended so that every person leaving had the impression she had been here the whole time.*

"Hello," repeated Ellie. "It is so nice to meet you. I look forward to being your neighbor."

Miss Puffenbarger smiled, revealing a set of even, white teeth.

Rose thought what a handsome woman she was. *Good hair. How I envy those women whose hair turns gray all at once. No mousy salt-and-pepper look like mine. Bet she was a no-nonsense sort of teacher. Believe it was English she taught. Interesting mole on her upper lip; almost a beauty mark.*

"I am happy that you will be up there on Two with Rose and me . . . and . . . goodness, I cannot begin to name all the other nice people. We are generally a quiet lot, but we are there for each other. Tell me, Mrs. Johnson, do you have a Max, also?"

Ellie laughed, her hearty guffaw causing some of the lingerers to turn and stare. "Oh, no, just a bird. A small canary with a very large heart: Vincent."

They continued walking from the Lounge area. Father Charlie bid good bye to each and hurried down the corridor to look for Lib Meecham and the promised book. Romero and Ernest were waiting in the hallway to gather up the chairs. Miss Moss had stated in no uncertain terms that the extra chairs were to be collected immediately and the Lounge restored to its original state. Neither Romero or Ernest had been informed of the photographers' arrival in the morning, but they had been directed to attend a 3:30 meeting in Miss Moss's office in the afternoon. Snippets of conversation reached their ears as the residents left the lounge. They surmised correctly that Miss Moss would have plenty to tell them.

"How do you stay so fit, Miss Puffenbarger?" Ellie asked the trim woman. "Do you have a secret you'd like to share?"

"Heavens, no," replied her neighbor. "I've been blessed. I shall be eighty in three weeks. The years have flown; it doesn't seem possible. Life has improved in many respects. My vision is 20-20 once again since my two cataract operations. I have a new set of dentures. My hearing and voice could be better. The students used to complain that I sounded like a record on the wrong speed."

"Eighty years young! You are remarkable!" Both Rose and Ellie shook their heads in admiration. Miss Puffenbarger's steel-gray hair was short and wavy and her complexion smooth and pink. Except for the mole, her skin was unblemished.

"Not remarkable, ladies. I find it hard to be cheerful all the time at eighty, or almost-eighty, when you know things are only going to get worse. But I try to put on my sunshiny-face. You will like it here, Mrs. Johnson. By chance, do you play golf?"

Ellie started to reply when the older woman continued.

"Golf is the one exercise I do enjoy. Can't be bothered with the regimented aerobics they keep pushing here. Perhaps we can get in a round or two before the temperature dips drastically. I admit to being a fair-weather golfer."

Ellie was delighted with this newly-revealed aspect of her neighbor in Apartment 212.

Golf? gasped Rose. *I simply don't believe it. Can it be she's on the golf course when I thought she was closeted in her apartment?*

Miss Puffenbarger smiled heartily, waved, and headed in the direction of the stairs.

Rose and Ellie stood in the corridor leading to the Bank and the mailboxes. They shared a silent glance.

"Rose," Ellie whispered, "this is peculiar. Miss Puffenbarger didn't seem embarrassed in the least about Miss Moss's admonition; almost as if she didn't hear it. And she looks as healthy as a horse."

"Even if the horse is almost eighty!" said Rose. "I told you, Ellie, this is one grand tour with all sorts of passengers climbing aboard."

Ellie looked at her new friend and rolled her eyes. "As Father Charlie just said, 'AMEN' to that!"

~~~

~~~

WYNSONG

E C H O E S

Lavinia Estelle Calhoun Whittington

LAVINIA WHITTINGTON—Vinnie—is Wynfield Farms' genuine Southern Belle. She was born on the Mississippi delta at her family's plantation, "Belle Bois." Vinnie's father was a pecan planter, hence "Belle Bois" refers to the 2700 acres of pecan groves that were home.

Raised in true Southern comfort, Vinnie shocked both her parents and siblings when she decided to go North in pursuit of a college education. A young woman of spirit, she decided against a "cloistered life among the moss and magnolia."

She proved herself capable of mastering the academic rigors of Vassar College (graduating *cum laude* with a degree in history), and of conquering the heights of the publishing world in New York City. For over two decades she held various editorial positions at the then fledgling *Vogue* magazine. With Vinnie's innate sense of style and immaculate appearance, it is not hard to visualize her among the ranks of fashion's finest!

Marriage to financier John O. Whittington, and three beautiful daughters, completed her charmed life. Now that she is widowed "after forty-three years of wedded bliss" Vinnie has moved to Wynfield to be close to her youngest child, Edith, who lives in Roanoke. When not playing bridge or checking on Wynfield Farms' "belle bois," Vinnie may often be found in the Library catching up on *FOOTNOTES'* assignments.

Although arthritis may confine Vinnie to her wheelchair most of the day, it does not confine her buoyant spirit, generous smile and the sparkle in her sapphire-blue eyes. And yes, she admits that pink is her favorite color and tries to wear "a touch of pink" each day.

Rose McNess

~~~
~~~

11

Arthur Everett poured himself a second cup of Ovaltine and carried it to his cluttered desk. He had six more pages of translations to complete before the weekend. He would not make the afternoon mail. *The old boys in New York will just have to wait.* He sipped his beverage and reflected on yesterday's meeting in the Lounge. And, especially, he reflected with genuine affection on the South Lounge itself.

Those myriad cases with species of fauna and fowl! Old Wynfield must have been quite a gentleman; taught himself taxidermy, or so the story goes. Probably studied abroad; doubt if they offered that at Harvard. I am sure that the Wynfields were the subject of scandalous rumors when news of his taxidermy practice got out. Not that it would have bothered Samuel T.! And look at the legacy he's left. Most interesting, those cases. I should replace some of the Latin nomenclature on more than a few; ink has grown quite faint through the years.

Arthur Everett was not disturbed by the news of the magazine's approaching invasion. If anything, he was oblivious to it. His tutoring and volunteer efforts were honed to a routine that did not vary unless an emergency arose. He arose each morning and dressed as if he were still part of a large corporation. No slippage in his regime.

But that other matter, about the meals. While he professed no burning admiration for Miss Moss, he did comprehend the difficulty of her position. The Dining Room was the crown jewel of Wynfield Farms. Why, unless someone was desperately ill, would that someone avoid it?

As Juvenal said in his Satires, "Nemo repente fuit turpissimus."

Still puzzling over the meal issue, Arthur Everett returned to the six pages that awaited his classicist's eyes.

~~~

Miss Puffenbarger was unhappy. She sipped black currant tea and nibbled at a Carr's wheatmeal biscuit. A large crumb fell from her lips onto the milky surface and instantly dissolved. Miss Puffenbarger drained the remains of the lukewarm liquid and looked with distaste at the sediment collecting at the bottom of the fragile teacup. She frowned.

"Large bites make many crumbs" had been one of Mother's dictums. Mealtime was always such an ordeal. Mother made it plain that every bite was a sacrifice to grow, to buy, to prepare. Waste of food, no matter how accidental, was not tolerated in the childhood I remember. Neither was any show of affection. But there was always Sister! We were there for each other. Could either of us have made it alone in that cold, desolate house? Yet now . . . with the swarms of visitors crawling over Wynfield . . . what am I to do?

"Wynfield is my inheritance! I deserve this life. I shall rebel against the injustice of the situation." Miss Puffenbarger sat upright and spoke resolutely to Renoir's insipid little girl holding a watering can in the reproduction above the loveseat.

Miss Puffenbarger's resolve ebbed as she considered the possibility of an impending confrontation.

"Life is sunshine and shadow, little girl. I *must* find the sunshine."

~~~

Albert Warrington pursued his morning ritual of inspecting the brass on the Hepplewhite chest. This morning he was more deliberate than usual.

"Drat! Drat and double-drat!" he exclaimed aloud. "Photographers, reporters, extraneous people from Richmond poking and prying into residents' private lives. Why in the name of heaven didn't the Board put it to a vote by the residents as to whether we wanted magazine exposure. Certainly Wynfield does not need publicity. Miss Moss. She is responsible! That woman will stop at nothing when it comes to getting her name and her job in the press."

Yesterday's meeting had clearly disturbed Albert Warrington. He had moved to Wynfield Farms for privacy and the luxury of fewer responsibilities. The invasion by photographers was clearly a breach of his, and others', privacy. He felt sure he was not the only resident disturbed by Miss Moss's announcement. Last evening at dinner he had joined Rose McNess and the newest tenant, Mrs. Johnson. Neither of the ladies endorsed the project; in fact, both were extremely reluctant about the entire business. Miss Moss had been catching people in the Reception Hall and asking them to "dress up a bit during the day," and "gussy up for the evening meal." She clearly did not want the photographers to catch old folks *really* at home, with their hair down, so to speak. Musn't look as if we had gone to seed.

The thought of *hair* made him peer closely into the antique shaving glass. *Good! No haircut needed yet. An uninterrupted day of work.* He turned his full attention to his briefcase.

~~~

Vinnie Whittington sat before the dressing table and gazed at her reflection in the tall mirror. Her skin was near parchment in hue and translucent in value. She smoothed the imported *Helia D* cream around her eyes and over the flattering rounded bolsters of her cheeks. Her nose was neither wide nor narrow, but long. With a practiced touch she applied a darker-than-skin color toner that effectively abbreviated this aberrant feature. *Medium Rose Madder* lipstick emphasized rosebud lips and a light dusting of *Summer Blonde Facial Powder* completed the morning
~~~

routine. She combed her luxuriant white hair back from her face and fastened it loosely in a French twist. Tired from the exertion of patting, smoothing and twisting, Vinnie sat and looked in the mirror once again. *Never let one's appearance falter! Haven't I always preached that to the girls?* She smiled and opened her blue eyes wide. Vinnie Whittington was a pretty woman with flawless skin but the first thing that people always noticed about her were her sapphire blue eyes with the brilliant fire of exotic gems.

She eased herself from the low stool into her wheelchair and rested; her breathing was rapid after this small effort.

My dressing gown will simply have to do until late afternoon. I have no appointments today. "VV" can just go jump as far as I'm concerned! Even thinking about pulling clothes over my head makes me tired. Of course, I should go pay a call on the new resident. Seems like a nice sort. Southern background undoubtedly accounts for that. Yes, I'll just sit here and drink my tea until I am feeling strong again. All of these intrusions . . .

A loud knock shattered Vinnie's daydreaming.

And once more: *Knock-knock.*

"Coming, coming!" she sang out, wheeling toward the door.

When she opened the door there on the floor sat the largest, most succulent-looking pineapple Vinnie had ever laid eyes upon.

"What in the world!" She looked across and down the hall. Rose McNess had her trash basket in front of her door. Not Rose! And certainly not Miss Puffenbarger. *And I don't even know Number 209. It must be from William! Of course . . . William!*

Just as Vinnie was retrieving her prize Major Featherstone appeared at the door of his apartment. He wheeled toward Vinnie with a smile on his face and a bouquet of fresh flowers across his knees.

"Vinnie, my dear! For *you*!" He flourished the huge bouquet with an exaggerated ducking of his head.

"William, you romantic old fool! They're just magnificent!" Vinnie was burying her nose in the cascade of pink and white stargaze lilies, freesia, blue Dutch iris and tiny white rosebuds. "All of my very favorites! You couldn't have known. And you shouldn't have! But the pineapple. Why the pineapple, William?"

"Ah, my dear, you have forgotten. The pineapple is the symbol of hospitality. Today is the day, Vinnie; today is the day."

Vinnie, remembering, puckered her rosebud lips and winked at the Major, as they both rolled into her apartment and closed the door behind them.

~~~

~~~

WYNSONG

E C H O E S

Major William Edward Featherstone

"Light as a feather, heavy as a stone!" That is what you'll hear when introduced to Wynfield's "whirlwind in a wheelchair," Major William Featherstone, U.S. Army, Retired. He brooks no misunderstanding of his name.

The Major has military blood running through his veins. From the generous sweep of his silver mustache to the tips of his gleaming boots he is every inch West Point graduate, career army man, World War II veteran (2nd Armored Division). A bad hip confines the Major to his wheelchair these days and prohibits his organizing all of Wynfield's residents into a marching unit.

The Major has never married but has a host of nieces and nephews on whom he dotes.

Major Featherstone says that his days at Wynfield are "too short, far too short for all I have to accomplish." This consists of challenging all comers to fierce battles on the chess board, reading every volume of history in the Library, and cataloging the trees on the grounds.

Major Featherstone, we salute you!

Rose McNess.

~~~
~~~

12

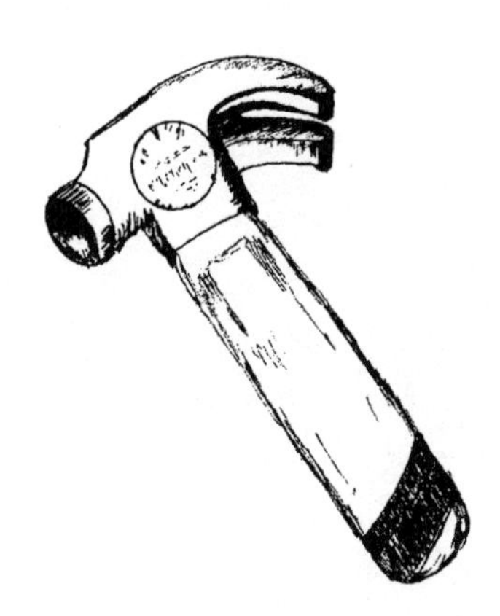

"Rose! Rose!" It was Ellie, her voice thick with morning huskiness, but unmistakably Ellie.

Rose opened her door to a distraught Ellie Johnson.

"Rose, I seem to be always barging in on you in the early morning. There is something going on in the room next to mine. Moving, scraping, thuds. Who did you say lived there? It really is a racket; started about seven."

"My goodness, Ellie. You have the quietest of neighbors. Vinnie Whittington. Remember, you met her in the Reception Hall yesterday? You don't suppose she's fallen? She's not crippled, just has poor circulation. But she can move easily for short distances. Bed to wheelchair, chair to table, you know. We'd better go check. Is it a real ruckus?"

"Doesn't she have the same call devices we have?" asked Ellie. "She could certainly ring for assistance . . . unless she's another one too proud to ask for help."

"Vinnie is proud but she's not stupid," said Rose. "I think we'd better get over there and listen. Maybe the noise has stopped by now."

Rose and Ellie stepped into the hallway. As Rose was pulling her door shut, a loud ***CRASH*** erupted from the apartment in question. This was followed by a second, a third, and then a ***BANG***. Rose and Ellie froze. Miss Puffenbarger opened her door a splinter, spotted Rose and Ellie, and hurried forth to stand with them.

"What is g-going on?" timidly inquired Miss Puffenbarger, her face solemn.

"We are afraid to guess," stated Rose. "But if we don't investigate I can tell you someone who will! And soon!"

Rose moved first. She walked swiftly to the door of Apartment 211 and putting her left ear to its surface, stood and listened for a moment. She heard the tinkle of glass and the dull thuds of heavy chunks falling to the floor. She could also smell plaster dust that was seeping through cracks around the door frame.

"Vinnie! Vinnie! It's me, Rose McNess. Can you hear me?"

There was no answer from 211. The only sounds Rose could distinguish were quiet scrapings, as if a heavy object were being shifted from one spot to another. Then she heard the *crunch-crunch* of wheels moving toward the door.

"Well, at least she's still mobile!" Rose cried to the pair behind her. "I can hear her chair coming this way."

No sooner had she spoken than the door to Apartment 211 opened. Sitting in their respective chairs, smiling at the trio gathered in the corridor, were Major Featherstone and Mrs. Lavinia Whittington. The two were as comfortable and congenial as if they were greeting midnight carolers on Christmas Eve. A fresh pineapple rested in Vinnie Whittington's lap and she cradled a huge bouquet. Major Featherstone's right hand clasped Vinnie's left one; his other hand held the most lethal hammer Rose had ever seen.

"We have decided to live together," said Major Featherstone, simply and without a hint of his usual affectation. "Sorry if we made too much of a disturbance. Didn't mean to worry anyone. Honestly didn't think this wall would be such a problem."

"The *wall*?" gasped Rose. "Don't tell me . . ." She could not finish the sentence.

"My dear Rose. I am removing the wall between my apartment and Vinnie's. It's a matter of logistics. Two wheelchairs in one small apartment would never do. This way, we'll each have our own place and be together. So sorry, Mrs. Johnson; I should have warned you, I know. But I also knew that if I told anyone, Miss Moss would be up here in a flash. She'd forbid this. Was the noise *fearful*, my dear?" He looked at Ellie apologetically. . . .

"*Fearful*, Major." Somehow Ellie knew that this answer would please the Major. "But do not give it another thought. I am an early riser. I am so happy for you and Vinnie!"

"Soon to be MRS. Featherstone!" proclaimed the Major.

"Now, William, it's my turn," drawled Vinnie. "Do you see how he started this proposal? With a pineapple and posies! A pineapple, as you know, is the symbol for hospitality. And the lovely flowers signify love. I found the pineapple on my doorstep this morning; answered a knock, looked; no one there, but this bounty! Isn't he romantic? We figure that it will take our families a long time to get used to the idea that their octogenarian invalids are going to marry. That is why we decided to make this move *now*. Our time is too precious! When they arrive for the ceremony another month may have passed. And who knows how many good months we can hope to have together?" Vinnie Whittington rolled her large, expressive blue eyes and smiled at each of the ladies standing open-mouthed before her.

"Major, Vinnie, I think it's just grand! Now, how can we help with demolition? The more you get completed before Miss Moss gets wind of this, the better. I love nothing more than a conspiracy! Tell us what to do!" Rose expounded enthusiastically as she looked past the couple and saw the pile of debris and hunks of plaster in the room.

"Thank you, my dears, thank you. Vinnie and I can manage. I have engaged Romero for the morning, and if need be, Ernest. Romero has been in on this; he's an engineer, you know, or rather *was*, back in El Salvador. He came up to check the wall supports and the electrical wiring. Actually, this is his hammer; brought it up last week."

"You are a sly old fox, Major," commented Ellie. "You have had this in the works for weeks, I suspect!"

"Absolutely. *Tempus fugit* when it comes to my Vinnie!"

"We should let you get back to work," concluded Miss Puffenbarger. "My very best wishes to the both of you."

They each said their good-byes, hugging both the Major and Vinnie several times and promising to be on the alert for Miss Moss.

"I'll close your door, Major," called Rose, watching the couple wheel back to their daunting task.

"My God! Have you ever?" asked Ellie. Her turban was crooked; the Major had bussed her vigorously when she had leaned over to give him a congratulatory hug. "Now I've seen everything! Those two old nutters can barely get around in their wheelchairs and now they're teaming up! Wait 'til I write Denver! Everyone will think I've come to 'Sin City of the South'!"

"Or," added Rose primly, "you could write all about 'Sex and Scandal on the Second Floor'!"

The two friends clutched each other in silent mirth. Each knew that if they let one giggle escape there would be no way to stifle the onslaught.

"Oh, Rose," Ellie croaked hoarsely, "you don't think, you *aren't* suggesting . . . "

"Ellie, I think our conversation stops now! '*Keep the bedroom door only ajar* . . . ' said Henry James. They shall, and so shall our conversation, if you follow me."

They grinned goofily as they stood in front of their respective apartments.

"Actually," Rose continued, "I think it's all pretty wonderful. Confined to a wheelchair, knocking down an entire wall just to gain access to your lady-love, living in sin . . . all at the tender age of . . . eighty-something? Talk about romance. We've got it right here!"

"To be sure! Wynfield grows more surprising day by day! *Nothing* like this was promised in the brochures! Sorry, gotta run, Rose. I'm expecting my movers today. Let's hope! After such an auspicious start—what else could happen?"

"And I've got to walk Max. Also, I promised Mary I'd take her for shots. See you later."

Ten minutes later Rose left with an impatient Max. She looked forward to the clean, crisp morning.

She thought to herself, *How could I have possibly imagined that today was going to be simply another day? Major Featherstone and his Vinnie! How many years do they hope to have? There's that word again, Max: hope! Maybe I should adopt a new slogan for my tours: "Hop on Rose's Tours with Hope." Ha!*

~~~

~~~

E C H O E S

Eloise Worthy Summers Johnson

Dude ranches, Stetson hats, ski resorts, golden aspens . . . do these remind you of Denver, Colorado? Good! Now you can reminisce about them with our newest resident, ELOISE JOHNSON (Mrs. Lanier Nelson Johnson) who has just moved into Apartment 209. Ellie (as she prefers, no, insists, on being called) arrived Thursday morning after journeying from the Mile-High City. She and her late husband "Duke" spent many autumns in the Shenandoah Valley because of his association with V.M.I., so our beautiful fall colors were no surprise to her.

Ellie admits to a weakness for good books by English mystery writers, a challenging game of bridge or backgammon, the color "melon," travel and travel talk, rainy days and hats.

When you meet this lovely lady with the quick smile and green eyes and a true peaches-and-cream complexion, be sure to extend a real Virginia and Wynfield welcome to her and Vincent, her canary.

R. McNess.

~~~
~~~

13

October 24

Dear Children:

I understand from Annie that you are worried about your old mother! Sorry I have not written in a long time. I am alive and well; how is that for a good report from the Old Folks Home?

Wynfield is keeping me busy and becoming more like HOME every day. I never seem to know where my time goes. The other day one of our residents tried to rob a bank (no luck) and was returned in the Sheriff's car--in hand-cuffs. Can you imagine the ruckus that caused? And an army of photographers from *Virginia Venues* magazine has invaded the place. Look for Wynfield Farms in the Winter issue (January?) when we'll be featured. We're proud of the honor but right now it is more of a nuisance. Longhaired chaps wearing earrings and sloppy sandals lurk everywhere. They shoot dozens of photos, ask hundreds of questions and never seem to go away.

One of my neighbors up here on Two—Major Featherstone--just demolished the wall between his apartment and his lady friend's so they could live together--with more room for both their wheelchairs!

And of course my tour business thrives! Interesting new member, neighbor across the hall from Denver. I think we shall be good friends. No dog, just Vincent the canary. I think I mentioned that I am reviving the newsletter. It was pathetic when I moved in, and now people really read it. Not a best seller but the circulation is soaring. Ha! Ha! Have ordered 400 daffodil bulbs. Don't worry--I'll call for volunteers to help plant them. And some of my Wordsworth Club pals might want to come out and help, too. It's our 106th year, did I tell you that? (Not the average age of the members--the Club's age.)

Must run. We are having a huge gala on November 19 and no, I am not Chairman, you'll be glad to hear.

My old Smith-Corona is performing at top speed and I hope the 3rd carbon is not too pale for you, Paul. My 16 year old Chevy Nova is performing well, too. I'd be lost without it!

Max sends woofs to all, especially the grandchildren. Hugs and kisses to all,

Mother.

P.S. I promise I'll write soon, again!

ECHOES

Doctor Robert Preston Lesley

It is always good to have a doctor in the house! ROBERT LESLEY (". . . please put in your column that I am retired; I am not advertising!") embodies the fine qualities one associates with the Hippocratic oath. This quiet, soft-spoken gentleman has enjoyed life at Wynfield Farms for three years.

After a busy career of forty-five years as general practitioner, Robert Lesley is now taking time for his hobbies. He has given up his passion for growing roses but is still an active "birder." In addition to bird watching, Bob is also crafting miniature furniture and researching genealogies.

It has been rumored that Bob Lesley has a powerful baritone and was active in informal singing groups for years. By his own admission he has 'feverish feet' and loves to dance. Recently his son John gave him a state of the art computer. That may pre-empt all other interests if our good doctor gets hooked. Bob Lesley has already mastered the word processor and e-mail. Watch out, Wynfield!

R. McNess.

~~~
~~~

14

Kate Alexander spread both arms across her desk and struggled to maintain a cleared area for her calendar and telephone. Two "VV" photographers huddled across from her, simultaneously inking copious notes in their thick notebooks and stealing admiring glances at the pretty receptionist.

Phrases such as *zoom lens, sunlight filters, boom, gaff, switchable formats, slow sync, 35-60 millimeters* were tossed around as easily as the words to a familiar nursery rhyme. Several canvas duffel bags, tripods and a collection of cameras rested on the floor beside the photographers.

"Is that it, gentlemen?" inquired Kate. She directed her question first to a longhaired youth and then to the older of the pair, a lanky man whose face was all but obscured by dark wraparound glasses and a baseball cap. Kate was adept at handling male ogling, no matter what the age of the male.

"Uh huh," replied Long Hair. "Gotta start somewhere. Boss'll be after us if we don't."

"That's great, Miss Alexander," added Baseball Cap. "South Lounge, Library, Chapel: all facing East. Morning light."

"No, no, not the Chapel," Kate noted hurriedly. "That's in a restricted area behind the East Wing. You'll have to set up special lighting in there. Do you have permission?"

"Oh, we're cleared," said Baseball Cap. "Thanks for the thumbs-up. And the Music Room is West, correct?"

"You got it!" said Kate, hoping they would soon collect their gear and be on their way. "You did say this was to come out in the Winter issue, didn't you? Will you have to come back and shoot Wynfield after the first snowfall?" Intimations of a return visit made Kate hesitant to even broach the question.

"No ma'am, not to worry. We'll do mostly interior for the spread in the magazine. Catch some brilliant color on one of the good weather days and let the readers imagine what it will be like in the snow. That's why we're here every other day. We develop and print our shots at night and if they don't turn out, we redo them when we return. Gotta redo the greenhouse; too much light there. Think you could give that Jocey person a call?"

"I'll be happy to. While you are shooting the Lounge I'll contact Jocey."

"Thanks, Miss Alexander. You're a doll. Come on, Judson. Get your gear and move it."

Kate slumped back in her chair and watched with resignation as the pair loaded their equipment and ambled down the hallway.

Rose came down the steps to the Reception Hall just in time to see the two photographers vanish in the direction of the South Lounge.

"Hard work is it, Kate?" teased Rose.

"I'm exhausted! No one asked me about this magazine project. If I'd known what big babies these men are, I would have vetoed it. I've had to spoon-feed them every inch of the way."

"Sorry, Kate. I hope we'll all think it has been worth the hoopla when the issue hits the newsstands. Until then . . . know that I'm thinking about you! With crossed fingers!"

Kate giggled—oh, that lively, lovely bubbling giggle—and Rose realized she was beaming like a schoolchild as she turned her attention to the matter of locating Mary Rector.

She did not have to search far. Rose spotted Mary on the bench beside the front doors. She was sprawled heavily in the corner, cushioned by her girth beneath the window. Bright sun streamed through the small panes, turning her frowzy hair into a cap of millions of short electrical circuits wired into her scalp.

Oh, if they only were, thought Rose, seizing the image.

"Mary, Mary," Rose called gently, patting the older woman's plump shoulder. "Mary, I'm here for our adventure. It's me, Rose McNess."

"What . . . what? Rose? Rose! I knew you'd come. I told Kate you'd be here. Do we take the bus? Will we see the police today?" Mary woke instantly, obviously with full recall of Rose's promise.

"Of course I'm here. Didn't I promise? And I brought you a surprise for later. No, we don't take the bus, Mary. We'll stroll on back to the Clinic for that flu shot. We can't have you getting sick this winter."

Mary's ears had caught the word 'surprise' and she stumbled to her feet. She spied the aluminum packet in Rose's left hand and smiled. Rose gripped Mary's elbow as they crossed the lobby. They were passing Kate Alexander's desk when Miss Moss's door burst open.

How in the world did that woman know that I wanted to avoid her this morning?

"Mrs. McNess," hailed Miss Moss, "you are not going outside with Mary, are you?"

Well, what if I am? thought Rose defiantly. *I think I shall!*

"Why, as a matter of fact . . ." Rose began, thinking she might as well confess her innocent destination to stave off further inquisition.

"Oh, no, Rose, that will never do. The photographers from "VV" are here, snapping from every angle. It would simply not do to have poor Mary wandering through the pathways like a . . . demented person. Why, what sort of image would that give Wynfield Farms?"

"Mary Rector is not hard of hearing, Miss Moss. She's occasionally confused, but her hearing is quite acute. Please. And as a matter of record I am escorting her to the Clinic for her flu and pneumonia shots. *As you specified at yesterday's meeting*."

"Oh, Mrs. McNess, I don't know what to say . . . It's just with the press and photographers all around, one cannot be too careful. I do want everything to go smoothly. It's our image to the outside world we must preserve, you know."

Miss Moss appeared for a moment as if she were going to follow Rose and Mary down the corridor. Rose tucked Mary's arm under hers and marched off with alacrity to avoid this possibility.

"You do understand my position, Mrs. McNess . . ." The Voice trailed after the two women but Miss Moss did not attempt to accompany them.

If she thinks Mary's image would muddy the waters of the magazine, wait until she gets wind of the Major's escapade. That woman! Image. It's all she can think about. What about a compassionate image?

"Miss Moss is not a kind person, Rose," volunteered Mary. Her voice was low, dispirited, and Rose had to lean close to hear her words. "I know she doesn't like me. But I've paid all my fees and I don't cause any trouble, do I Rose? The Bank didn't let me visit my money but that wasn't my fault, was it?" She looked pleadingly at Rose with eyes wide and full of agony.

"Indeed not, Mary," returned Rose with as much animation as she could muster. "You have many, many friends at Wynfield and I am pleased to be among them." *Can't say the same for Miss Moss, that's for sure.* "Why, here we are already."

A tall, attractive young man at the Clinic desk smiled jauntily at the two women.

"Two more customers? Welcome, ladies. I'm Dr. Williamson, specializing in flu shots today. Names, please?"

"I'm going to cheat you out of one customer, Doctor," said Rose. "Got my flu vaccine last week and I certainly do not need another lifetime pneumonia shot. Just shots for my friend, Mary Rector."

"Come with me, Mrs. Rector. The nurse will check your records and we'll have you out of here in no time. Getting near chow time, isn't it?" He led Mary behind a screen to another cubicle in the Clinic.

What a reassuring manner that young man has. Senses that Mary is a bit dusty in the attic. So glad she's got a pleasant person for this visit.

Rose sat in one of the ladder-back chairs in the vestibule to wait for her friend. She was enjoying this minute of quiet and allowed her mind to calm down after seething over Miss Moss's communications. She removed her bifocals and clasped them tightly in both hands.

I shall practice my patience. Rose concentrated, eyes closed, as she had learned to do years ago while raising three teenagers.

"Mrs. McNess? Are you ill?"

The deep voice startled Rose and she looked up wildly. Her glasses clattered to the floor. Doctor Lesley had just entered the Clinic. He inquired again, "Are you ill? Here, let me get those," he said, stooping for her spectacles.

"Dr. Lesley! You startled me. No, I am not ill, just wool-gathering. And waiting for Mary Rector to get her shots. The nice young doctor has Mary back there now. Sit down, won't you?"

Bob Lesley was one of Rose's—and everybody else's—favorites at the retirement home. Rose had heard it said that when he closed his practice, men and women cried openly. He had been a beloved physician in Roanoke for many, many years and people could not imagine life without him. When his wife died four years ago he had taken less than a year to sell his home and make the move to Wynfield.

"Thank you; don't mind if I do. I'll wait for Mary with you. Just wondered how the shots were going. If everyone was coming in as they should. I've heard dire reports from Atlanta on the projected flu for this winter. It frightens me, when prevention is such a simple thing."

No wonder he was so beloved, Rose mused. *He is such a caring person, and it shows. I wish Tom and I had known him when we moved to Roanoke.*

"Doctor Lesley!" Rose said suddenly as a thought occurred to her.

"Please, Rose, it's Robert, or Bob. You call me Bob and I shall continue addressing you as Rose. A lovely name, incidentally. I used to grow roses, you know."

"Oh? I didn't know, Bob." They both enjoyed a companionable laugh. "But this is a professional question. Perhaps you'll want me to switch back to 'doctor' when you hear what I am about to ask you."

"Try me, Rose."

"You know Mary Rector, and about the trauma in her life. Trauma which is, I am convinced, responsible for the sad state she's in. Behind that face, inside that pitiful dumpling of a woman, is a smart person. Is there any mild medication that could be prescribed for her? She is not crazy, but if she continues to live in this delusionary state, she will be. I feel so helpless."

"You help Mary more than anyone here, Rose. And I share your deep concern. It has bothered me, too. Guess I've gotten used to playing hooky from medicine, though, or I might have done something about it before now." Dr. Lesley's broad face was craggy with wrinkles of worry as he talked with Rose.

"What about her son, Rose? Didn't I hear that he had brought Mary here?"

"Brought her and dumped her, as far as I can tell. Never been back. Mary's not so far gone that Wynfield can't handle her situation. She doesn't cook, so she won't burn the place down. She's just so . . . so vacant. Vacant. That's the word. I guess I hoped you would know of a magic pill to cure the Marys in the world. And in particular, our Mary."

"She may need long-term therapy, Rose. To force her to come to grips with the reality of her missing daughter. That won't be easy. I cannot do that, but I'll be glad to talk to her. I'll even try to get her to come birding with me. Now, there's salvation for the soul!" Bob Lesley's eyes lit up at the thought of his favorite outdoor diversion.

"Oh, thank you . . . Bob. It's providence that we met this morning. I dreaded approaching you; so many people don't want to take on anyone else's troubles. Not that our lives are so full we can't carry a little extra baggage."

"Why, what do you mean, Rose? My calendar is practically full! There's this fool Fete, the magazine invasion, holidays approaching before you know it. Who could be busier than we Wynfielders?"

They shared another chuckle poking fun at themselves before Dr. Williamson and Mary reappeared.

"All through are we, Mary?" asked Rose solicitously. "Didn't hurt much, did it?"

"It did hurt, Rose, but he said I did just fine. He doesn't know where Suzanne is either. Wouldn't she like him, Rose? Such a handsome young man. But Suzanne's fellow is a looker, too. Thank you, Doctor."

"It was a pleasure, Mrs. Rector. Now keep well this winter." The young doctor hesitated as if he would like to question Rose about her friend, but Rose led Mary from the Clinic. Turning, she waved from the doorway. Rose knew that Bob Lesley would seize this opportunity to discuss Mary with Dr. Williamson, and perhaps get some hint for treatment.

Rose escorted her friend to the Dining Room for the cafeteria style lunch. She chatted with Mary about the simplest happenings in Wynfield life. Was Mary making plans to attend the upcoming Fall Fete? Had Mary heard Father Charlie's gray parrot quote Edgar Allen Poe? Would Mary like to have her hair shampooed and set in the Wynfield salon? "I'd be so happy to introduce you to Becky. She's a wizard with scissors and I know she would be tickled to meet you, Mary . . .

"I'm going to leave you now, Mary. I don't eat lunch down here. But I'm sure you can manage just fine. Ummmm. Smells like Brunswick stew to me. And those delicious biscuits!" Tantalizing whiffs of simmering chicken, okra and tomatoes filtered into the hallway leading to the Dining Room. Rose was wavering.

"Thank you, Rose. Thank you. I've had quite a trip this morning. Maybe next time we can take the bus together. Will you do that with me, Rose?"

"We will do that, Mary, and that's a promise. But not today. Oh, I nearly forgot: your surprise! A few of my homemade

'Ranger' cookies for you. Save these for your dessert, Mary." Rose spoke clearly and slowly to her friend before watching her step timidly into the noisy Dining Room and join the line forming for the noon meal.

I am going to do everything in my power to help that poor woman, Rose promised herself. *Short of letting the responsibility for her smother me. Poor Mary! But at least I have a pal in Bob Lesley. Bob Lesley and Rose McNess versus Mary's son and Miss Moss.*

~~~

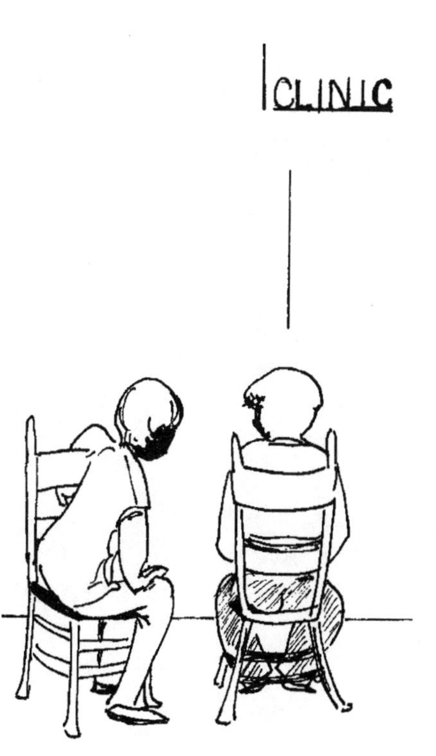
~~~

E C H O E S

Henrietta Cora Puffenbarger

HENRIETTA PUFFENBARGER practically came home when she moved to Wynfield. Her parents, part of a large wave of German immigrants settling in Pennsylvania, moved to the Shenandoah Valley just before World War I. Henrietta says she has Puffenbarger cousins from Roanoke to Reading. She grew up on her family's farm a mere ten miles from here and vividly remembers picking berries near the lake in Montremont Gardens. "We walked barefoot in the lane from our farm to the main road and we'd wonder what the Wynfields were going to do next. They were always building something here--either Old Man Wynfield or some of his relatives--and it had to be the biggest and best for miles around!"

Henrietta attended Teacher's College in Farmville and returned to teach English in the local high school. Now retired, she has brought her talents and quiet manner to Wynfield. Henrietta is a whiz at crossword puzzles (works them in ink), and also Whist and Patience. She keeps abreast of events in the literary world. Saturday afternoons will find her next to her radio in Apartment 212 listening to the Metropolitan Opera broadcasts. She does not miss a single one.

R. McN.

~~~
~~~

15

So absorbed in his walk and the nameless tune he was humming, "The Prowler," marching down the second floor corridor, nearly collided with Rose McNess who was stepping along from the opposite direction.

"Oops! I *beg* your pardon, Mrs. McNess! My little woman keeps telling me I'd better keep a sharp eye open! Did I bump you?"

"Heavens no, Mr. Jenkins. My fault; I was a hundred miles away. Please, it's Rose. I'm Rose and you're Bob. Let's don't be so formal around here!"

"Well, thanks, Rose. I appreciate that."

"I've been meaning to call you," continued Rose, always believing in *carpe diem*, "to see if I could interview you and Mrs. Jenkins for *Wynsong*. Could I come and chat for about ten minutes for a profile?"

"I'm flattered, Rose. When?"

"Well, it can't be this week but I'll give you plenty of notice. Residents seem to like reading about one another. I promise my questions don't probe too deeply."

"I'll clear it with Esther. Miss Moss called us about that magazine coming up for pictures and we told her 'no.' Invasion of privacy. What do you think?"

"It is, and I do not like it one bit. But we are stuck with it, I fear. The penalty we pay for living in this gorgeous place. Sorry to detain you, Bob. How many miles so far?"

"Quite all right, Rose. This will be mile three when I return to our apartment. I'm certainly not going to walk the lower corridors with the cameras lurking all about. See you later!"

Rose was poised to enter her own apartment, thought better of it and turning, knocked on Ellie's door. *Wonder if her furniture arrived today? Awfully quiet in there.*

"Ellie, Ellie, it's me, Rose. Are you decent?"

The door opened to reveal its occupant swathed in billowing gray chiffon with matching turban. The latter was swirled around her head until it ended in a vertical puff. Ellie's face was slathered with a thick, white creamy substance that smelled of lilac and fresh cucumbers.

She looks, Rose thought, *exactly like an ice cream sundae*!

"Oh, Rose, you caught me. No moving van today, so I have decided to take advantage of this extra time and give myself a beauty treatment. Like it, dear?"

"Ellie, you are a breath of fresh air! Love your get-up! Can I do anything for you before I retreat to write some letters?"

"Thank you, Rose, nothing whatsoever. The Major and Vinnie brought over a peace offering about an hour ago. Think they were feeling guilty about the noise. They insisted on giving me a bottle of Virginia wine and a tin of cheese wafers. I said I'd save the nibbles for cocktail hour but I dived into them for lunch. That and a cup of tea; I did have a huge breakfast."

"And your furniture?" The apartment was still as bare as it had been four days ago.

"Oh, the movers called. They're in St. Louis and should be here tomorrow."

"You are far more patient than I," offered Rose.

"What's my hurry? I'm here safely, until they carry me out. I can wait another day for my possessions. Besides, when my stuff does arrive I'll never have time to indulge in all my creams and lotions. You don't want a neighbor you're ashamed of, Rose!"

"That will never happen! I'm delighted you're here, Ellie, wrinkles, warts *and* wigs!"

Rose backed out of the doorway, blew Ellie a breezy kiss, and returned to her own home across the hall. She placed her trash basket directly under the apartment number. Max looked up from his bed and waved his tail in a desultory manner.

"Max, what a morning! Tell me what I must do about Miss Moss! I can't let her raise my blood pressure every time she speaks. If Miss Moss would just practice some discretion before opening her mouth! Maybe I'm too sensitive. Do you think I'm too sensitive, Max?"

The Scottie had been listening to his mistress speak and pricked up his ears at the mention of his name. He cocked his head and looked at Rose in total sympathy.

Rose watered the Boston fern on the dinette table and hung her cardigan in the closet. She found two stale wheat-crackers in the kitchen cabinet and quickly ate them as she put her electric kettle on for a cup of tea.

"Thank goodness Annie gave me this teakettle, Max. I like plenty of hot water if I'm going to make tea, more than what I can heat in the microwave. These automatic kettles should be standard issue in every apartment. They are, in English hotels."

Once more Max gazed at his mistress in complete agreement.

"Max, I had better get busy. Tons of news for *Wynsong* this week: another juicy profile and the Fall Fete, not to mention the *Virginia Venues* arrival. That really is an honor for Wynfield. I'll give Miss Moss plenty of credit in my article; maybe that will soften her up." Rose sighed audibly. "My 'to do' list, Max, grows longer by the hour. Where does time go?"

Rose took her tea cup to her "office": the walnut gentleman's desk on which rested her ancient typewriter, *Roget's Thesaurus*, and the latest edition of the *American Heritage Dictionary*. The latter had been a gift from her journalist son, Rob, when he discovered that his mother's spelling was nonexistent. "Just you wait until you're my age, Rob," she had told him. "Word skills are often the first things to go!" The desk was positioned opposite the bed, so that Rose had her back to the Wynfield view that she loved. This was her way of saying "when I sit down here it's to work and not to daydream!"

She polished the lens of her glasses with a tissue before haphazardly shoving them on her nose and pulled out a creased page from the drawer. She studied it for some minutes.

```
          TO DO - OCTOBER
Finish profiles—Lib M., Dr. Lesley, Jana,
   Major F.
call Jenkins for interview?
PLANT tulip bulbs; permission? call
   Wordsworth gals?
Check Mary R—new coat? Haircut?
WRITE KIDS! stamps for Tom
Volunteer for Fall Fete
Car inspection date- ?
```

Well, I have accomplished very little so far. I did finish the profile on Jana and I just have to type the Major's. Why didn't I mention a coat to Mary this morning? I'll go shopping with her next week; there's time. . . . Certainly can't do anything about those bulbs if they haven't arrived yet. What possessed me to order 400? I'll get Romero to help me, and some of the Wordsworth girls . . . those daffodils will be simply beautiful along the path to the lake . . . Wordsworth's "host of golden daffodils" . . . waving in the breeze . . . and some in the woods, too. I won't need to buy any more airmail stamps if Tom's on his way home. . . .

Rose's mind was whirling. She skimmed her "to do" list and found a dozen other subjects that needed her attention but now she focused on the typing she had assigned herself this afternoon.

Think I'll ever run out of news, Max? Might run out of profiles, but news, never. Not on this tour! Maybe I'll have a wedding announcement before long. Guess I'd better not mention their cohabitation. Wonder how long they think they can keep Rolling Stone in the dark? Not very long, that's my wager.

With a satisfied grunt Rose finished the Major's profile and placed the copy on the thesaurus. She felt her efforts deserved to "season" on a place of honor. She typed a brief article regarding the upcoming Fete and made a mental note to chat with its Chairman this evening. There were many questions and ideas concerning this event that Rose wanted to discuss with the formidable Mrs. Keynes-Livingston.

Mrs. K-L. is undoubtedly one of the brightest people here in Wynfield. I may like her very much when I get to know her better. If I do! Why does she intimidate me? I'm shrinking, yet she seems to grow taller every time we meet. Silly me; my imagination.

Rose stretched and felt the desk chair's hard seat bite into her not-so-well padded derriere when the telephone rang. Max sat up and barked at the unexpected noise.

"I hear it, Max, don't worry. Hello? Rose McNess here."

"Mrs. McNess, it's Kate Alexander. You have a package down here, at the desk. Would you be able to come for it? Or . . ."

"A package? Oh, for heaven's sakes. What can it be? No, I mean, yes, certainly I'll be down for it. Right away. Do I need to sign anything, dear?"

"Oh, no. I'll take care of that, Mrs. McNess."

She has a lovely telephone voice. I'll skip along and pick it up. Did I order another audio book? I know! The bulbs are here! At last! I'll get Kate to store them until I can plant them this weekend. No point lugging 400 bulbs up and back down again.

Smoothing her hair and taking time to smear on a trace of lipstick, Rose waved to Max and trotted from her apartment. When she entered the Reception Hall, Kate Alexander was absorbed in filling out forms at the desk. There was no package in sight.

"Oh, Kate, thank goodness my bulbs have arrived. It is planting time . . ."

A familiar voice cried "Gan!" and a tall, bearded, handsome young man stepped from behind the Chinoiserie screen and started for Rose with outstretched arms.

"Tom? Tom! It *is* Tom!"

Rose embraced her oldest grandson and in a wink he had lifted her up and swung her around the room as she protested that she was too heavy for him.

"You are a sight for sore eyes, Tom! I can't believe it's really you! That beard! And you've gotten taller! Oh my, how you look like your grandfather! I may shed a tear if I'm not careful. Or faint from this excitement. I'm thrilled to see you, Tom." Rose hugged Tom tightly and kissed him soundly on both cheeks.

"Kate, did I tell you about my grandson in Japan? Of course I did. Well, this is he!"

"And I have had the pleasure of delivering your package, Mrs. McNess," blushed Kate. "He insisted on the surprise; he's very persuasive."

"Gan! You never mentioned the younger generation here at Wynfield Farms! Miss Alexander is a real bonus!" Tom was staring at Kate with undisguised admiration in his blue eyes.

"Tom, this is too good to be true. Do you have time to come up to my apartment for a visit? Oh, there is so much I have to ask you. . . . I don't know where to begin. Say you'll stay a minute, please?"

"Of course, Gan, I planned on it. Not too long, but time enough for a chat. Besides, I have to see old Max, and your apartment. This layout is some kind of swank. Huge by Japanese standards."

Rose noticed that Tom winked at Kate as he turned to follow his grandmother up the stairs.

"So you like the looks of our receptionist, Tom?" inquired Rose. "Kate is a superior young woman, and smart, to boot."

"I gather," said Tom. "She's way ahead of me, halfway toward her Master's."

"Tom! You've been here barely half an hour and you already know her academic credentials?" Rose was curious and delighted by Tom's interest in Kate Alexander.

"She was working on a paper at her desk. One of her course papers and I couldn't help reading the title as I was waiting for her to dial you. We chatted a bit. Watch out, Gan, I may become a regular here at Wynfield. Think they'd give me a job? I'm unemployed!"

They both laughed at this prospect. As they approached Rose's door Miss Puffenbarger was leaving Number 212. Her eyes stared vacantly and her expressionless face revealed nothing. No semblance of the smiling, cheery countenance that had greeted the Featherstone-Whittington uproar of the morning. Rose decided against introductions.

"Hope she's not your typical neighbor," whispered Tom as they entered Number 208.

An ecstatic Max hurled himself at Tom. Then the little dog stood on his hind legs and danced and whimpered joyfully. He nosed the boy's pockets in hopes of finding a treat, then ran and fetched his toy for Tom to throw.

"Same old Max! He does remember me, Gan!"

"Of course he does!"

"How old is Max now," asked Tom, "ten or eleven?"

"Twelve, soon thirteen. On Halloween, remember?"

"That's right; Halloween. Say, Gan, this is really nice. I mean it. But where is all your furniture? Haven't you been here almost six months?"

Rose doubled over in chuckles. "Seven, Tom. And this is it. I'm fully unpacked, dear."

"But you had a house *full* of stuff. This looks like my freshman dorm room. What happened?" Tom was walking around Rose's apartment, exploring the alcove for the bed, the closets, the tiny kitchen, her "office."

"Your old Smith-Corona! Gan, we've got to get you on-line! Has Dad talked to you about a lap-top? We must move you out of the dark ages!"

"Now, Tom, my antique typewriter does everything I ask of it. Don't try to sell me on a computer. I am set in my ways in some things."

"Bet you still have your old Chevy Nova, too. How many miles, Gan? Hit that hundred thousand yet?" Tom settled his lanky frame deep into the depths of the wing chair and draped a long leg over the arm rest. He smiled contentedly at Rose, thinking that two years had changed her very little. A few less pounds, a few more lines, hair about the same. Still perky, still energetic, still in command.

"My Chevy Nova enjoys perfect health, Tom, despite the

efforts of your mother to upgrade me to a heavier car. Which of course I am not about to do." Rose rather enjoyed her ongoing battle with Annie, knowing that a strange new vehicle would never replace her beloved familiar wheels.

Rose pulled up one of her kitchen chairs and perched on the edge. "Tom, I will tell you what I have told your mother and the other children. I have spent too many years being possessed by things, even things that I collected and loved. Right now, in my bonus years, I don't have time to dust and catalogue and polish and worry about the extras. I want to spend my days *living*! And I do! Your mother has boxes packed away for you and the other children; she'll explain. But enough about me! Tell me about your trip home. Siberian Express and everything!"

Tom digested what his grandmother had said and began, "That's right. Traveled by train across Russia to Kiev, then Budapest, Vienna, Paris, London. And I flew to New York from there. I think I'm still in a time-warp. Six days on the train with practically zero sleep, then catnaps the rest of the way. But I feel great! Fascinating trip; can't wait to get my pictures back. I have slides of the Russian countryside you won't believe. . . ."

Rose and Tom talked nonstop for another thirty minutes. Rose felt her head spinning with the excitement of having her grandson safely home. Suddenly she stopped mid-sentence.

"Tom! Where are my manners! Guess what I made this week?"

"Not 'Little Strangers!' "

"One and the same. Wait, let me bring the box." Rose hurried to the cabinet and retrieved a large and dented cookie tin.

"Gee, Gan, you didn't give away everything. Still the same old box." Tom reached in and helped himself to a handful of the moist oatmeal and coconut concoctions that Rose called "Rangers." The children had long ago dubbed her "Queen of the Rangers."

"This is such fun, Tom, but I don't want you to overstay your time. Did you hate to leave your school in Machida? And your faculty housing?"

"My school, yes. A special place. Really neat people, the

faculty, the boys and girls. I even got a pretty good lacrosse team going."

"Was your apartment about this size?"

"Gosh, no. Just a six-tatami size, which translates into the smallest possible for a single faculty member."

"And how big is a tatami, Tom? Approximately three feet by six?" Rose was intrigued by this unit of measurement.

"That's about right. I had all the room I needed and all the things I needed. Sort of like you, Gan, in this apartment."

"A lesson in life, Tom. I think your years in Japan served you well!"

"Correct as always, Gan. Gee, I'd better hustle. Wish I could stroll over the grounds with you and Max but I'll save that for another day. Beautiful here. I didn't even know Wynfield existed until Ma wrote that you had decided to move. It's really in the country but I made it from Roanoke in about forty minutes."

Rose decided that she had better not address the issue of who determined her move here.

"Say, Gan, who's the geezer out prowling along the road when I came in? All dressed up and carrying a briefcase and poking along the side of the road like a bottle collector."

"That," sighed Rose, "is our Yale graduate, Mr. Albert Warrington. What he does and where he goes is a mystery. Might *be* collecting bottles. He may be an avid recycler."

"And the stork in the pith helmet coming out of the woods as I turned in the gates? Who is she?"

"Mrs. Keynes-Livingston. Tom, you're going to think Wynfield is full of zany eccentrics if you judge us by the few residents you've seen! You're just not ready for this Western culture!"

"They just looked odd, Gan. Sorry, probably your best friends. They may think I'm the wild man with this beard. What do you think about the beard, Gan? Does it go or stay?"

"Let me ponder that question, Tom. You know I think you look good any way. Actually, it is rather distinguished. I may just get used to it."

They hugged and Tom scratched Max vigorously behind his ears.

"Think you can find your way down? There's just the one flight of stairs at the end of the corridor. And I bet Miss Alexander would like a farewell wave from you!" Rose added this last remark jokingly but she had the distinct impression that Tom would stop and say good-by to Kate.

Tom grinned back and waved to Rose as he headed down the wide corridor.

~~~

~~~

ECHOES

Katherine Starr Alexander

KATE ALEXANDER is practically a household name at Wynfield Farms!

Kate not only manages the main desk in the Reception Hall but calls and cancels taxis, makes appointments, finds lost pets, remembers birthdays, answers incoming calls of inquiry and radiates charm and goodwill while she is doing this.

Kate's welcoming smile gives new meaning to the morning at Wynfield.

A graduate of Hollins College, Kate is currently doing graduate work at Virginia Tech in the field of psychology. She is a native of Hickory, North Carolina, but says that now she feels like a "real Virginian."

Kate, all of us here at Wynfield hope that you are a "real Virginian" and will remain here at Wynfield Farms!

R. McNess

~~~
~~~

16

Tom Brewster loped the length of the corridor and raced down the stairs to the Reception Hall in three minutes. To his intense disappointment the cute redhead was engrossed in a lengthy telephone conversation and did not glance up as he slowed his pace and crossed the large room. He paused for a second on the front steps, hands shoved into his jeans, and wondered if he should return and speak to the receptionist.

Nope. Better get moving. Got to move my stuff out of the living room before Ma has a fit. And I have to stop by the camera shop on the way into town. Wow! What beautiful trees. Magnificent foliage. Resembles one of the Temple parks near Machida.

Tom walked to Visitors' Parking where the sugar maples offered a dazzling display of popsicle orange and lemon yellow, each out-sparkling its neighbor with broad strokes from Mother Nature's paintbrush.

"Awesome!" he exclaimed. "Bet Ma hasn't seen that!"

My guess is that there is some good hiking around here, too. Of course the Wynfield residents don't indulge but anybody else could. Over there somewhere is House Mountain, and wait . . . I bet that's Tinker a little to the south . . . Sure it is.

Excited at the prospect of these hiking possibilities Tom climbed into his mother's car and started out of the parking lot.

He passed Rose's faded gray Nova sitting snugly in the corner of Residents' Parking.

Good old Gan—she's a real tiger! he thought with a smile.

~~~

From her window Rose watched Tom cross the driveway until he got into Annie's Volvo and drove off. *Such good long strides; he bolts across the ground just like his granddad!*

What a surprise! And a shock for Kate Alexander, too! Wouldn't that be something if Kate and Tom . . . there I go again. Matchmaking already! But I have always been so fond of Kate. I hope Tom asks me for my opinion.

A soft whine at her side alerted Rose to look down at the upturned muzzle of her pet. Max's brown eyes were fastened on her.

"Oh, Max. I guess you think I've forgotten you today. You're right; it's time for your afternoon walk. Almost four o'clock!"

Rose reluctantly left the cozy, seat-worn comfort of her favorite chair and stretched. *It's a good thing I've got you, Max, or I'd just vegetate all afternoon. We both need fresh air.*

"Let me make a call or two, Max, just quickies, and then we'll go. I promise."

Max, accustomed to this tone, stretched out in his "rug" position" by the door and began his patient wait.

This day is too special to let it slip by without celebration. I'll have Ellie over, and Bob Lesley. I owe him. And Miss Puffenbarger; she seemed so down. And the lovebirds, of course. The Major does make a great martini! And this is a martini night!

Rose made four calls. Her friends were home and eagerly accepted Rose's invitation for drinks at 6 P.M. She hung up after chatting with Vinnie Whittington and found herself jittery with anticipation.

"Why, I feel so good I think I'll include Mrs. Keynes-Livingston. I did tell her I'd meet and go over plans for the Fete. Maybe we can chat or at least set a time for a meeting. Yes, I shall call her. She's not one of my favorites, but who knows? Nothing is going to cast a shadow on *this* day!"

An astonished Mrs. Keynes-Livingston accepted at once.
~~~

Somehow I don't think she gets many calls like this. I may be breaking the ice . . . or precipitating a thaw, Rose thought.

"Max, just one more. Sorry. But I can't exclude Lib Meecham. She's your friend, too, remember? She's been so helpful to me in the Library and besides, she saved me a seat at the table the first night Ellie was here. Lib? Rose McNess here. Are you free tonight . . . ?"

Rose's party now numbered eight, including herself. It was by tacit agreement that if residents had evening gatherings they began promptly at six and ended at seven, with guests continuing on to the Dining Room unless other plans had been made.

"Let's go, Max," called Rose, pulling on her windbreaker and snapping Max's leash. "This is going to be quick."

In the Reception Hall, Rose paused a moment at Kate's desk. Kate was just hanging up the phone and she turned to smile at Rose.

"Why didn't you tell me your grandson was so handsome, Mrs. McNess?"

"Well, I don't like to brag too much . . . but he is kind of nice looking, isn't he?"

"And so interesting! Why not a slide lecture in the Lounge when he gets his slides all developed? I bet everyone would enjoy that."

She's absolutely smitten! Smitten, in one afternoon. The younger woman was looking dreamily at Rose.

"Good idea, Kate. I'll talk to Tom after he gets settled. I assume he'd be willing. But I'll have to see what Miss Moss will let us schedule."

"I think she just better let us schedule him," replied Kate testily. "After all, he is your grandson."

"We'll work on it, Kate," promised Rose, leading Max outdoors.

The pair tramped for an hour. Max turned over every leaf that had fallen during his absence. He flushed a pair of mourning doves by the lake and spooked a small rabbit beyond an Alberta spruce.

Rose inhaled deeply, drinking in the crisp air and the showy brilliance of the sunshine-yellow maples that were at their peak. Two hawks swooped in wide and lazy circles over the hills to the South. A jet flew overhead. Its roar exhausted rapidly and a skiff of a wind quickly dissipated its contrail, leaving Rose to wonder if she had imagined this modern intruder of the heavens. A distant *chuff-chuff* of a farmer's tractor meant that the fields were being worked, probably for the final time before frost. *That could be the Puffenbarger's farm. Miss Puffenbarger told me that she grew up within walking distance of Wynfield.*

Small birds searching for autumn's seeds and berries darted among the manicured shrubs and thatch, their noisy chirping reminding Rose of a group of pre-schoolers on a picnic. Except for Max's constant rustling and these natural sounds, it was a hushed world in Montremont Gardens.

Next time Tom comes I will insist that he walk with us. My favorite time of the day; at least, today it is!

"Enough, Max. Treat time." At the magic word, "Treat," Max turned and trotted obediently toward his home in 208.

"Actually, Max, it's treat time for Mother, also!" Rose was still exhilarated over Tom's visit and the prospects of the approaching evening. "I'll stop and beg Faye for a bag of ice. I've got that tin of Smithfield ham spread in the pantry. Pity I don't have any of Tinnell's ham biscuits in the freezer. Oh, well. Do I have crackers? Of course, I always keep crackers. I've got gin; one lemon will be ample, olives . . ." Rose was so immersed in the inventory of her pantry that she did not see Albert Warrington coming up the driveway until they very nearly crashed into one another.

"I'm so sorry!" she exclaimed, collecting Max who had somehow wound his leash around her legs in the confusion. "Bob Jenkins keeps telling me I should reduce my hazards! Hope I didn't upset your papers . . ." Rose was staring at Mr. Warrington's briefcase. It was bulging. Perceptively bulging with one buckle not latched.

"No, no; no harm done. Nothing amiss." Albert Warrington spoke amiably. "Just finishing your walk, are you? Lovely day today! Perfect fall day. Yes, indeed. Going in now, Mrs. McNess? After you."

"Rose, please. And yes, we are going in. I wonder . . . I'm having a few of the second-floor residents in for a drink before dinner tonight. A celebration, really. Would you . . . care to join us, Mr. Warrington?"

Rose impulsively blurted the invitation before thinking. She was often guilty of this.

"Why, that's very kind of you, Mrs. McN . . . Rose. But I really cannot this evening. I have a great deal of reading to catch up on. Some other time, perhaps? So kind of you to ask." He tipped his camel-hair cap as he looked at Rose with an expression of relief mingled with gratitude and backed away as she and Max preceded him into the Reception Hall.

"Some other time! Have a good evening!" burbled Rose cheerily to the departing figure as she hustled to find Faye.

Ice in hand, she climbed the steps to her apartment.

Why in the world did I ask Mr. Warrington to join us? Mr. Warrington! Notice he didn't ask me to call him Albert. I asked him for the same reason I included the Livingston woman: still don't know her first name. Here I go, playing tour leader. Where in the world has Mr. Warrington been all day? I watched him leave Wynfield at dawn and Tom said he saw him along the roadside when he drove in. A bit peculiar? He certainly didn't look perturbed. If anything, he seemed euphoric. Another puzzle, Max?

~~~

~~~

ECHOES

Ernest Norton

The tall, khaki-clad figure wielding a saw, clippers, wheelbarrow or shovel pops up just about everywhere on the Wynfield Farms' grounds. If that figure happens to be wearing an Atlanta *Braves* cap you can be sure it is ERNEST NORTON.

Ernest has worked at Wynfield Farms for more than thirty years. While he did not know Samuel T. Wynfield, Sr., he knew and respected his grandsons and their families. The Nottingham Corporation's smartest move was to retain Ernest, who has first-hand, feet-wise knowledge of almost every inch of the estate. Golfers among us have Ernest to thank for keeping the greens in tip-top shape. Gardeners may wonder how the flower beds stay weeded, mulched and trimmed so precisely. Wonder no longer: Ernest does it! In addition to his many outside assignments Ernest makes sure the wood bins are filled for the roaring fires we enjoy and that the elevators function properly.

Ernest is a native of Botetourt County and lives nearby with his wife, Hazel. (Hazel is the talented lady who makes and delivers those delicious sweet potato pies we enjoy every week!) Their two children are grown and married.

Ernest, if only each of us had your common sense and energy!

-R. McN.

~~~
~~~

17

At 6 P.M. sharp, Ellie Johnson knocked on Rose's door. She carried an open can of Macadamia nuts in her left hand and a chubby jar of giant olives in her right.

"Thought you could use a few necessities!" she called happily as she nibbled.

"Ellie, how thoughtful! Come on in; let's get down to serious matters here," invited her hostess. Rose had changed from her daytime "uniform" of cardigan and slacks into one of her three remaining "best" dresses: navy wool crepe with long sleeves and pleated skirt. A thin gold choker at the modest neckline was her only accessory.

Another knock announced Vinnie and the Major, who rolled in noiselessly in their wheelchairs.

"Rose, you are lovely to do this!" exuded Vinnie. "Your apartment is so spacious . . . with just the right homey touches!"

"My children call it downright *bare*, Vinnie, but I like it this way. Family pictures carry all the past memories I need. I can't wait to see how you arrange *your* living quarters; it makes so much sense to remove that wall. Less wall space but more chair space." Rose was conversing with a beaming Vinnie when three other guests arrived simultaneously and she hurried away to close the apartment door. She was conscious of the noise factor on the second floor, despite the thickness of the walls. Then she realized that almost all her guests lived on the second floor; there was no one left to disturb. At that moment Henrietta Puffenbarger walked in, resplendent in long, dress-Gordon kilt and starched white shirt. An old-fashioned oval cameo anchored the tens of vertical tucks marching across this woman's shelf-like bosom.

"Come in, Miss Puffenbarger! What a handsome kilt! We have started without you, but just barely. We renegades are having martinis but I also have sherry, wine, bourbon, Scotch . . ."

"And I am the bartender," called the Major. "Light at a feather, heavy as a stone . . . same in hand as in name. What's your poison, m'dear? And I for one shall address you as Henrietta!"

Everyone should have a Major Featherstone as a neighbor, thought Rose. *He sparks every gathering!*

"Please do, Major. And I should like Scotch, please. Single malt if Rose has it. On the rocks, please, with just a splash of water."

"Bravo, Henrietta!" Rose exclaimed. "I'm proud of you! I'm a devotee of single malt also. Martinis are my *celebration* drink only. Tell me, did you fall for malts *and* kilts on a trip to Scotland?"

"Actually, no; single malt was Papa's drink of choice. He insisted I try it when I turned twenty-five and I've drunk nothing else since."

"He was a wise man, Henrietta," solemnly intoned the Major as he handed her a chunky glass of the pale amber Dalwhinnie.

"I want to ask you about your handsome kilt, and your family farm, but first . . . does everyone have a drink?" asked Rose, looking at the crowd of nine in her small living room. The assembled group raised their glasses to signify the affirmative.

"Then I would like to propose a toast," said Rose. "Actually, two toasts. The first salute is to our friends: Major Featherstone and Eleanor, rather, Vinnie. And to our first wedding in Wynfield Farms. To the Major and his lady: long life and much happiness!"

The friends all clinked glasses, whooped a loud "Cheers!" and sipped happily.

"Next," continued Rose, raising her voice above the resumed conversations, "I should like to propose a toast to my grandson, Tom. He is not among us this evening, but he has just returned safely from two years in Japan. To Tom!"

"To Tom!" chorused the residents.

The noise level in the apartment increased fully ten decibels after the last toast. Well-wishes were exchanged. Rose was questioned about Tom's arrival and future plans. The possibility of a slide show lecture was embraced enthusiastically. Rose observed Dr. Lesley chatting animatedly with Ellie. Of the nine present, only he had not really spent any length of time with her since her arrival. *They'll enjoy one another. I won't mention Mary tonight; thinking about her makes me feel guilty!*

Lib Meecham was spreading ham paté on thin wheat-crackers. Completing the task she slipped among the guests to distribute the salty delicacies and to exchange chit-chat.

Mrs. Keynes-Livingston was standing apart. Surveying the scene she reluctantly admitted to herself that she was flattered to be included.

"Mrs. Keynes-Livingston," Rose called to the stork-like woman standing in the corner near Rose's "office." "I cannot for the life of me remember your first name, *if* I've ever known it. But please call me Rose."

"I'm Frances. Never Fran or Franny. But Frances; I'd be flattered if you would call me Frances.

Frawn-ces, Rose echoed silently. *Why, she is thawing . . . and actually smiling! I may like her more than I thought. Hope I can remember to pronounce it the way she does: Frawn-ces, Frawn-ces.*

"I told you I would be happy to help you with the Fete, Frances. I hope Miss Moss is not making it too difficult. Giving you some leeway, as it were. I'll be happy to meet with you any time you suggest—other than tonight, of course." Rose realized that she was prattling without pause or hesitation—a phenomenon compared to the minimal conversations held previously with Mrs. Keynes-Livingston.

It's that tall woman-short woman complex I have, admitted Rose to herself. *Tall women simply put me off. And they shouldn't.*

If people were flowers, Frances Keynes-Livingston would be an amaryllis . . . and I? . . . a clover. . . .

In the midst of her speculations Major Featherstone noisily tapped his empty glass and immediately captured everyone's attention.

Gosh, is it seven already? Rose looked at her watch. *Don't want to make all of us late for dinner. We'll look guilty enough going in all rosy and giggly!*

"Ladies and gentlemen," began the Major, "Eleanor, my Vinnie, and I have something to tell you."

Every eye in the room was on the attractive, white-maned, retired Army man and the diminutive lady with the astonishing sapphire eyes.

"Miss Moss has gotten wind of my morning capers and is taking our case to the Board next week for 'review of action.' What I have to tell you, rather, ask you, is whether or not our action has disturbed you and would you be willing to sign a petition on our behalf? Not very well put, I'm afraid, but you do grasp the situation?"

"Major," asked Mrs. Keynes-Livingston, "isn't a Board review rather *after* the fact? That is, you have removed the wall and are ensconced, as I understand it."

"To be sure, to be sure," replied the Major. "And I have calculated removal expenses and cosmetic repairs *to the penny*. And have the check ready to place on Miss Moss's desk in the morning. My move—*our* move—in no way presents a financial expense to Wynfield Farms. It is just that I have committed the unforgivable in Miss Moss's eyes: I have broken a rule by breaking down a wall. I have rebelled against conformity! Seniors just don't do that!"

The room erupted in a roar of indignation. Everyone talked at once, offering advice to the Major, then to Vinnie, and hastily signing the carefully crafted petition that the Major had withdrawn from his pocket.

"Something should be done about Miss Moss," offered Lib Meecham. "The woman is a square peg in a round hole. I just know that she is not a happy person."

"She is transmitting her unhappiness among us, or trying to," added Henrietta Puffenbarger.

"Certainly a psychological study in moods," contributed ever-professional Dr. Lesley.

"Well, I've been here less than a week and she has been pleasant enough to me," said Ellie. "Maybe because I *am* new and haven't caused her any problems . . . yet."

"Do you plan on causing problems, Ellie?" asked Bob Lesley.

The room burst into gales of laughter and happy talk once again.

Again Major Featherstone tapped his glass.

"Speech, Major, on the knotty problem of Miss Moss!" cried Rose.

"I yield the floor to my lady," responded Major Featherstone gallantly.

"Well," began Vinnie Whittington in a dulcet Southern voice as thick as Mississippi's Natchez Trace, "I'd simply like to add a tiny bit to what each of you already knows so well. Life is ninety percent hope. The other ten percent is hard work. The Major and I figure between us that we are rich in hope. We look forward to pooling our resources, our mutual hopes, and having many good seasons together. We look forward to our families gathering to bless us in our union, but, as I told some of you this morning, a month of waiting at our age is a long time."

"Hear! Hear!" A soft cheer of approbation flew from the crowd.

"Vinnie," said Rose, "if you tell the Board exactly what you have just told us, they can and will do nothing to you and the Major. And I say who cares what the board does to Miss Moss!"

Hope, hope, hope! thought Rose. *The fuel that keeps us going*!

"Rose, I think we should forget dinner and order pizza," offered Dr. Lesley. "Fat content be damned. This is too good a party to break up."

"Alas, but break up we must," replied Rose. "And we'd better leave right now. Don't want the wrath of you-know-who to come down upon us. I've upset too many of her well-laid plans already. Time, everyone; just leave your glasses on the counter. Thanks *so much* for making this a memorable celebration!"

Good-byes and more kisses were given to the Major and his lady who rolled on toward the elevator as the remainder of the group headed for the stairs. All continued talking animatedly as if they had never seen each other before.

Rose sighed happily. She knew that the gathering had been a success. The timing had been perfect. She and Frances were now friends; perhaps not chums, but friends. Ellie had had a chance to talk with Bob Lesley, and Henrietta Puffenbarger had blossomed!

Who would have thought she drank single malt? And I never got a chance to ask about that stunning kilt.

Rose stole a glance at her neighbor. Miss Puffenbarger was chatting enthusiastically with the good doctor, and gesturing with both hands, a large opal ring prominent on her right hand.

Something clicked in Rose's head. *There's something unusual about that ring. What is it?*

Rose shivered. A slight tremor, a premonition, swept over her, closing out Ellie's chatter at her left. She was trying to reconstruct her first meeting with Miss Puffenbarger.

It had been upstairs, in the corridor. She had sensed then this same vague mood of uneasiness. *What is it? Why does she make me feel unhinged?* Rose asked herself. Fragmented thoughts crowded into her brain.

Shaking her head as if to brush off the cobwebs, Rose and the entourage entered the Dining Room after the prospective bride and groom.

What a tour group I've got now! Genuine romance aboard the "love boat"!

~~~
~~~

ECHOES

Frances Garnett Keynes-Livingston

When Wynfield's first "Fall Fete" takes place, it will be right and proper to recognize the driving force behind it: FRANCES KEYNES-LIVINGSTON.

Tireless gardener, shrewd card player, devoted mother of three—all apply to Frances. While "home" was mainline Philadelphia (Ardmore) for most of her life, Frances has been happily settled in Virginia for almost ten years, four of these at Wynfield. Her children live in the Old Dominion so it was natural for Frances to move South to be closer to her brood.

Frances' talent for organizing activities and events has long been recognized by churches and community groups to which she has belonged. She never seems to run out of ideas or energy, and has the ability to convince others around her that it is FUN to become involved in her latest project.

After hearing just a few of Frances Keynes-Livingston's plans, I'm sure the "Fall Fete" will be a rousing success!

-R. McN.

~~~
~~~

18

Max's persistent grunts roused Rose the next morning. She sat up in bed and looked at the sky: brilliant blue and cloudless.

"Who says weather doesn't affect your mood, Max? On a day like this I can take on the world!" With a bound Rose was up. She made coffee, dressed and was out the door with her pet for a vigorous constitutional.

It's even too early for Kate, Max! Rose missed the pretty receptionist who had not yet arrived. *She is the first person people see when they walk into Wynfield Farms. And what a fine impression she makes! Always so courteous and sweet with all of us elderly persons. Her smile is worth a King's ransom!*

Rose and Max stepped down the wide steps and onto the gravel drive. The Lombardy poplars were swaying and waltzing in the gentle breeze, showering the beckoning promenade with leaves of gold and gray-green and umber. "This morning we're going in a new direction, Max. I just feel like something different."

Long accustomed to his own routine and predetermined routes, Max stood still and looked at his mistress for a minute as if to ask, "Are you sure about this?" Then he trotted along eagerly, anticipating new scents that lay outside the gates of Wynfield Farms.

The air was fresh. Rose could sniff maple leaves, sumac, just-plowed fields. Birds were trilling early morning serenades. She stopped to watch a scarlet cardinal tease a seed loose and then fly off to one of the tall cedars bordering the road leading from the Wynfield property.

"I share Ellie's feelings, Max; I'd be lost without bird song. Thank heavens for good hearing . . . so far!"

Max was too busy investigating new smells to look up.

Rose was happily replaying last evening's party and was content to let her companion lead her astray. *One thing's certain: we got no further in solving the problem of what to do about Miss Moss. It's the old tale of "belling the cat." Everyone agrees that something must be done, but no one is volunteering for the job. I'll avoid her for the next few days. When we meet again, I'll put forth a concerted effort to be nice.*

Mrs. Keynes-Livingston has the Fall Fete under control; we don't need Miss Moss to consult with us . . . Oops! Can't forget my 9:30 meeting this morning. Last night was one of my better ideas, if I do say so! And that Henrietta Puffenbarger is more of a riddle than before. She must have serious bouts of mood swings. I'm just glad she was "up" last night!

Rose and Max walked another quarter mile before turning and retracing their path back to Wynfield. Suddenly, Max stopped. He refused to budge, straining at the leash and sniffing furiously at the underbrush.

"What is it, Max?" Rose asked. "Do you see a chipmunk?"

Rose stepped cautiously into the ground covering that Max was probing with his nose. The little dog's tail was quivering wildly and his investigative efforts were becoming more frantic with every step he took.

"Why, it's a rabbit's nest, Max. Didn't burrow this time, did they? Little bits of fur still sticking there; some animal's gotten the babies, I'm afraid. Not a very smart mama to build where it was so exposed." Rose was as fascinated as Max.

"What's this?" Rose spotted a knotted cloth pushed under

some adjacent briars. Stooping to retrieve it, she held it limply by its corners and saw a monogram along one side: "A.C.C.W." Even though the piece was damp and soiled Rose knew fine linen when she saw it.

Too big for a handkerchief. A hand towel? Yes, that's exactly what it is, a fine linen hand towel. A.C.C.W. . . . *why, it's Albert Warrington! I remember his full name from my interview. All those family names he was so proud to tell me about. Albert Warrington's hand towel in a rabbit's nest! Max, you are a regular detective!*

Rose chuckled out loud. She stuffed the damp towel in the pocket of her red windbreaker and gave Max's leash a determined tug.

"Enough, Max, if you want breakfast." Reluctantly the Scottie turned and walked docilely beside his mistress.

One more knot to unravel, she thought. I don't even want to contemplate the possible motives for his towel being out here in the field!

The sharp *beep-beep* of a horn warned Rose and Max to jump even further to the shoulder.

"Mrs. McNess! Didn't mean to frighten you! Hop in! I'll give you a lift!" It was Kate Alexander arriving to begin her workday.

"Kate! How grand to see you! Glorious morning, isn't it?" Rose waved and smiled at the scrubbed, beaming face leaning out the car window. "Thanks, but you know Rose's Rule 'Never ride if you can still walk!' We need the exercise; see you inside in a few minutes!"

The young woman saluted briskly in response and the car sped around the corner toward the estate.

"Max, you are not the only one who needs breakfast. Coffee, coffee; it's calling me."

Rose's recent discovery, the soggy, dirty material in her pocket, was, for the time being, quite forgotten. Frances Keynes-Livingston had said 9:30 sharp in the South Lounge and Rose intended to be on time.

~~~
~~~

The two women spent a full hour discussing the upcoming Fall Fete.

It was apparent to Rose, as Frances Keynes-Livingston talked logistics and minute details, that Frances was a veteran of chairing such celebrations and was in total command of the operation. She was the Commander-in-Chief and Wynfield Farms was her battleground. Rose was happy to sit and listen and offer a minimum of suggestions.

I don't even know why she roped me into this event. She doesn't need me!

"Frances, may I ask you something?"

"Certainly, Rose; I value your input."

"It's not about the Fete. It's your lichens."

"My lichens?"

"Yes, all the lichens you collect. What do you do with them?"

"I am trying to categorize by age and algae the numerous classifications of lichen represented in the limestone-influenced growth in the Shenandoah Valley. Lichenology was my specialty in college and graduate school. It is, my dear, an addictive pursuit. One learns the most fascinating things from the growth on a rock or tree trunk."

"Why do I suspect you are Bryn Mawr. Am I correct?"

"You are! And you, Rose . . . Smith? Wellesley?"

"Wellesley! And Hollins. I always enjoyed picking up courses at Hollins."

Their educational backgrounds thus established, the two continued their planning.

"You know, Rose, Miss Moss is utterly incapable of utilizing the minds here to their best advantage. Not her own nor those of the residents. We have some fine intellects among us. Why, Miss Moss envisioned the Fall Fete to be a sort of 'forest festival,' outdoorsy and pagan. Virtually a carnival. Can you imagine the absurdity of it? That is why I said yes to chairing the blasted affair. I am determined that Wynfield's Fall Fete will be a dignified performance. Do you ever feel like shaking your fist at that woman?"

"There are things best left unsaid, Frances," replied Rose, glancing at her new acquaintance. "Thank heavens you did say *yes*! She'd trample over anyone with less spine than yourself! Besides, you have a real gift for organization; I appreciate that. Looks like the Fete will bring out the best in everyone. I had no idea we had such musical talent here at Wynfield."

"You are avoiding the subject, Rose, by being exceedingly tactful. But I sense that you share my jaundiced view of Miss Moss." Frances halted, frowning. Unspoken words dangled in the air between the pair. "Yes, musical talent we have in abundance. And readers. Arthur Everett is splendid with Shakespeare. And he has asked Lib Meecham to read a scene with him."

"*Romeo and Juliet?*" joked Rose.

"Next year!" shot back a smiling Mrs. Keynes-Livingston.

"Now, Rose," began the lady with the pearls, "here is the thing I think only you can accomplish. You are the one person at Wynfield who seems to communicate with Madame Zdorek. Your love of animals, perhaps? Do you believe you could persuade her to sing for us at the Fete?"

Rose's mouth flew open in amazement. "Me? You think I could persuade her to do what no one else has been able to do the entire three years she's lived at Wynfield?"

"She was extraordinarily famous, you know," continued Frances Keynes-Livingston as if she had not heard Rose's protests. "Had a glorious operatic career before the war. Berlin, Dresden, Leipzig, Budapest, Prague. She sang in all those cities. I looked her up in the *Who's Who of 20th Century Musicians*. Would you mind asking her, Rose?"

"Oh, I realize she's quite a celebrity! I did that profile on her, you may remember, for *Wynsong*. But would we be doing her an injustice? Perhaps her voice is gone. She is, after all, up in her eighties. I hate to use the word 'old' . . . but that is what she is."

"I have a feeling we might be surprised, Rose. And, if she does not want to actually *sing* for us, she could play one of her recordings and talk a bit about it. How does that strike you?"

"Excellent, Frances. But how about the accompanist? The

piano is here, but who plays well enough to accompany a diva of Jana's caliber?"

"Ha! I thought you'd never ask. Don't you remember? Betty Gehrmann studied at Julliard, taught piano for thirty years. And I'll personally take charge of getting the piano tuned. Immediately. I've already secured Betty's services for the Fete. All that remains is for you to get Jana to sing!"

"You've thought of everything. Wait a minute, maestro. What is this blip: 'Musical Welcome'? Betty again?" Rose was reading Frances Keynes-Livingston's notes. "And here, 'Musical Interlude.' Do we have other hidden treasures?" Rose looked at Frances quizzically.

"Not hidden. I've just never had the chance to reveal it," replied the Chairman shyly.

"You play?" asked Rose. "The violin? Viola? Oh, I do envy you!"

"The accordion," said Mrs. Keynes-Livingston.

"The WHAT? Accordion? I've never known anyone, no, not *anyone* who played the accordion! I've just heard, and seen it done, on television . . . looks terribly complicated and difficult, all that fingering . . ."

"Well," her companion replied archly, "*now* you know someone who plays. I studied the accordion throughout my childhood. I hated it at the beginning, and then it became my best friend. When I reached adolescence and became so tall and gawky, *and* homely, I found that it ensured my being asked to all the parties. And I had something to do with my hands. The boys loved the accordion. Never mind that I was never asked to dance; it was more fun being the star! Teenage years are so awkward and cruel. I would have been an absolute wallflower had I not played my way through."

"Frances, I just have to confess." Rose looked at Frances Keynes-Livingston and spoke, a tinge of awe in her voice. "I have been intimidated by you ever since our first meeting. No, no, don't say anything. Intimidated mostly because you are everything I am not: tall, well-groomed, calm, coordinated, but mostly, *tall*. And willowy. I was convinced you grew up like a beautiful hot-house flower, supremely happy and living a life of luxury. To hear you speak of awkward times . . . and to know you play that bulky instrument . . . well, I am flabbergasted!"

The other woman laughed, causing Rose to do the same. Their joyous outburst eclipsed the hint of a strain that had hovered since the beginning of the meeting.

"My husband was not proud of my playing, so essentially I gave it up during our marriage. I had very few opportunities to show off, shall we say, for a long period of time. But once you learn the fingering you never forget. I spend many a long evening playing in my room. I try to be a mouse about it. Thank goodness the walls are so thick; I pray my neighbors think it is regular music on public radio . . . or old re-runs of the Lawrence Welk show!"

"Frances, you will bring the house down! You and Jana! Now—what else can I do to help?"

"Programs, Rose. Will you be able to type the programs for us? And add a touch of your art work at the top? Miss Alexander has promised to make copies for us."

"Consider it done. Let me have your notes and I'll hop to it. And I'll stop by Jana's room and see if I still have any powers of persuasion left in me."

"Perfect!" said Mrs. Keynes-Livingston. "If only we could dispense with the ghastly cases in this room. The room resembles a laboratory. Did you realize that Mr. Wynfield captured all the beasts right on these grounds? And preserved them?" She gestured with long arms at the display cases dotting the paneled walls.

"I did, Frances, and they are part and parcel of the tradition of this place. As indigenous as afternoon tea time. I'm afraid the Board would be unforgiving if we even hinted at covering them up for our gala!"

"Ah, well," sighed Mrs. Keynes-Livingston. "At least you know that I consider them offensive and unappetizing. Thank you, Rose. And I have a bit of a confession to make to you. I've been wary of you, the way you settled in immediately, made friends with everyone, got the newsletter revived. I envied your easy way with people. I'm glad you agreed to work with me on the Fete. It has thrown us together and I, for one, feel better for it. I'm actually looking forward to this affair now that you're on board!"

"Same here!" repeated Rose, preparing to leave the Lounge.

Wynfield's Fall Fete, Rose thought, *is going to be memorable!*

~~~

After dinner Rose climbed into bed before nine. She dozed contentedly with the morning paper, unread, spread out on her blanket. Max's snores, sonorous and regular, suddenly shifted to piteous whimpers and puppy-like yelps. Rose woke with a spasm that sent the paper skittering to the rug.

"That's OK, Max; it's all right. I'm here. Mother's here. Go back to sleep."

Probably dreaming of those bunnies he didn't catch.

The thought of bunnies reminded Rose of the mysterious hand towel, still soaking in a bowl of bleach and cold water in the bathroom.

If it hasn't dissolved, she thought. Goodness, this has been a long day. I'm so tired my toes ache. Hmmmm. How shall I present the towel to Albert Warrington? If he's too shy or too busy to come for a drink, I'm certainly not going to bribe him with his hand towel! "Mr. Warrington, here is your hand towel that I found in the field half a mile away!" Too stilted. Too embarrassing. He may not even realize it's missing. A genuine quandary. But one that is not going to leave this room.

Now fully awake Rose looked down at the paper lying beside the bed.

No point reading today's paper when it's almost tomorrow . . . I'll try to go back to sleep . . . I never did see Jana; must try first thing in the morning . . . And was it just today that Annie called about dinner? Saturday night? Or Friday? Saturday, I think . . . must have circled it on the calendar. At least Ellie's all moved in . . . jammed in is more like it. No wonder it took four men to haul her furniture all the way up here . . . but she values my opinion
~~~

and it was a challenge to try and fit all the pieces in . . . that took most of the afternoon . . . I bet Ellie is one tired chicken, too!

Rose was lost in a deep brown study of things done and things left undone.

I'll never feel comfortable calling her Frawnces . . . she's forever Amaryllis.

~~~

~~~

E C H O E S

Madame Jana Paleta Zdorek

When a well-groomed, apricot toy poodle trots past your door you can be sure that MADAME JANA ZDOREK is not far behind! Madame Zdorek and Mille Fleurs, both natives of Prague, The Czech Republic, are virtually inseparable. How they came to the United States and to Wynfield Farms is a tale too long to tell in these pages. It is a saga of intrigue and romance. If that piques your interest, introduce yourself to Madame Zdorek and let her tell you this fascinating story.

Madame Zdorek has been singing professionally since her early twenties. She studied at Karlova Univerzita (Charles University) in Prague and made her musical debut at the famed Stavoske Divadlo ("Theatre of the Estates") in that city. This is the same theatre where Mozart premiered *Don Giovanni* in 1787. In her debut, Madame sang the role of Zerlina from that same opera. She has performed in Berlin, Dresden, Leipzig, London, and New York City, always to enthusiastic crowds, and has received rave reviews from the harshest of critics.

Madame Zdorek's apartment is a treasure trove of memories. Photos, books and recordings share equal space with natural *objets d'art*, revealing her deep love for the gifts of the environment.

Madame Zdorek, you are one of Wynfield Farms' treasures!

-R. McN.

~~~
~~~

19

Lib Meecham and Dr. Lesley were engrossed in a large portfolio of prints spread across one of the wide oak tables in the Library.

"*Gift from Anonymous Donor*," read Lib. "They're priceless. Look at the detail on each engraving. Hand-colored, signed and numbered. The signature says 'M. Orrell.' Probably around the same time as Audubon. Can you imagine giving away something like this?"

"I can," replied Bob Lesley. "Where does one display such prints? Surely not framed and hanging in a private living room. A library is a perfect home for them, where masses can see and enjoy. I know I shall."

"And where someone else's insurance policy will keep them protected," added Lib. "I understand the estate's annuity provides all the insurance on this place: fire, theft, flood, vandalism. Pretty generous of old Wynfield."

"You are a practical woman," said the genial doctor. "Handsome, aren't they? How many in this collection?"

"Twelve. Romero is cutting heavy plastic for each page so that we can display them around the room."

At that moment, Rose, refreshed and recharged after a dreamless night's sleep, appeared. She had decided to short cut through the Library on her route to Madame Zdorek's first floor suite. She greeted Lib and Dr. Lesley with a "Good morning, one and all!" and stopped to see what they were inspecting so intently. The pair welcomed Rose and beckoned her to look at the exquisite botanical prints arrayed before them.

Preoccupied with her mission, Rose made properly admiring remarks before turning to the Librarian and saying, "Lib, I've just met with Mrs. Keynes-Livingston and I'm delighted you've consented to participate in the Fall Fete. I knew there was an ardent thespian under literature's still waters!"

Lib blushed and jostled Dr. Lesley's arm, saying, "And have you heard about the good doctor's talents?"

Rose feigned ignorance.

"Dr. Lesley, Father Charlie and Major Featherstone are devotees of the D'Oyly Carte, the keeper of the Gilbert and Sullivan operas," Lib offered. "In fact, they know the words to almost all the operas. Which ones are you going to highlight for us, Robert?"

"We hope to present lively renditions from both *Penzance* and *Mikado*. Depending upon our accompanist, of course. *And* the prospective bridegroom!"

"Oh, I think he'll be up to it," laughed Rose. "Eleanor will see to that!"

"Rose, thank you for the other evening. A swell party! We need get-togethers like that more often." The doctor spoke enthusiastically, his eyes twinkling.

"Yes, Rose. It was so thoughtful of you . . . and so typical! Thanks so much." Lib Meecham, too, was warm in her gratitude.

"I enjoyed having you," responded Rose. "What I cannot abide are those huge affairs where there is so much noise you have to lean onto your neighbor like a sailboat in a storm and everyone shouts and you still can't hear. And if you *do* hear it sounds as if everyone is talking with a mouthful of mashed potatoes. I much prefer an intimate group; just friends."

She smiled her good-bye to the pair and continued briskly on her way to Kate's desk.

"Kate, would you be a dear and ring Madame Zdorek's apartment for me? My glasses have slipped down into the bottom of this purse and you'll save me at least three minutes if you could . . ."

"Certainly, Mrs. McNess."

She handed the receiver to Rose who listened to three rings, then a sultry voice asking "Yess, who iz eet?" The sibilant sounds recalled a bird song Rose had heard on one of her recent walks.

"It's Rose, Jana; Rose McNess. I was wondering if I could come by for just an instant. I'm in the Reception Hall and could be there in a jiffy. That is, if you're not getting ready to walk Fleur . . ."

"Eet would be my pleazure to greet you," replied Madame Zdorek.

"Fine," said Rose. "I'll be up in a second."

She replaced the receiver carefully. She observed that a basket with daisies, pale blue Dutch iris and miniature pink rosebuds stood beside Kate's nameplate.

A new addition, Rose thought.

"Lovely flowers, Kate. They brighten up the entire room."

"Thank you, Mrs. McNess. They do, don't they? You know who sent them, don't you?" Kate asked, her face becoming as pink as one of the rose buds.

"I could be silly and say, 'Heavens, no idea' . . . but I have some gumption, Kate! I may be resting, but I'm not rusting! Tom?"

"Oh, yes!" bubbled the now red-faced young woman. "Such a pleasant surprise. He really is a dear, Mrs. McNess."

"I could not agree more, Kate. Now, if you'll excuse me, I must run up and chat with Madame Zdorek!"

Turning, she asked, "Oh, Kate, have you seen Mary Rector today?"

"Oh, sure, Mrs. McNess. She took the second bus into town, the ten o'clock. There were six others on it this morning. Six or eight, I'm not sure. Did she have an appointment?"

"No, I'm positive she didn't. Just went along for the ride . . . as usual. I can't seem to stop worrying about Mary."

Kate spoke confidently. "Now don't you worry; Ernest is aware of Mary's habits. Tell you what. I'll give you a ring when she comes in."

Rose felt a wave of relief sweep over her.

"Kate, you're special! Please do! Thanks so much." Rose blew the receptionist a kiss and hurried off to keep her appointment with Madame Jana Zdorek, the "Queen of Prague."

~~~

Madame Zdorek opened the door to her apartment at the first knock.

"Cum een, Rosa, cum een! You are welcoming!"

Rose found Madame Zdorek's Czech accent charming, and also the way she jumbled English, French and German in her conversation. Only when she began talking rapidly—which she did often—were her words unintelligible. Usually there were scatterings of English phrases so Rose could, with some concentration, follow the gist of the conversation.

"You weel hav' café, Rose? I am so pleesured you are here. Un moment; the café is all ready. Down, Mille Fleurs . . . Rosa, you know!"

"I adore your café, Jana. You know that's my weakness! Come here, Fleur; let me love you."

Rose sat in a huge, overstuffed, over-fringed upholstered chair. The fabric, a once handsome, expensive satin in broad stripes of gray and cobalt, was now dull and tired, with patches of loose threads dotting the arms like a bad case of chicken pox.

A miniature apricot poodle jumped into Rose's lap and snuggled down for a nap. Moments later it leaped nimbly to the floor to trail into the kitchen after her mistress.

Rose looked around. All her hesitation and doubts about calling on Jana Zdorek vanished. This apartment was a true reflection of Jana's heritage, her career, her obsession with nature. It was a lifetime's collection as bedizened and eclectic as its occupant. Yet no one object jarred or crowded or overshadowed the next.
~~~

The living room walls were painted a deep pewter color. This neutrality provided the perfect foil for Jana's art collection: varying sizes of oils, mostly landscapes, with wide and deep gilt frames, alternating with somber engravings of cathedrals and opera houses. These served as silent witnesses to the array of two loveseats, three chairs (each equally as large as the one now enveloping Rose), and a scattering of pier tables, floor lamps and a glass-front what-not cabinet.

A giant, square Bechstein piano, centered in front of the long windows at the far end, proudly held pride of place in the room. Rose had heard that it took six men four hours to move the behemoth into Wynfield. She believed it.

Rose was beginning to count the vases of peacock feathers, clutches of autumn leaves and bird nests perched on top of almost everything when Madame returned.

"What a pity Max and Fleur can't be friends, Jana. We could have such fun walking together. But Max doesn't think he's a dog; ergo, he won't associate with other dogs. His hard luck!"

"And who knows what theese dogs theenk?" nodded Madame Zdorek, bearing a silver tray upon which rested a steaming brass coffee urn and two thin porcelain cups and saucers. "Do I recall you dreenk it *schwarz*?"

"The only way, Jana," confirmed Rose, waiting as her hostess situated herself on the plump loveseat and handed her one of the fragile cups.

"I knew Rosa to be, to have, the beest of taste in café," said Jana. "Ees the best, *n'est-ce pas*?"

They nodded and smiled in agreement, both sipping the scalding, thick coffee.

"In my next life, Jana, I want your artistic skills. Your arrangement of everything is . . . lovely? And unique! Those Roman shades are smashing! Your Bechstein might well be resting on the proscenium at an opera house. It is perfect with the handsome shades as backdrop."

"Ach, my luffy new shades. Rosa, you say alvays what Jana luf to be hearing."

Now or never! Rose trembled with anticipation at her question.

"Jana, I have a big favor to ask of you. Bigger even than the interview you granted me last month."

"That eenterview! You made Jana sound . . . *trés marvelous! Eine Linzertorte mit Sahne*! *Ach!* I seent copies to neece in Praha. Madame Jana—een the paper, at my age!"

"Well, now I want you to do something else for me, 'at your age.' What makes you think you have cornered the market for *age*, Madame?" Rose faced her friend squarely and looked into her eyes as she said this. She found her grin becoming contagious.

"Rosa, Rosa, I am having suspeects of you!" laughed Jana. "What can I do possible for you at theese times?"

Rose gulped. Then she blurted: "Sing for us at the Fall Fete on November 19!"

"Seeng? Seeng? Ach, Rosa, *c'est impossible! Mais non chérie . . . impossible!*"

"I knew you would say that, Jana. But let me tell you a little about the Fete. It won't be in a large auditorium—just the South Lounge. The piano there is actually quite good. In fact, Mrs. Keynes-Livingston is going to have it tuned just before the Fete. Your audience would be just your friends here at Wynfield. And you have a lot of those! Well, maybe a few extras, but a small, friendly audience. Plus, all the performers are your Wynfield peers. It would not embarrass you; it would be such a treat for everyone to hear a professional! You are the only real star we have!"

Rose knew she had better stop her runaway gallop and let Madame Zdorek try to absorb the facts.

"You are the flattereeng, Rosa," Madame Zdorek began, "but theese would be breaking my vow of sileencing for all so many years . . ."

"But didn't you tell me last month that you still pulled your recordings out to play when you felt really homesick for Prague? And sang along with them? We wouldn't expect a full repertoire; just one or two simple selections. Of your choice."

Rose hoped that her friend was wavering.

"I'll tell you what, Jana. Promise nothing today. Just think about it. I'll accept your decision, whatever. Maybe in a day or two you'll call me. How does that sound?"

"Absoluement! You make me young, Rosa. Such eneergetic. I weel sleep on it, Rosa; I call you in the morning. Is all right?"

"That's all I can hope for, Jana. Perfect. Now, thank you for the cafe. Delicious as usual. I better get back to my Max. Au revoir, petite Fleur!"

"Au revoir, Rosa!" waved Madame Zdorek.

~~~

Madame Zdorek closed the door, and leaned against it.

"Rosa, Rosa, *mein Wunderkind! Lieber Gott!*"

She walked slowly to the Bechstein. Gnarled but immaculately manicured fingers swept over yellowed keys. She brushed an imagined crumb from the top of the instrument and then turned away. She straightened the engraving of the Wien Stadtopernhaus and stepped back to verify her adjustment. Only after she had returned the café tray to her kitchen and cleared its counters did Madame Zdorek sit down to ponder the unponderable.

~~~

That Rosa—ees so much the mule. Mein Herr Professor say neever sing after seexty . . . he vould not like! Madame Zdorek closed her eyes and recalled every minute detail of her first meeting with the handsome Professor in Prague. He had plucked her out of the large choral group he directed at the University and asked her to sing a solo. Later, as they had walked across the Charles Bridge to her parents' home, she had listened raptly to his every word. *Alvays a meal before a performance . . . neever take small opernhaus just to seeng . . . save yourself for very best . . . leave beezness to manager . . . neever seeng after seexty* . . . She had heeded his advice until now . . . but perhaps, just perhaps, for Rosa, for her new friends, she would bend his rules. And hers.

~~~
~~~

WHISPERS

The Wynfield Farms Library has just received a magnificent gift from an anonymous donor. Twelve large hand-colored botanical prints, each signed and numbered by the artist, are on display in the Library for your enjoyment and study. The artist was M. Orrell, probably a contemporary of John Audubon. Our Librarian, Lib Meecham, is sleuthing through the stacks here and at the local colleges in order to learn more about M. Orrell. There seems to be a paucity of information about the man (or woman).

Romero Quintero did a masterful job of mounting the prints under protective lucite so that we may enjoy them without fear of their disintegration.

Our horticulturist, Jocey Ribble, of course, is the artist responsible for the look-alike botanical display as you enter the Library.

The gift is the latest of many additions made recently to the Wynfield Library that only increases its value and charm for each of the residents of Wynfield Farms

For a visual feast, stop by the Library and treat yourself to a visit with the Orrell prints.

-R. McN.

~~~
~~~

20

Rose entered the Reception Hall at the same time that Mary Rector and the other bus passengers bustled through the front doors. From their cheerful faces Rose could see that nothing was amiss. Indeed, the group appeared to be in high spirits and great good humor.

"Rose!" shouted Mary, waving to her friend "You will never believe what we've just done!" She was lumbering across the hall toward Rose, eyes sparkling, her ever-present large, white imitation leather handbag thumping against her thighs.

"No, indeed, Mrs. McNess," spoke Henry Weintraub, also a passenger, "we have certainly had an adventure!"

"What in the world, Mary?" asked Rose. She was wary of hearing the answer, but realized that Mary didn't often look this blissful . . . or sound this lucid.

"We got Ernest to take us to the apple orchard! And we bought apples and cider and apple butter for everybody! My Suzanne loves cold cider. I want to have it icy cold when she gets home tonight."

"And what else did we do, Mary?" prodded Helen Sutton, another member of the morning's outing.

"We were wicked! Ernest had to stop for gas. You know, at that store in the village. Not the regular service station. The one that sells food and hats and drinks and all sorts of chips . . . "

"The 7-11," prompted Helen.

Rose knew the store. It sat at the crossroads leading to the village and to the largest apple orchard in the vicinity. She could picture the scene: Mary wandering aimlessly among the candies and chips and soft drinks with a few coins in her purse.

"But we didn't buy any food, Rose. While Ernest was putting gasoline in the bus, we went inside and . . . gambled! Here, I could win a million dollars! And I will! I feel lucky. Yes, I am going to win. I picked the numbers myself." She rummaged in the depths of the voluminous bag and pulled out one crumpled green ticket for Saturday night's lottery drawing.

"And I bought one for you, Rose. You aren't mad, are you? See, there's your name: Rose McNess. I used all my favorite numbers. Here, this is yours."

"Oh, Mary, thank you! I'm touched, truly touched!" Rose felt hot tears gathering behind her eyes. "You shouldn't have spent your money on me, Mary," she scolded tenderly as she took the crumpled slip from Mary's outstretched hand.

"Weren't we the wicked ones?" asked Henry Weintraub, chuckling to Rose and John Lowman. "Of course," he continued, "Ruth is going to skin me alive when she finds out. She thinks the lottery is a big scam. Resents every dollar I put down for it. One of these days . . ."

"You're going to win . . . BIG!" Rose finished for him. "I hardly think occasionally playing the lottery is corrupting all your values, Henry. Look at the lift it has given Mary! Besides, when you do win, you and Ruth can visit all those grandchildren!"

"But I am going to win, aren't I Rose?" Mary's brows were knit with worry and her eyes had the anxious, pleading look of an orphaned fawn. Her brief venture into reality was rapidly slipping into the void of forgetfulness, of never-was, of disturbing dreams, and fantasy. The scrunched features in her flaccid face and the down-turn of her mouth belonged to a person other than the laughing, merry creature who had walked through the main doors a few minutes ago.

How can reason fly away and evaporate so swiftly? Rose asked herself. She looked at the dull, doughy, untidy woman grasping at her soiled sweater. *At least she has had four hours of carefree happiness. Away from Wynfield and the photographers. Wouldn't Miss Moss be in a tizzy if she found Mary like this? And in the Reception Hall!*

"Now, Mary Rector, you listen to me," giggled Rose, determined to keep her voice and conversation light. "Of course you might win. And I might, too. And then we could share with all our friends. Just the way you've going to share those apples. Ummmm. Where are they, incidentally? Is Ernest carrying them in for you?"

Apples was the operative word. Mary's face brightened perceptively. Once again she returned to the Wynfield world. Apples were more tangible than the elusive millions. Apples she could see and smell; the lottery was a fleeting escape in a five-minute fantasy.

As if on cue Ernest and Romero came through the side entrance of the hall pushing a wheelbarrow overflowing with shiny, fragrant Winesap, York, and Grimes Golden apples.

"What a picture!" cried Kate. She had been an observer to all of the previous exchange. "Let's put this precious cargo right in front of my desk. That way we can share with everyone who comes in. What do you think? Will that be all right with you, Mary?"

Good girl, Kate! Rose marveled again at the young woman's sensitivity. *She is deliberately involving Mary in this important decision. Mary thinks she is the one who discovered the orchard. I bet it was that nice Henry Weintraub who bribed Ernest to drive out there. Probably for Mary's sake.*

The others followed Ernest back to the bus to collect their cider.

"Mary, I'll bring your cider up to your apartment," called John Lowman. "I'll put it inside your door before you can say 'winesap.' "

"Such nice people," whispered Mary, looking after the jolly group dispersing. "Daughter is going to like them."

"Mary, I'm going upstairs now," said Rose. "Let me walk up with you. Unless you want to ride the elevator. I know you're tired after all the fresh air."

"Oh, no, Rose. The sunshine felt good. It was such a pretty place. You must go with me next time . . . you and Max. Max could run and run. Did I tell you I had a dog back at the farm? Good old Shep. Mr. Rector loved that dog as much as I did. My son had Shep put to sleep. Said he smelled. Just came and took him and put him to sleep. Just did it, came and took old Shep." Mary's eyes spilled tears that coursed down her cheeks and collected on her wavering chin.

Put him away just the way he put you away Mary! Rose recalled her one and only glimpse of Mary's son. *Tall man, crook-nose, thin; looked as if he was always reacting to an unpleasant odor. Wore a brown suit of listless wool serge. Why do I remember that detail about a perfectly heartless individual? He looked the type to put a dog down without any provocation. And not even his dog!*

Rose's eyes were moist as she bade her friend farewell after seeing her safely into the apartment and placing peanut butter and crackers on the small table that Mary used for her snacks.

That, and a cold glass of cider, will make Mary an excellent lunch, thought Rose, who suddenly realized that her own tummy was hollow.

"Now, Mary, I have not forgotten my promise to you. I will take you into Roanoke next week and we'll talk to the police. But you've had enough excitement for one day. For one *week,* in fact. Why don't you rest this afternoon? Then by dinner time you'll feel so much better. Take a long, hot bath, and rest. Does that sound like a good idea?"

"Thank you, Rose. Now that I am sitting down . . . I am tired. Shep and I are tired. My feet hurt. I'll look for Suzanne after I rest. Thank you, Rose. You are so good to me."

Why does she make me feel so worthless? I perform a simple act of kindness and she thinks I am Mother Teresa. She needs so much love! And she needs people to talk to, and to talk to her, and listen to her. Mostly listen. Mary requires so little; perhaps that is why she is overlooked and goes around peeing in folks' apartments to attract attention. Remarkable mass, the human mind. Mary was clear as a bell back there until the clouds rolled in and she began searching for her lost daughter. Golly, I'd better get back home; Max needs me almost as much as Mary does. And if I don't grab a bite to eat soon, I won't be there for either Max or Mary!

~~~

~~~

E C H O E S

Arthur Talcott Everett

"Suaviter in modo, fortiter in re"

"Gently in manner, strongly in deed": this phrase aptly describes ARTHUR EVERETT, a true classicist and scholar. He advocates classical study for everyone, and Tuesdays find him tutoring in the local high school. Wednesday evenings are dedicated to assisting with the school's Latin Club activities. He ranks playing bridge as his next-favorite occupation and many mornings he may be found with a regular foursome in a sunny corner of the Lounge.

In between his regular commitments, Arthur translates Latin manuscripts for a private firm in New York City. Arthur is a native of North Carolina but his late wife, Genevieve, was a Virginian and the couple spent many happy years in the state when he was active in the publishing business.

Arthur declares himself perfectly content at Wynfield Farms, where ". . . there is always plenty to do with such interesting people . . ."

-R. McN.

~~~
~~~

21

"Gentlemen, I shall pocket my winnings and return to my lady love. As usual, it has been a pleasure taking your money." Major Featherstone saluted his three companions, wiped a nonexistent particle of dust from the toe of his gleaming boot, twirled his mustache and wheeled away from the game table and out through the doorway of the South Lounge.

"That son of a gun!" exclaimed Father Charlie Caldwell. "He takes our money every time! Two rubbers and I didn't win six cents!"

"Perhaps," considered Arthur Everett, "we should start playing Chicago bridge. When I belonged to the Shenandoah Club in Roanoke we always played *Chicago*. Stakes are higher; perhaps the Major wouldn't be so carefree then with his bidding. *Voluptates commendat rarior usus*, and the such."

"Now Arthur," cautioned Bob Lesley, "you know my knowledge of Latin is confined to the medical profession; I don't follow you completely."

"All I was suggesting, my friends," obliged the Latin scholar, "was that the Major might consider the advice of Juvenal. He counseled moderation in living well. Literally, what I offered was

"Rare indulgence increases pleasures." With higher stakes, the Major might exercise more judgment in bidding and when he did win, it would be ne *plus ultra*. That means 'the acme,' Bob! Indeed, we just may not be challenging the Major's card skills as we should be doing."

Bob Lesley chuckled. "Somehow, with the Major's new living arrangements, I don't think we need to worry about his wanting to play bridge with the three of us quite as often as before."

"I agree, Bob," laughed Father Charlie. "Unless we play *con amore*. I, for one, don't mind giving up a tenth of a cent a point in exchange for a couple of hours of his wit. Razor sharp mind, his!"

"I'd better write down today's scores if we're going to keep a running tally," said the doctor.

"By all means. For the time being, let's assume he'll be back next week. What did he take today: two dollars and thirty cents? I can almost hear the gears gyrating in that tactician's mind as he bids!" chortled Arthur Everett.

Father Charlie sat back and looked around him. Playing cards in the South Lounge was one of the more pleasurable benefits of the Wynfield life. The atmosphere was palpably, undeniably English upper echelon. *Old Wynfield had probably visited one of the private clubs on London's Pall Mall and insisted on this reproduction*. Father Charlie studied the Stubbs oils over the Adams mantle. *Early paintings, perhaps? Not a terrier in either canvas and most of Stubbs' later stable pieces have dogs. Of course, Miss Moss would correct me on this but . . . He looked at the Kirman. I do know that's early. None of the recent looms come close to being so large. Probably early '30s. After the old man had died*. Father Charlie turned to the glass cases protruding from the salon's perimeter. They were permanently affixed to the paneled walls. The inhabitants of these transparent prisons gazed out at the world with fixed and beady stares. *A rather Dickensian touch if you ask me*, thought Father Charlie.

"Gentlemen," he said aloud to his companions, "I want to ask you something that has been bothering me. I am familiar with the Wynfield peculiarities, but do you think the late Mr. Wynfield actually preserved all the species we see before us in this room?"

"They say," replied Arthur Everett, who of the three had lived at Wynfield Farms the longest, "it was his avocation in his latter years. A consuming passion. He captured or collected here on the estate every specimen you see in the cases, and practiced his skills of taxidermy back where the Crafts' Shop is located now. And you've reminded me; I need to replace some of the labels on many of these cases. Ink has faded on many of them."

"Well, I don't know about you," noted Father Charlie sardonically, "but occasionally they give me a severe case of depression. I try to read the paper in here every morning but some days I have to give it up and go to my apartment. Today of course, with the sun streaming in, coupled with the presence of my associates, the specimens are of no consequence to me."

"Thanks, Charlie," beamed the genial doctor. "I certainly would like to know who has the time to keep the cases spotlessly clean. It would depress me, too, if this place took on the appearance of a musty old museum. I've been in a few of those in my time. But these cases are polished to perfection every time you step in here. They rather remind me of a perfect frame around a jewel of a Dutch painting. Say, a Vermeer."

"Whoa, Bob!" came the hearty response from the rector. "If I didn't know for a fact that you'd just viewed the Vermeers in Washington I'd say you were name dropping. Or big into the visual arts. Excellent analogy; I'll keep it in mind. I am genuinely fond of this room. None other like it in the place. Perhaps you're the one we should thank for the dusting of the cases; I know the cleaning gals can't get to it daily."

"Not I, Charles," denied Bob Lesley. "You'd have to be either totally taken with these creatures or crackers to maintain the gloss on these cases every single day."

" 'Crackers'—that's a term applicable to just about any of us," joked Arthur Everett.

He pushed his chair back and stood. "Gentlemen, I hate to leave this scintillating conversation but I have a tutoring session in thirty minutes. I must be on my way. Anything I can purchase for either of you while I am in the village?"

"Sure you are not off for a haircut, Arthur?" teased Father Charlie.

"*Misericordia*!" groaned Arthur Everett, rubbing both hands over his shiny pate. "You know what they say, Charlie, grass doesn't grow on a busy street!"

The three men automatically burst into uninhibited laughter, and none louder than the completely bald Arthur Everett. He left the South Lounge with a smile.

"A fine man," commented Father Charlie. "He would have made a superior churchwarden in any parish. He probably has served as warden; I must ask him next time we talk."

"I agree completely," continued Bob Lesley. "Excellent mind. Not only a student of the Mother Tongue but a Shakespearean scholar as well. He and Lib Meecham are reading at this Fall Fete."

"So I understand. And speaking of the Fete, Bob, when do you propose we get together and rehearse our contribution? Have you been going over any scores?"

"I have, but I confess I start listening to my old recordings and before I know it, I'm sound asleep. I never thought Messrs. Gilbert and Sullivan would lull me to sleep!"

Father Charlie looked at the kindly doctor and said, "I think you've earned a few catnaps, Bob! How long did you practice? Did I hear forty-odd years?"

"Forty-eight. But that is no excuse for nodding off when I've promised to do something! Actually I've made a few notes. Think we can whip our vocal cords into shape by November 19? That's only two weeks away. Did you mention getting together at your place this Sunday evening?"

"If that time is good with you. I'll fix a light supper for the three of us. Sunday night is fairly skimpy here, anyway." Father Charlie suddenly sat up and whistled in surprise. "Oh, my, I forgot about the Major's Vinnie. Think I should include her, Bob? I thought we could talk about the selections during supper, then practice for about an hour afterwards. Featherstone will be reluctant to leave Vinnie for that long. What do you think, my friend?"

"Definitely include Vinnie, Charlie, if you think you can manage," replied Bob Lesley.

"Of course! No problem! Why did I even wonder about it? In fact, four is easier than three when you're cooking. I'll have to keep Caesar in the bedroom, though. He does not like the ladies."

"Are those African parrots genuinely satisfactory? Other than their dislike for the female?" Bob Lesley mistrusted anything with feathers. He and his wife had shared their lives with a series of English setters during fifty years of marriage. He could not imagine becoming friendly with a walking, talking fowl.

"Caesar is!" answered Father Charlie. "He's all the company I need in my retirement. I like the thought of someone needing me, but not too much. I also like the thought of having someone in the house, but not interfering with my reading or cooking. Yes, Bob, Caesar suits me fine!"

"And didn't I read that the African grays live close to seventy-five years?" queried his friend.

"That's right. Caesar is forty-two. When I go, Caesar goes to a nephew in Norfolk. An unmarried nephew, I might add!"

"Would that all decisions were that simple!" exclaimed Dr. Lesley. "And speaking of decisions, I promised Rose McNess that I would talk with Mary Rector. Note that I did not say 'consult.' The other day at the Clinic, when Mary was there for her shots, the young doctor and I chatted."

"And?" posed Father Charlie, well acquainted with Mary's sad history.

"We reached the same conclusion. 'Benign senility,' aggravated by severe mental trauma. Not much you can do for that sort of thing, except what we're already doing. Rather, what Rose McNess is doing. Rose seems to be the one looking out for Mary."

"She didn't look out fast enough yesterday," quipped Father Charlie. "I had a visit from Mary and she left me with a wet rug. Poor soul! But I agree, Rose is a real spark plug. If you have a project, call Rose! Want something done, call Rose! Rose is one of the exclamation points in life!"

"Since she has been here at Wynfield, the tempo has picked up considerably. She keeps her word; I like that. And I better keep my word about Mary. This has been pleasant, Father. You can't imagine my joy in discovering that you not only play a decent game of bridge but that you've also succumbed to the allure of Gilbert and Sullivan!"

"Before you go, Bob, let me ask you something. What do you make of Miss Moss?"

Bob Lesley rubbed his sturdy chin before answering. His expression became grave. "I think," he replied thoughtfully, "that she's a dragon on the quiet, rather. Miss Moss presents more of a problem than ten Mary Rectors. She is a rather plain, post-menopausal woman who looks through the glass darkly."

Father Charlie nodded but did not interrupt.

"She is," Bob Lesley went on, "looking at the residents here and witnessing a preview of her own life. Solitary confinement. Only her past, present or future life cannot compare to the rich fulfillment enjoyed by any one of us. She sees nothing but gloom and doom and unconsciously inflicts the same upon all of us. Or so it appears. End of diagnosis. Off the cuff, you understand. Think I'm being too harsh on the lady?"

"Understood," emphasized Father Charlie. "What bothers me the most is the fact that she is a glaring misfit here. I won't go as far as comparing her to the serpent in the Garden; I like your image of the dragon much better! Someone should get to the Board; there has to be a personnel chief who does the hiring and firing. The woman is a menace. She might do a perfectly fine job in some other environment, preferably where she doesn't work with seniors. Who can we get to contact the big Board, Bob?"

The two men looked at each other for a half-second before speaking in one voice: "Rose!"

~~~
~~~

WHISPERS

Ranger Cookies

Many of you have asked for the recipe for my Ranger Cookies--here it is!!

Mix:
1 cup margarine (2 sticks)
1 cup white sugar and 1 cup brown sugar
2 eggs
1 Tbsp. vanilla

To this mix add:
1 cup flour, sifted with 1 teaspoon soda
1/2 teaspoon baking powder
1/2 teaspoon salt
MIX and MIX again, adding a bit more flour if it feels too sticky

To this mix add:
2 cups quick oats
2 cups Rice Krispies
1 cup coconut

Blend well: you might find your hands are your best mixers! Roll into walnut-size balls and place on lightly greased cookie sheet. Bake 12-14 minutes at 325°. (If you place balls about 1" apart they don't spread.) Let stand a bit before placing on cooling rack. Makes about 72 cookies. These are a family favorite! My grandchildren call them "Little Strangers."

-Rose and Max

~~~
~~~

22

The storm began with a boom of thunder that racked the windows in Wynfield's Dining Room. Monique and Jean had just served the filet of sole and were bringing casseroles of vegetables to the tables. They looked at one another with fear in their eyes. The room was silent. No glass was lifted, no fork raised. Lightning sliced the evening sky. Sheets of rain slashed against the building. The wind shrieked.

"Looks like we're in for it, ladies and gentlemen," spoke Father Charlie. "Would you please pass the rolls my way, Helen?" He looked around the table of eight and beamed. He knew that each person in the room wished for nothing more but to be safely back in his or her own apartment. But he knew, too, that routine must be maintained and he determined to do his part.

"After you, Father, if I may?" Ellie Johnson grasped the meaningful manner in which Father Charlie was methodically attacking his fish. She had witnessed some terrific storms in the Rockies, but that last splintering was unlike anything she had ever seen or heard.

"Just be glad none of us is out in this," Ellie added. Rather lamely, she admitted to herself. "I've sat through football games in rain and it's no fun. Felt like an eel after the first quarter."

"No symphony for me tonight!" cried one of the other ladies at the table.

"I should imagine they'll cancel if it's this bad in Roanoke," volunteered another.

"Remember what Noah did!"

"Have you ever taken any Elderhostel trips, Ellie?" asked Father Charlie, determined to change the subject from rain and weather to anything.

The lights in the Dining Room flickered, glowed, flickered again, and then went out altogether. The tapers on each table blazed steadily with a soft radiance and the atmosphere immediately switched from one of gloom to one of gaiety.

Everyone loves a party, Father Charlie chuckled, *and candlelight signifies a gala occasion. Splendid, because that's a gale-force hurricane raging out there. Bet ten to one some trees fell with that first crack. Ah! the roar of the auxiliary generators! Knew they'd kick in . . . lights will return in a moment.*

"Ladies, how lovely you all look in the candlelight!"

~~~

The tempest assaulted Wynfield throughout the night; the next day dawned dark and wet. Although no longer a downpour, the rain was still significant enough to make Rose question the wisdom of venturing forth with Max.

She had just started making coffee when the sharp ring of the telephone punctuated the morning quiet.

"This will be Annie, Max; you know her habits as well as I do."

My wake-up call! Did I survive the storm? And another tidbit about Tom! Should he save—or shave—the beard—the burning issue!

"Good morning! Rose McNess here," she spoke into the receiver cradled between her chin and left shoulder as she wrested a mug from the cabinet with her free hand.

"Mrs. McNess, Elvina Moss speaking," came the low and
~~~

funereal voice. "I wish it were a good morning. I hate to disturb you so early but you are the logical person to call. Mary Rector is missing."

Rose listened to the familiar, unmistakable timbre of Miss Moss's voice as it swelled, dropped to a murmur, then gained momentum once more in an on-going litany of Mary's name, the daughter's name, Rose's name. But the only words she heard were "Mary Rector is missing."

"Oh, Miss Moss, she can't be! She had such a good day yesterday! Have you looked all over . . . I mean in and out of the house?"

I am babbling like an idiot, thought Rose. *Chattering inanities, sheer craziness. Of course she must have searched all over or she wouldn't have called me.*

"Mrs. McNess, the police team is in my office as I speak. I phoned them at six this morning. I am calling because you know Mary's habits better than most of our . . . residents. Could you come down?"

"I am on my way," replied Rose, dropping the receiver and the mug at the same time. The thick pottery shattered at her feet.

"One less mug to wash, Max, and thankfully not full!" she hurriedly told the Scottie. The terrier looked up at his mistress with questioning eyes.

She can't be missing. Momentarily lost but not missing. Wait a minute: did I see Mary at dinner last night?

Rose paused between snapping on Max's leash and grabbing at her red windbreaker. The hall-tree teetered as she yanked the garment free.

Come to think of it, I don't think I did. She agreed to rest yesterday afternoon. I confess I never gave her another thought last evening!

Rose and Max exited the apartment and padded silently down the corridor. *No point in alarming anyone else about this! Rumors will fly soon enough!*

As she approached Miss Moss's office Rose suddenly found herself overcome by the gravity of the situation. Ernest, Romero and two uniformed police officers stood just inside the open door, causing her to hesitate for a split-second. She gulped, and was grateful for having Max's leash clutched in her left hand and her stout walking stick in her right.

Miss Moss, every pinstripe in place, stood behind her wide mahogany desk. She appeared as thunderous as she had sounded.

"Gentlemen, this is Mrs. McNess . . . and her *dog,* Max. Mrs. McNess is the friend to whom I referred earlier. She has been attentive to Mary Rector . . . *more* attentive, I should say, than most of our other residents. She knows Mary's habits. Would you comment, Mrs. McNess?"

"Mary was a friend. That accounts for my attentiveness. As to her habits . . . let me think. I refuse to think she just . . . wandered away. What cruel irony!"

"Mrs. McNess is referring to the fact that Mrs. Rector's daughter also disappeared," Miss Moss explained to the officers. "I went over that matter with the gentlemen when they arrived this morning," she said to Rose.

"How did you discover she was missing, Miss Moss? You said you called the police at six this morning?"

"Mary Rector did not appear at the evening meal." The Director spoke slowly, icily, each word a hurled pebble rippling the surrounding hush. Listening to this statement, one had the distinct impression that Miss Moss knew every action of every resident of Wynfield Farms. She continued, in the same monotone. "I called her apartment at nine last evening. No reply. I retired, but at 11 P.M. found myself unable to sleep. I fixed myself a cup of warm milk and read for an hour. Then I decided to try Mary's apartment once more. Inconvenient or not, I wanted to ascertain her whereabouts. Again, no response. That is when I asked Ernest and Romero to come over."

"Then you've been looking for her, I mean, searching, since midnight?" questioned Rose. The forlorn pair nodded. Both men looked exhausted and grubby.

"Yes, Mrs. McNess," said Ernest, speaking for both of them. "We been over every inch of the building, the outbuildings, the grounds . . ."

The older of the two policemen shifted forward slightly. He

had a strong face; his skin was the exact color and texture of an English walnut and his chin jutted forward. The brown cloth of his uniform stretched across the expanse of his belly. Patting this anatomical feature with a gesture that seemed more habit than nerves, he directed his attention to Rose. Rose was grateful that this was not the same païr who had returned Mary from her attempted "bank robbery."

"Mrs. McNess, do you know of any spot on the Wynfield grounds that Mrs. Rector liked to visit? Any bench that was her favorite? Any grove of trees?"

"Officer, to my knowledge Mary Rector seldom walked these grounds. My dog and I are out two or three times a day, and we know just about all of Wynfield Farms. But never, never on our walks have I run into Mary. She rode the bus at the drop of a hat. Surely Ernest has told you about the trip yesterday morning. Mary was ecstatic! She had a glorious time. I've never seen her so buoyant as when she came back with the apples . . . "

Ernest brightened at Rose's recollections of the orchard adventure.

"Oh, yes, ma'am, I told the officer about that. Miz Rector, she just laughed all the way out and all the way back. Just like a little girl. Didn't even talk much about that daughter, either."

"Then you would not say she was unduly depressed yesterday?" asked the officer.

"Oh, no, sir. No more'n usual. Maybe not as much as usual," reflected Ernest.

"I can verify that" Rose said. "I spoke to her as the group was getting back yesterday, just before lunch time. In fact, I walked up to her apartment with her and saw that she got in safely. I got her few lunch things out and I suggested that she might rest until dinner time."

The officer addressed Rose once more. "Then perhaps you are the last person to have seen Mary Rector before she disappeared."

"No, I doubt that," mused Rose. "John Lowman, another resident who had gone on the orchard outing, was going to deliver Mary's cider to her apartment. I distinctly remember thinking that Mary was going to have a good lunch: peanut butter crackers and cold apple cider. Yes, John Lowman. I don't think he would have just left the cider and gone on his way. Knowing John, he probably knocked, took the jug in, and may have even put the cider in Mary's refrigerator. John is a sweet man; he'd do that for Mary. Yes, talk to John Lowman."

"We'll interview Mr. Lowman. Meanwhile, would you care to accompany me, Mrs. McNess, as I search the grounds once more?"

"Gladly, officer. If I don't exit soon, Miss Moss will make Max and me disappear for rude violation of her Persian carpet. Come, Max."

Turning and looking back, Rose asked, actually stated, "You have no objections to my accompanying the officer, do you, Miss Moss."

"By all means, Rose. Your help is invaluable."

With her heart sinking at the prospect of what she feared was inevitable, Rose realized that Miss Moss had just used her Christian name for the first time.

The Rolling Stone has become the Rock of Gibraltar, admitted Rose. *I give her that! And beneath that calm facade she is worried sick about the magazine people learning this juicy tidbit. Well, that is secondary to finding Mary . . .*

~~~

Led by an eager Max, the unlikely pair—thin, shivering Rose and the tall Sergeant with a paunch—left the office. The younger officer remained with Miss Moss who was now dialing John Lowman.

"Now you just go your usual route, Mrs. McNess," the Sergeant told Rose. "It will help me get a better handle on this place. Did Mrs. Rector have many visitors?"

"None. Absolutely none. Other than the one son who brought her here, she had no family or friends. Or at least she never said she did. I feel sure she would have mentioned family members to me if there were any. I told her enough about mine!"

Rose walked in the direction of the gardens. And the lake.
~~~

Max ignored the additional company, though Rose noticed that he was marking the shrubs less than usual. *Dogs sense tension. He knows something is just not right.*

"Officer, have you checked the lake?" Rose asked.

"No ma'am, we haven't. We did a thorough check of all those dark bushes around the main building, then re-checked the outbuildings. That took most of our time until you met us in the office. Would you like to wait for me while I go ahead and give the lake a look-see?"

"Officer, you are very kind. But I am up to this. And I have a terrible feeling of foreboding. Although I can attest to the fact that I've never seen Mary anywhere near these gardens, I have a terrible premonition."

"Let's hope you're wrong, ma'am. I'm Sergeant Connell, by the way. My partner back there is Sergeant Wilkes. Sorry I didn't introduce myself before. I got caught up in this search . . ."

"Thank you, Sergeant Connell. I'm not a stickler for etiquette. I do prefer working with a person rather than just a uniform. You are being quite kind. I really am scared to death for Mary. She can't have survived the night out here; I believe the temperature was thirty-something. She's not used to the cold. Besides, she never wears a coat . . . oh, I shouldn't sputter on like this. Just a moment, Sergeant. My glasses have completely fogged over. Let me just give them a swipe . . ."

"This mist will get to you," said Sergeant Connell as he waited for Rose to clean her glasses and shove them back on her nose.

Max strained at his leash as the pair circled toward the eastern edge of the murky water. Deep shadows darkened the entire area. No morning sun shot the surface to send prisms of color dancing across the rippling waves. Golden maple leaves and remnants from copper beeches floated haphazardly: fall's leftover souvenirs. Small twigs and branches littered the once-pristine reservoir, now a sepia engraving of a fish pond of the ancients, long in disuse and longer deprived of attention.

Brrrr, shivered Rose, *that was more thunder I just heard.*

"Bet this was once a private fishing preserve for old man

Wynfield. I've heard stories about him. He must've been quite a sport." Sergeant Connell looked speculatively at the scene before him.

"You're exactly right, Sergeant. I've heard the same. It really is one of Max's and my very favorite places. Max is no water dog so there's little worry of his jumping in. It's calm down here . . ."

Rose, too, was scanning the lake and surrounding area.

"Oh, Sergeant . . . look! Over there, to the left . . ." Rose was pointing and walking rapidly to the left corner of the site.

"I see, Mrs. McNess. Won't you stay here, please?"

Rose was already ahead of Sergeant Connell.

She and Max were the first to reach the outer edge of the water. The body of Mary Rector bobbed weightlessly in the pitch-black. Mary was face down, and a scattering of leaves had all but obscured the pale sweater. Her arms were outstretched and Rose could see the handle of the bulky white pocketbook entwined securely around her right wrist.

"Oh, Mary, Mary, I am so sorry."

"This is the missing person, then, Mrs. McNess? Can you make positive identification?"

"Oh, yes, Sergeant. She's wearing exactly what she wore yesterday. Mary rarely changed. The pocketbook will give you the proof, Sergeant. She carried everything in there. Oh, Mary! What do we do now, Sergeant? Can I give you a hand in getting her out of there?"

Sergeant Connell thought to himself that he had seen some tough customers in his career but none could compare to this petite, gray-haired grandmother at his side.

"I can manage, ma'am. All we can do is get her out and I'll radio for the ambulance."

Sergeant Connell had waded into the pond and was grasping Mary's body under the armpits. He lifted the lifeless form and then backed slowly towards the shore, half-carrying, half-dragging the sodden burden. When he reached a level, grassy area he carefully positioned the body on the soft turf.

"Can't have been in there too long. Features aren't distorted. Looks almost peaceful, doesn't she?" The officer turned to study Rose, to see what effect this retrieval had made. *Surely this little lady doesn't see dead bodies every day,* he concluded correctly.

"Peaceful. That is a perfect description, Sergeant. Mary does look peaceful. At last. She has had such a . . . well, help me find the word I want . . . unsettled, tragic pursuit for the past twenty-plus years. Now, at least she can sleep and not have to wake up and start searching all over again. Sergeant, you may think me hard, but I can feel only blessed relief for Mary Rector. I never would have wished that she would die in this manner, but I am thankful that the past no longer haunts her. Case closed, Sergeant, on Mary and her missing daughter."

"You're one in a million, Mrs. McNess. Thank you for coming this morning. I guess I never do get used to finding dead bodies. Especially someone about my mother's age."

"Sergeant, aside from Max, you are the nicest companion I've had on my morning walk since my husband died. And I mean that as a compliment! Now, hadn't you better get on your radio and call the station? And one more thing, does Miss Moss have to be involved?"

"Right. I'm calling now. Sorry, I will have to talk with that woman again."

The sergeant was interrupted by Rose's short "Ha!"

"I don't mean to be disrespectful, Sergeant Connell, but that is precisely the term that Mary often used for Miss Moss. *'That woman!'* Miss Moss thought that Mary Rector didn't quite fit the image of the classic Wynfield Farms resident. Mary may have been addled, but she was still shrewd enough to figure Miss Moss's motives. Yes, of course you'll have to deal with Miss Moss. And she'll have to deal with Mary's son."

"Why don't you go on back, Mrs. McNess? I'll get Sergeant Wilkes to come down here and wait with me. It won't take the ambulance long. They'll take the body to the morgue in Roanoke, of course. Autopsy, forms, all of that. After the squad gets here I'll come up to Miss Moss's office. No need for you to wait around. Besides, you're probably getting chilled." For the first time the

Sergeant noticed that Rose was wearing only a light windbreaker. The air held a chill and she was bound to feel it's nip.

"Thank you, Sergeant. I am a little cold, come to think of it, but I think it's my feelings about what has happened to Mary as much as the weather. You're right; you don't need me any longer. You'll be gentle with her, won't you? Putting her in the ambulance?"

"Of course, Mrs. McNess. And . . . thank you."

The two shook hands somberly. Then Rose knelt down beside Mary. She straightened the stringy, limp strands of hair, tenderly brushing away the collected leaves. She pulled the yellow cardigan over her chest, fastening the bottom button as Mary had always done. Making sure that Mary's skirt covered her knees, she patted the sallow, sagging cheek of her deceased friend.

"Good-bye, Mary Rector. 'For I reckon that the sufferings of this present time are not worthy to be compared with the glory which shall be revealed in us.' Just a little message for my friend, Sergeant. Good-bye, again. Come, Max."

Sergeant Connell punched his remote radio and, waiting for Wilkie to pick up, waved to the departing figure heading up the path. He watched Rose walk stoically, retracing the steps they had taken not a half-hour previously. He noted that her shoulders were square and her head was high, the way a practiced sailor reads sea breezes.

Rose and Max walked silently toward the main building. Max trotted obediently at his mistress's side. No chipmunks were chased this morning. The little black dog was chastened, his normally merry tail drooping.

"Come on, Max. I feel miserable, too. Poor Mary! We'll miss her, you and I, and you'll miss those treats she always found for you!"

At the magic word "treat," Max stopped. He looked up at his mistress with his knowing look as if to say, "No more treats and no breakfast either?"

"Let's face the music first, for only a minute. Then we'll go home and I'll give you a special breakfast. I'm tired just thinking of all the hullabaloo this is going to cause. Not the least of which will be dealing with Miss Moss . . . Where did that Bible verse come from, Max? Did you ever hear me quoting *Romans* before? And yet I could remember all of that verse back there with Mary . . . What is the rest? 'But if we hope for that for what we see not, then do we with patience wait for it . . .' "

"Mary, Mary. You've waited so patiently for Suzanne; I hope and pray she's there with you now. That is my prayer, Mary Rector."

~~~

~~~

WHISPERS

FOOTNOTES

FOOTNOTES meets Tuesday afternoon at 3:30 sharp in the Library. Our gracious Librarian, Lib Meecham, will guide us through Edith Wharton's House of Mirth. Please come! Remember that the only requirements for membership in this literary group are a desire to read better-than-average books, a willingness to examine your opinions about the book, and a promise to bring an occasional cookie. Meetings last approximately two hours; you'll be home in time for the evening meal.

FOOTNOTES--for the book lover in you!

R. McNess

~~~

PATHWAYS

The landscape of our lives changes daily.
We breathe the air of unsullied plains
and walk footworn paths of familiar miles.
No hill in sight, no jet trace above.
The blue blackboard of sky envelopes
with a boring sameness that we welcome.
Without warning looms a boulder Sisyphus might
have pushed.
and another, and another.
Treasured landmarks shift, crumble, disappear.
We are thrust into our selves. Is this an incubus
that will never end?

Rose McNess
~~~

23

Nov 2

Dear Mom:

I'm at work so this won't be long. What's going on up there in your neck of the woods? Heard about the hurricane that tore though Virginia. National news mentioned Roanoke the other night and I thought about Wynfield. Any damage? Tried to get Anne but no one home there and you are never at the number I have for you. Are you OK? Let us hear!!! Sue and the kids send their love.

Love,

Paul.

P.S. PLEASE consider getting a computer with e-mail; we call this stuff snail mail. And please get an answering machine! I've tried calling six times!

~~~

Dear Children--

Sorry that it has taken me soooo (sorry--my o sticks) long tooo write. I
~~~

didn't realize we got national news coooverage with our recent hurricane. What a stoorm! It didn't seem nearly as bad ooout here where we are--this IS a sooolid house, you knooow--but the rains and winds were fierce. Looots of trees down on the estate and the usual debris. I am OOOK Max and I huddled together in bed all night. But ... MY CAR IS FLAT! Smashed like a bug in a windshield! My belooved little Nova! I'd be more upset if a real tragedy hadn't happened that very same night. OOne of my friends here at Wynfield wandered off and drowned in the lake! Looosing my car is very small stuff in coomparison to that. I'll tell you all about it when we talk, and I PROMISE to call after our big celebration is over (Fall Fete on Nov 19). Annie's Jim has set up app'tment for the insurance man tooo looook at my tin can. I might get a few hundred dollars for the recycled metal! Ha!

Know that I love each of you and that your Old Mother is FINE!

Looove and xxxxx,

Moother.

~~~

~~~

WYNSONG

IN MEMORIAM

Mary Elizabeth Greenway Rector

Mary Rector, Wynfield Farms' first resident, died Thursday. The widow of Ebert T. Rector, she is survived by one son, Ebert T. Rector, Jr., of Pottstown, Pennsylvania, and a host of friends here and in her previous home of Winchester.

Mary Rector had unfailing good humor and a beguiling smile. She wished to be a friend to all and looked forward to the beginning of each new day. Though her recent years had been filled with tragic loss, she looked forward expectantly to a bright tomorrow.

Everyone in the Wynfield community hopes that Mary's tomorrow brings her deep happiness and the lost sheep she had been seeking.

A private burial will be held in Pottstown. A Memorial Service will be held in the Wynfield Chapel, on Tuesday morning at 11 o'clock. Father Caldwell will officiate.

Wynfield Farms will miss Mary Rector.

"When darkness appears and night draws near,
And the day is past and gone,
At the river I stand, guide my feet, hold my hand,
Take my hand, precious Lord, lead me home."

~~~

"Precious Lord, Take My Hand," Thomas Dorsey.

The words of this lovely hymn echo our prayer for you, Mary.

R. McNess

~~~

24

I will lift up mine eyes unto the hills;
from whence cometh my help.

The familiar and comforting words of Psalm 121 echoed against the plain stone walls of the Wynfield Chapel as the assembled residents read responsively. A somber Father Charlie led the reading with a vigorous voice. The square, airless room was packed, and Rose could see that Romero, Ernest, Jocey, three of the kitchen staff and even Miss Moss were forced to stand in the tiny transept.

"Mr. Wynfield must have thought that his heirs weren't going to be big on church-going," whispered Ellie. "This place is not as big as my closet!"

Father Charlie read the Lesson: Romans, Chapter 15, verse 13:

"*May the God who gives hope fill you with great joy, May you have perfect peace as you trust in him. May the power of the Holy Spirit fill you with hope.*"

"He sure hit the nail on the head with that one," came Ellie's hoarse whisper once more. "I don't know of anyone who had a more tragic life than Mary, do you, Rose?"

The homily was brief. Father Charlie elicited chuckles as he recounted Mary's fey quality, the innocent visit to her money that resulted in near-arrest ("Miss Moss isn't going to soon forget that!" chortled Ellie), and the happy hours in the orchard that last day. Rose stole a look at the Weintraubs and the Lowmans who sat to their right on the second row.

"Hope is what we celebrate today; hope that our friend Mary is home at last, rejoicing in her reunion with Suzanne, Mr. Rector and our Lord."

The service concluded with the Lord's Prayer, two verses of "Onward, Christian Soldiers" which everyone sang lustily, and a vibrant, prayerful benediction: "Go in love and love one another. Amen."

"*Amen*!" repeated Rose. *And I sure hope Miss Moss heard that benediction!*

Ellie and Rose filed out slowly, each lost in her own thoughts and memories.

What did I tell Ellie when she first moved to Wynfield? That I'd filled up my emptiness with hope? Well, that's exactly what I must do now. Fill my grief and emptiness with hope of Mary's happiness.

Rose fixed the image of peaceful, sleeping Mary indelibly in her mind; it became the lodestone of her thoughts in the days ahead.

~~~

Miss Moss had been her usual efficient self, and had shown unexpected concern.

I will tell the harridan that her efforts have not gone unnoticed. Perhaps she'll be my next project, thought Rose.

Miss Moss had met with Mary's son when he arrived at Wynfield and had dispatched Ernest and Romero to help him clean out Mary's sparse apartment. She agreed with Rose that a memorial service for their late resident would be appropriate, sooner rather than later. Ebert Rector, Jr., had shipped Mary's body back to Pennsylvania for the burial.

Probably a pauper's grave. The son inherited every penny of Mary's pitiful estate, and I doubt if he even puts up a headstone.
~~~

Did for Mary as he did old Shep. Rose sighed, thinking of the dour, long-faced man with the jowls of a Basset hound whom she had passed in the Reception Hall. *Wonder if he was even courteous to Kate.*

The other residents were sympathetic but reserved in their comments. These came more in the form of confidential, comforting murmurs to Rose rather than blatant inquisitions. Most of the residents had a surprising ability for avoiding any discussion of life's inevitable finale, either by drowning or other disaster. The "D" word was rarely heard.

Henry Weintraub and Rose concluded that Mary had been so pleased with the cider she had decided to go looking for Suzanne, to take the jug to her. John Lowman had placed Mary's cider in her refrigerator. It was not to be found in the apartment. *If Henry and I are correct, thought Rose, that gallon of cider is sitting at the bottom of the lake.*

~~~

Anne Brewster offered to postpone the family gathering on Saturday evening, but Rose was adamant that it be held as planned. "Annie, this was a tragedy, and an unexpected tragedy. But I am sincere in my belief that Mary is now, finally, eternally at peace with herself and God. What we need now is a little gaiety and fun in our lives!"

The evening was superb to the last detail. Jim Brewster cooked a magnificent leg of lamb, his martinis were wickedly dry, and Anne's dinner left nothing to be desired. The other children were full of pep and conversation, and Tom's slides of Japan were fascinating.

Bravo, Tom! I feel as though I had just spent two years with you—and the sumo wrestlers and the smiling school children in their neat, navy uniforms! Let me sign you up for a slide presentation at Wynfield. We'll be mobbed!

The entire Brewster clan chimed in with remarks about Rose's car or, rather, what had been Rose's car. Jim Brewster had arranged for Rose's insurance agent to give her an appraisal of the flattened platter that rested in Webster's garage in Fincastle.
~~~

Anne and Jim advised Rose to take the settlement and enjoy the pittance she would receive.

"The Blue Book value of a 16-year old Chevy Nova, even in top condition, is negligible," added Jim. *I know that!* thought Rose.

"You really *don't* need a car anymore, Mother. Didn't you tell me that the Wynfield bus goes practically everywhere?" *Annie loves deciding what's best for me!*

Tom and his siblings were downright irreverent in their jibes and suggestions: "Why not get a Moped?" "Say, a Harley's even better! That'd shake 'em up at the funny farm!" "Or a Mustang; now that's a great car. Heavier car? Don't settle for less than a Beamer!"

Rose smiled and listened and wondered if it wasn't about time for her to be getting home.

~~~

Rose was particularly grateful for Ellie Johnson during the days after Mary's death. The laughing, effusive newcomer from Denver had quietly but firmly become an integral part of Rose's life. She was solicitous without being gummy, empathetic and yet pragmatic. Enough so to concur with Rose that Mary's sad situation had come to a timely, if tragic, end. Ellie had joined Arthur Everett's hilarious quasi-bridge group and was substituting for Betty Gehrmann every other Thursday in a more serious four-some. She had volunteered to help plant the 400 daffodil bulbs and, at Mrs. Keynes-Livingston's invitation, signed up to help decorate for the Fall Fete.

Ellie has been accepted, mused Rose. *She's a good listener; that's a big part of her success. How rare it is to develop a really satisfying friendship this late in life! What did Simone de Beauvoir say about female friends . . . they look to each other for "the affirmation of the universe they have in common." How true! With Ellie I can let my hair down, and she . . . well, she can "de-wig" in my presence any time!*

"Max! My heavens! I'm woolgathering again. It's Monday morning. You know that, don't you? Let me have a sip of coffee, then we're off for our walk. Not too long this morning, though.
~~~

That Fete is creeping up fast! 'the Fast Fall Fete'; how does that sound, Max? Or the '*Last* Fall Fete'? Even better, eh?"

Her chuckle was interrupted by the telephone.

"That will be Annie, Max; I should have called her. Won't talk long, I promise."

"Good morning, Rose McNess here."

"My goodness, Mother," said Anne Brewster, "you really sound *with it* this morning, and it's Monday, too! All I could do was drag myself out of bed this morning, much less put on a cheery voice. Sleep well?"

"Like a baby, dear. Still savoring that wonderful dinner Saturday evening. As I told you yesterday, you and Jim outdid yourselves. It was such a treat to see everyone! I *almost* hated to come home."

"Mother, I know I've told you that you can stay over any time. Perhaps Christmas?"

"Thank you, Annie, I will when I really need to. But I do have obligations here. And weighty ones today. Our upcoming Fete, you know; I can't chit-chat this morning."

"I know, Mother. And I'm sick that we'll miss the big event. But you know Tom will be there with bells and whistles! I wanted to thank you again for the lovely flowers you sent. That was not necessary, you know that. But they are perfectly beautiful. Jocey did a marvelous job, didn't she? The arrangement is so airy and open, with all those natural woodsy pieces among the hot-house flowers. Wynfield is lucky to have her, don't you think?"

"Absolutely, dear, and I'm lucky to have you, but I really do have to go. Max has been practicing his patience by the door."

"Bye, Ma; love you!"

"Love you, too, dear, and thanks again! Bye-bye!"

Max, attuned to this morning ritual, had assumed his waiting position.

"Quiet, Max," Rose whispered, snapping on his leash. "We're the only ones in this end of the hall to creep out at dawn." She finished pulling on her windbreaker and pulled the door behind her. She strongly suspected that Annie's early-morning phone calls were to ascertain if her mother were still alive. *What would*

Annie do if I let the phone ring more than three times some morning! Would she panic? Wake up Miss Moss? She's a sweet daughter, but paranoid about my well-being.

Hearing a slight murmuring, Rose glanced over her shoulder toward Apartment 212. *What in the world is Miss Puffenbarger doing up—and out—this early?*

Rose stopped in her tracks, bringing Max up short as she did. She pivoted on her heels to confirm what her cursory glance had caught.

In the open door of Apartment 212 stood two Miss Puffenbargers! Indeed, two ladies identical in appearance stood in the doorway. Each had white hair slicked to the back of the head, each was approximately 5'5" of solid build. Each wore a blue-green plaid wrapper and tan pigskin slippers. Identical twins!

Rose advanced upon the pair.

"Shhhhh!" whispered one of the ladies. "Shhh! Come in, Rose, please, and let us explain."

"Yes, do. Please come in," whispered the second Miss Puffenbarger.

"I am . . . flabbergasted!" whispered Rose in return. Let me walk Max then I'll come right back up. *This* requires some explanation! Just be glad Miss Moss doesn't live nearby! I'll be back in a second!"

Rose and her dog strode rapidly to the stairs, down, through the Reception Hall and out the side door. Her mind was whirling.

Identical twins! And I do mean identical! This explains the meals requested for upstairs, the extra goodies Henrietta takes up after dinner. Or was it really Henrietta? Perhaps this explains why sometimes she was up, sometimes, down. Mirror image twins! My goodness, it does pay to get up early in the morning!

"Max! Max! Are you tending to your business? Good boy. Now let's go get breakfast. I'll feed you and leave you; this is one mystery I'm happy to see solved!"

Rose hurried back inside. Once in, she scurried past the reception desk. Although it was far too early for either Kate or Miss Moss, Rose was taking no chances.

Climbing the back steps, Rose met the Prowler.

"Whoops! Sorry, Bob! I almost made you wish you had gone outside this morning. I didn't mean to be so clumsy."

"You're not clumsy at all, Rose," returned Bob. "You're just preoccupied with your friend's death. So sorry. Everything else going along all right?"

"Quite, thank you, Bob. I'll be more careful about my hazards in the future! Can't go around knocking into people!"

Close call, Max!

Rose and Max entered 208 stealthily, taking caution to open and close the apartment door to keep noise to a minimum. This was not the time to alert every resident in the hall to the new neighbor. Or was she that new? How long has she been here?

While Rose was considering this development, she was mixing Max's breakfast bowl, adding the meat, vitamins, kibbles. She prolonged the ceremony of preparation in order to ruminate on the situation next door.

"OK, Mr. Piggy, here you are. I am going to leave you now. *Bon appetit*!"

Max was already eagerly eating his one meal of the day and did not look up as Rose let herself back into the hallway.

She knocked softly on the door of Apartment 212.

"Henrietta, Miss Puffenbarger—its me, Rose."

The door opened at once, as if the crying woman had been standing and anticipating the knock. "Oh, Rose, thank you for coming," sniffed Miss Puffenbarger. "If we had to be found out, I'm so glad it was you who did it. What in the world are we going to do?"

". . . are we going to do?" The question was a duet by the pair.

"Well, ladies, I've got to sit down for starters," said Rose. "And if you were to offer me a cup of coffee . . . "

"Sister! Where are your manners? Coffee, of course, and muffins. Freshly baked this very morning! Apple and cinnamon."

"How could I refuse?" replied Rose. "You never told me you were a pastry chef, Henrietta."

"Harriet. Harriet is the baker in the family. She concentrated in Home Economics, you know."

Fortified with cups of scalding coffee served in flowered Rosenthal china and warm and sugary apple muffins, the trio settled back on the settee and chairs in the Puffenbarger apartment.

Seeing them together, I can tell the difference. Henrietta's face is fuller. Her cheeks are round, and her opal ring is on her right hand! I thought there was something unusual about that ring! I had seen an opal ring on Harriet's left hand, but I couldn't make the connection. Harriet doesn't really resemble Henrietta all that much Her face is longer. She's got a mole on the right upper lip. Hardly a mole . . . and she's the one who never smiles. And that ring is on the left hand! But their hair is the same shade, and slicked back into the old-maid school-marm style . . . Rose was mesmerized by the pair sitting opposite her on the Victorian loveseat.

Henrietta Puffenbarger was the first to speak. She had dried her eyes and the sniffles were ending as she sipped her coffee.

"When we decided to move to Wynfield, we thought we would get two apartments, right next to each other. But when we talked to Miss Moss, there were no two studio apartments side-by-side. Miss Moss insisted we look at the two-bedroom, over on West. But we each wanted our own space. Besides, those are far too expensive for our budget. So Sister stayed home for a while, and came over only on weekends. Then she sold the home place and had to close immediately. It seemed silly to rent something so I . . ."

Miss Puffenbarger was, Rose perceived, wound up, and the words kept tumbling out.

"So you invited Harriet over for a visit . . . and she never left?" guessed Rose, quickly getting a word into the lengthy explanation.

"Actually, she came in early August, when I had that summer cold. I felt miserable and Sister knew how to take care of me better than the Nursery would have done. You see, Rose, we've always been together. I just can't think of being separated now . . ."

Henrietta's eyes were brimming, and her lips quivering.

"Do you think we have been terribly deceitful?" she asked in a surprisingly firm voice. "I've paid for every extra meal. Faye has taken care of that. I had to let Faye in on it from the first. She's been an angel . . ."

"Did you ever think of approaching Miss Moss about the situation again?" asked Rose. "I mean, the woman is not completely without heart. She actually surprised me when Mary died. Or maybe you *don't* know. She has actually been very sympathetic."

"That woman is a toadie," shot back Harriet Puffenbarger. "I know her type. She toadies to the Board, toadies to the wealthy residents, toadies to those photographers. I worked with school administrators just like Miss Moss. Talk to her? Absolutely not!"

Rose was astounded at Harriet's acerbic voice. Ever practical in the face of disaster, she tried again. "There are two certainties here as I see them. Number one, you can't continue to keep up this charade of being *one* person. It's too difficult. Besides being so confining for the both of you, you are cheating yourselves. Think of all the years ahead you can enjoy *together*! Number two, these studio apartments are definitely NOT made for two people. Why, Max and I get in each other's way occasionally. And he's just a little fella!"

The two ladies laughed heartily at the mention of Max, particularly as a "little fella." Good humor dispelled the rain cloud. The apartment was, temporarily at least, suffused with sunlight.

"So . . . this is what I propose that you do." Rose's mind was spinning out ideas. The twins leaned forward in unison, listening intently.

"You know that Mary's studio apartment is vacant?" The twins nodded.

"And do you know who has the studio apartment right next to Mary's?"

"No!" Again in chorus.

"One of the nicest people at Wynfield. Easy disposition, low-key personality, rarely gets ruffled. Think a moment, ladies."

"I don't mingle as much as Henrietta, Rose. I can't imagine who you are describing."

"Father Charlie!" shouted Henrietta. "Father Charlie and his parrot live next to Mary. Rather, where she did live."

"Correct," said Rose, suddenly feeling smug. "And he has only been there a short time. Can't be too set in his ways. I have a plan for what you should do."

"Oh, Rose," cried Henrietta Puffenbarger, "what would we do without you? I . . . we . . . can't tell you what this means . . ."

"Now, Henrietta," spoke Rose sharply, "if you start sniffling again, I'm going to leave. We've got to take action immediately or Miss Rolling Stone will let that place go to another. Here's what you must do."

Rose's business-like tone, adopted for nay-sayers and magazine salesmen, stopped any thought of tears that either twin may have harbored.

"First of all, Harriet, you must leave and re-enter. Reapply to Wynfield. That should be no problem. Kate Alexander should have your first application on file. I'll speak to her on the quiet.

Rose paused. *What am I getting into? Can I actually pull off this caper?*

"Meanwhile, I shall go and talk to Father Charlie. Somehow, I think I've got the easy part of this puzzle to fit together. How does that sound to you, ladies?"

The Puffenbarger twins were effusive in their expressions of delight. There were hugs and kisses and napkins filled with warm muffins urged on Rose for her "little fella."

"I think, Harriet," continued Rose, turning as she opened the door to the hallway, "I would try to slip out during the noon meal. Use the East door. Miss Moss always eats an early lunch in the dining room. I'll go down promptly at twelve and catch Kate. She can pull your application. That way you will be out of here, can go somewhere to change clothes, and then return. Your car still fairly reliable, Henrietta? And I'd call for an appointment with Miss Moss. That will make it sound really legitimate."

"Rose," cried the Misses Puffenbargers, "this is turning out so well! Not the sad ending we both had feared."

"Don't count your chickens, ladies . . . ," retorted Rose. Then, impishly, she smiled and continued, "but I think it will work!" The sun shone at full strength.

Rose fairly fled to the privacy of her own apartment.

"Max! Where are you, old man? Here, a bit of a treat for you. Home baked! We'll share. You will never guess where the muffins came from! Nor would I have until an hour ago. Whew! Who ever thought that life at Wynfield could be so full of curious twists and turns? Now I've got to call Father Charlie and see if I can charm him into moving. Max, would you like to have a small gray parrot living next door? Every cruise ship needs at least one!"

~~~

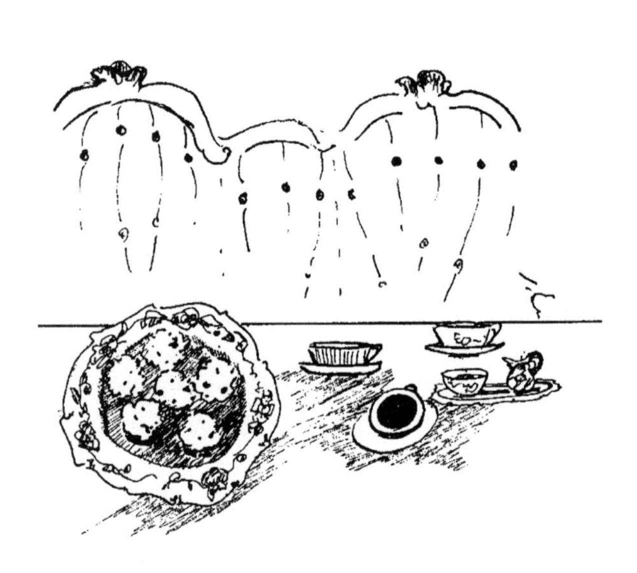
~~~

E C H O E S

Harriet Alberta Puffenbarger

If you think you are seeing double these days . . . you ARE! HARRIET PUFFENBARGER has just moved to Wynfield Farms to join her twin sister, Henrietta. For nearly eighty years these ladies have been inseparable; now they live side by side in studios on Two West.

Harriet Puffenbarger studied Home Economics at Teacher's College, Farmville, and returned to the family home after graduation. She managed the Botetourt County Farm Extension Department for six years before settling into her first love--teaching. She and her sister taught at the same local high school for nearly thirty years before retiring! In addition to her skills in the homemaking area, Harriet also enjoyed coaching girls' field hockey. That may account for her being an enthusiastic fan of the Roanoke *Express* Ice Hockey Team and an even greater booster of her idols, the Boston Bruins.

Harriet enjoys baking (try her apple-cinnamon muffins!), fair-weather golf and a good mystery to read in rainy weather.

Wynfield Farms welcomes Harriet. We are so glad you are here!

-R. McN.

~~~
~~~

25

Virginia Venues photographers were shooting every day. Long Hair and Baseball Cap appeared regularly with various pieces of equipment either slung over their shoulders or draped around their waists. What could not be carried was dragged. If the Library was the first stop, they took the necessary shots and then hurried off to their truck, leaving the extra equipment piled in one corner. Lib Meecham, at first entranced with "those hard-working young men," found her patience wearing thin as residents stepped warily through the labyrinth of equipment abandoned near the mystery section.

Miss Moss's standard boom to every resident was "Just a few more days, just a few more days." This had been her standard rejoinder for nearly three weeks. Miss Moss was clearly entranced by the magazine's visit and positively preened when the Editorial Assistant required her help on various aspects of the assignment. Rose's apartment had escaped the photographers' lens ("Heaven's sakes! a picture would make it look like a prison cell!"); Ellie Johnson's had been shot from every angle. Ellie had enjoyed the entire day of "VV's" invasion with its duo of long-haired young men and two copywriters Peals of laughter had rolled out of Number 209. ("I can't wait until publication! My friends in Denver will never believe this—a cover girl at my age!") The photographers rejected Jana Zdorek's eclectic atelier in favor of Mrs. Keynes-Livingston's elegant quarters. ("I have no objections to having my home in print; I am living in the manner to which I have always been accustomed.")

During the day, the crew roamed the Wynfield grounds. Rose did agree to being photographed while walking Max, "but only if you take it from the back and from a long distance." The Dining Room, the Health Unit, Comfort Fit, Crafts, even the scenario of 400 spring bulbs being planted were all recorded for the public and posterity.

Upon reflection, Rose decided that the magazine's visit, albeit intrusive, could not have been better timed. It deflected the spotlight from the everyday happenings that ordinarily would have turned Wynfield Farms into a swarm of curious, rumor-buzzing bees. Better still, it kept Rolling Stone totally preoccupied with presenting the best possible image at all possible times.

Consequently, Mary's death was handled with tact and taste by everyone. The Memorial Service had been held purposely on one of the magazine's "off" days. Mary Rector's name was rarely mentioned. *Just as if one of my tour members had decided to return home,* thought Rose.

And what Rose had privately begun to call "The Great Migration" had gone virtually unnoticed by all except those intimately involved. Rose had approached Father Caldwell on the subject of switching apartments, and the move was effected two days later. He and Caesar were now happily ensconced in Apartment 212. Rose was delighted that Father Charlie was also a morning walker. She and Max were occasionally joined by the pastor on their early strolls.

The Puffenbarger twins had moved into their two studio apartments and were as blissful as newlyweds. Harriet Puffenbarger's admission to Wynfield Farms had proved to be a mixed blessing with unexpected consequences. Henrietta was so delighted to have "sister" in close proximity that her entire countenance changed from dour to dimpled—at all times! This resulted in the residents never knowing if they were talking to Harriet or Henrietta. The twins handled the confusion with nonchalance ("It's been the same all our life—we fill in for one another") and Miss Moss, ironically, doted upon them. Harriet Puffenbarger's prior assessment of Miss Moss stuck like a tick in Rose's memory. It did not surprise Rose that she often heard Miss Moss asking if anyone had seen the Puffenbarger twins—"I would so like to make sure the other twin is happy here." The old gals learned early how to elude Miss Rolling Stone.

In Apartment Number 208 Rose was relaxing in her chair, soaking up the view from her window and reflecting on the events of the past two weeks. It had been too long since she had merely sat. Merely sat without notebook, pen, book or lists in her hands. She closed her eyes and tried to concentrate. Each day blurred into the next. *I need to slow down, stop! Each hour is so precious, I want to wring every drop out of it! I want to savor the seconds, the minutes of living!*

"Kate and Tom," Rose spoke aloud. "Max, did you hear me?"

The Scottie hunkered down even more soundly in his bed, his left ear twitching in response.

"Kate and Tom," Rose continued, "may be getting serious."

Mmmmmmmm. Great confidant you are, Max! But they are seeing each other. That counts for something! Why, when Tom showed his slides on Japan, Kate practically shoved everyone into the Lounge. Subtly, of course. And each time Tom comes up here on the pretense of seeing me, he's had more than a few minutes with Kate! Young love! Why should I be surprised at this turn of events? Why should anything surprise me anymore? After the Major and Vinnie Whittington! As if on cue, Rose, glancing out her window, saw the two senior lovebirds wheeling along the Wynfield driveway. Each was gesturing expansively toward the top of a giant oak tree that stood near the main gate. Rose thought, *Probably a kestrel they've spotted; I've heard they're compiling a count for the Bird Club.*

Rose looked at her watch. Two o'clock. She had promised Frances Keynes-Livingston (I really must force myself to use her given name, she thought, even if it doesn't come easily!) that she would meet her in the South Lounge ("Closed in Preparation for Fete") at 2:30 to go over the final arrangements of chairs. And she'd mentioned something about additions to the program; they would need to review the program one more time.

Rose fixed herself a cup of Earl Grey. *I'd better give myself some energy,* she thought. She mulled over her recent association with Frances. *I bet she was a dynamic board member, no matter what board. Once she has an idea, that's that. Unless someone presents a plausible reason why it wouldn't work. Trouble is, her ideas always work! They mesh. At least, in my limited experience that's true.*

Mrs. Keynes-Livingston had taken Miss Moss' idea of "Forest Festival at Wynfield" (a horrific vision of elves and jesters and merry bands jostling on the grounds,) and turned it into a dignified, entertaining celebration of talent. Everyone knew that, although she wasn't lifting a finger, Miss Moss would be on hand, the day of the Fete, to take credit for everything. Frances Keynes-Livingston was shrewd enough not to be bothered by this. With Miss Moss out of the way, Madam Chairman could move full steam with her promising ideas.

I bet this becomes an annual event. Rose sipped her tea and chuckled over the thought. *People usually have some talent to share. When we're gone, there will be others. Always are. Perhaps an actress will move in, or an aging actor. That's all we lack. Not much room for retired athletes; who wants to see someone swing a golf club or a tennis racquet? No, that sport will just have to develop a sideline. But I bet opera stars will be few and far between . . .*

Rose remembered that she had promised to call Jana Zdorek this afternoon. The *diva* had gracefully declined singing a complete aria ("There is neever worse theeng than patheetic croak of anteek voice box, Rosa") and Rose had thankfully agreed. The octogenarian had produced two 33" recordings of performances at La Scala and the Vienna Opera House. Jana would introduce the performances with a brief synopsis of the opera and her part in it, and then play a short segment ("neever tire-out ze audience") of the performance. Both Rose and Frances Keynes-

Livingston pronounced this perfection. They could count on the old trooper to turn in a professional twenty minutes.

Wonder what Jana has on her mind? Rose asked herself. *I'll call her right now before I meet with Frances.*

Rose practically fainted with relief at her friend's dilemma.

"Do I wear ze broun . . . or ze reed, Rose?" asked Jana Zdorek. "Ze broun eez my primo choise . . . but eet eez . . . how you say, 'mossy?' Weel it look reedeeculous to see old, old lady in ze reed?"

Rose exclaimed "Oh, no!" and "Not really" to her friend about the "mossy" condition (moth holes?) of her favorite dress, but assured her the red-for-passion would be even better.

"You will be the star, Madame Zdorek! With your white hair and lovely complexion you should wear red all the time. Anything else I can do? I'm going to meet the Chairman in the Lounge in ten minutes."

Assured by Madame Zdorek that there was "not ze cloud on my meend," Rose replaced the receiver with a laugh. *What a generous, funny lady! It's a shame all great talent can't age half as well as Jana. I'm so glad I'm the one to introduce her!*

"I shall be back presently, you sleepyhead. Max, did we wear you out this morning? Having Father Charlie along on our walks does make it more invigorating, doesn't it?"

Rose left the little dog snoring steadily as she closed her apartment door.

~~~

Frances Keynes-Livingston, pearls in place, was arranging an unwieldy armload of fall branches, bronze spider mums and tall, umber cattails into an equally unwieldy Chinese water jug.

"What one must do for one's fellow man!" she called out cheerfully as Rose entered the dim Lounge. "Aren't these colors heavenly? What do you think . . . over there on the chest by the red fox? Or . . . I say! Let's place them on the stand right inside the doors. More people will see them as they come in. A welcome sight!"

"I agree! Where did these come from, incidentally?"

"Your friend—Jana. Madame Zdorek. Don't they just look like her?" asked Frances.
~~~

"To be sure," replied Rose. "And they will go right back to her apartment after the Fete, or at least the branches and cattails will. To last forever."

"There. How does it look?"

The two women stood back to admire the huge arrangement, now dramatically shooting up in the oversize container. The effect was stunning.

"Frances, I bet you were the President of every garden club in Bryn Mawr. They must have hated it when you left Pennsylvania. That is outstanding!" Rose's admiration for her friend's handiwork was genuine.

"Thank you. No, they were probably overjoyed when I moved on. An organization is a sorry entity if it depends on one wheel to keep it running. Now. Look around. Chairs suit you? Romero and Ernest worked diligently: two aisles instead of one. Hard for those wheel chairs to scoot around with just a center opening. Do you think they've allowed enough room on the sides?"

Rose nodded. *Rhetorical questions. That's fine; I'm guilty of asking rhetorical questions, too.*

"We have this one change in the program, Rose, that I mentioned to you. Albert Warrington asked if he could participate; he called last evening. I almost dropped the phone. Asked if it was too late to become a participant in the Fete. Spoke in that *veddy, veddy* Yale voice of his. What could I say? It's just *where* to put him . . . *after* the Shakespeare and *before* Gilbert and Sullivan? Or before Shakespeare and *after* Gilbert and Sullivan? Tell me, what do you think? Honestly?"

Where indeed! Rose gulped. She mulled over the question before answering. "He should consider himself honored to be bracketed by either of the four men already on the program. That shy, sly fox! What in the world is he going to present?"

"He gave no hint, and I was so shocked that I didn't pursue it. In retrospect, I should have. But he wouldn't do anything mawkish . . . or tacky." Frances Keynes-Livingston fingered her large, luminous pearls distractedly and puzzled on the late addition to her long-completed program.

"Did I tell you how he acted when I returned his towel?"

Rose asked. She had hardly been able to conceal her astonishment at Albert Warrington's latest act.

"Towel?" repeated Frances Keynes-Livingston, looking bewildered.

"Yes, *towel.* I found a linen towel with his monogram embroidered on it. Found it, mind you, while Max and I were walking on the road to the village. I was as astounded as you are. I retrieved it, brought it home and washed it. Soaked it in bleach, as a matter of fact, then after it was dry, ironed it. And then I rang him to ask if I could pop up to see him a minute."

"And?"

"Well, he wasn't rude, but he didn't act too thrilled that I wanted to pay him a call," replied Rose.

"Probably had it in mind that you were going to seduce him," chortled Frances, trying to imagine someone rebuffing Rose.

"Only when I said I had found one of his towels and I was on my way out for a walk did he relent and say, 'Why, do come up, Rose—I'll meet you in the hallway.' That's what I call cool treatment."

"Distant," stated Frances Keynes-Livingston. "He is a distant, solitary man. Perhaps his being in the Fete is a breakthrough, sharing some unknown talent with his contemporaries. Madame Zdorek is rather thick with him. No doubt their mutual love of opera. Maybe she has coaxed him out of his shell."

"What in the world do you suppose he'll do? Magic tricks?" asked Rose.

Frances Keynes-Livingston burst out laughing. "If so, I say good for us! And good for Jana, too! Isn't that what we are striving for? A showcase of Wynfield's talent!"

"I say let's put him after the Shakespeare recitations and prior to the lighter side of the evening. That way he will sort of naturally lead into the Gilbert and Sullivan. They are good, incidentally! I've heard them practicing. And they are already talking about a weekly song fest!"

"Fine, if one happens to like Gilbert and Sullivan. It is not a favorite of mine. But that is the very fruit we hoped this Fete would produce, Rose. A natural outgrowth of people's talent that will bring people of like interests together."

"Then it suits you if he precedes the trio of Gilbert and Sullivan singers?" persisted Rose, who wanted to see Albert Warrington's name written indelibly on the program. *He seems so . . . what is the word . . . ephemeral? It would be just like him to forget or back out. Maybe I've been misjudging him. I've put wrong covers on books before. But if his name is in print . . . he won't dare walk out!*

"So be it," emphatically voiced the Chairman of the Fete.

Thus accomplished, the two women slumped with relief.

"I'll drop this by Kate Alexander's this afternoon. She's happy to do this on her computer. And the laser copies will be so much cleaner than my old Smith-Corona," said Rose.

After the weighty decisions had been put to rest, Rose and Frances Keynes-Livingston adjourned to Rose's apartment for a glass of excellent Amontillado and a plate of Anne's cheese wafers. Max's afternoon snores accompanied the hum of cheerful conversation.

~~~

~~~

ECHOES

Jocelyn Ribble

The tiny young woman with the green thumb responsible for Wynfield Farms' outstanding flower arrangements is JOCELYN LEE RIBBLE. Jocey ("I hate the formal version of my name. My mother named me after a heroine in an English novel") received her training in horticulture at the local high school and community college and has been at Wynfield Farms since the doors opened. Actually, before the doors opened as she was charged with installing sixteen fresh-flower masterpieces for the grand opening. Since that first weekend her fame has spread and her talent has only increased! Fortunately for Wynfield, she loves "her" garden and greenhouse and enjoys the artistry involved in creating her bouquets.

Jocey lives in Fincastle and drives the zippy red Range Rover that you see parked behind the gardens. The youngest of six children, Jocey is now the only child at home with her parents, Mr. and Mrs. Kenneth Ribble.

Jocey brings beauty to our lives every day!

-R.McN.

~~~
~~~

26

Saturday, November 19: the day of the Wynfield Farms Fall Fete. Rose woke early, scrambled out of bed and started coffee. Max emerged from his bed with a wake-up scratch and instantly detected a shift in the atmosphere. Telltale signs were evident: Rose's steps were quicker than usual, the clink of the coffee mug a notch louder, there was a noticeable absence of any treat. The little dog decided to follow his favorite scheme of garnering attention and became a rug. He extended himself full-length by the door of the apartment. Rose could not make a move without stepping on or over her pet.

By 6:20 Rose was dressed and in her windbreaker. She sipped her hot coffee and spoke to Max for the first time.

"OK, old fellow. You know exactly what day this is, don't you? That's right, the big celebration is tonight. I'll be gone most of the morning. You ARE going to be shortchanged. But then don't I always make it up to you after things return to normal? Come on, Max. Annie's not going to call. And we aren't going to wait for Father Charlie, either. Wait a sec, let me be sure I have some tissues with me."

Rose felt in the pocket of the tired red windbreaker. Nothing in the left pocket. The right pocket yielded a wadded packet of Kleenex and a slip of paper. *Did I make a list for something? Wh* . . . Rose smoothed out the note. It wasn't a note; it was the lottery ticket that Mary Rector had purchased for her.

"For goodness sakes, Max! It's almost like getting a message from Mary. This was her gift to me, on that happy, happy day. Seems like so long ago. Well, I'm sure this ticket is out of date now. Stirs up old memories, Max, I can tell you that."

Rose placed the ticket on the kitchen counter and anchored it with her mug. The pair padded down the hall and stairs to the Reception Hall and out the doorway. The only sounds heard were the muffled *boings!* of clocks announcing the half hour and the distant chatter of arriving kitchen help.

Most of the storm's destruction had been removed. Ernest and Romero, working with a professional tree service, had sawed, chipped, dug and hauled for the past two weeks. Gaping holes left by uprooted trees had been filled in and were now all but invisible under new mulch and a crazy quilt of leaves. The majestic alignment of Lombardy poplars fronting the driveway was missing seven members of its select "century club." Instead of a straight-as-a-die salute, the trees presented a sheepish and snaggle-tooth grin.

Mother Nature's way of pruning, thought Rose. *That applies to us mortals, too.*

"Brrr, Max. Don't linger. November is here with a vengeance!" Rose shivered.

There had been a light frost during the night and the wide lawns were covered with sliver-thin sheets of sparkling silver moisture. Animal tracks criss-crossed Montremont Gardens. The feeble morning light was the color of skim milk. *What did Matthew always call skim milk: "blue john"? Yep, the sky's "blue john" this morning.*

"Almost a moonscape, Max. Everything's the same color. Or non-color. Eerie. Hope it doesn't rain again. We've had enough of that for a while. November has never been my favorite month."

Jocey Ribble had worked diligently in restoring the flower beds to their pre-storm status. The borders were clean and plant markers stood rigidly at attention beside the beds of winter pansies. Rose noted that huge clumps of chrysanthemums fringed the edging along the facade of the main building. Two enormous urns flanking the portico held healthy, generously budded plants. *What did Jocey tell me that color was: Grenadine? Wonderful contrast in those mossy old urns. She hasn't gone for the quantity she had before the storm but I think the quality is better. I'll remember to comment when I pay for Annie's arrangement.*

Before the storm. People will use the storm as a gauge of time, Max. Same as the assassinations in the sixties. Before the storm I did thus and so. After the storm . . . when Mary disappeared. Yes, it will be a measure of our lives.

They walked until the first hunger pangs spurred their usual ramble and brought them around; neither Rose nor Max walked far on an empty stomach. They retraced their homeward trail in the moist grass, passing Father Charlie coming down the front steps.

Inside, Rose nearly collided (again) with Bob Jenkins retreating to the second floor.

Rose shook her head. *Some things never change, do they Max? Bob may say the same about me! Hope he doesn't lose sleep over the hazards I encounter daily! He'd be a peerless timekeeper on my tour!*

Safely back in her own apartment, having fixed Max's breakfast, Rose sat down to enjoy her coffee and granola and a quick reading of the morning paper. *For some reason, the news just is not as important as it used to be. Or maybe I'm so old that nothing is new anymore. Or at the very least, nothing shocks me anymore. Maybe I should watch television more regularly . . . but that's just as bad as the paper. I don't know . . .* She flipped through the pages, skimming the headlines and reading captions under the photos. Elections, run-offs, labor disputes in the Valley . . . lottery news. *Lottery news? I've never noticed this before! But then I've never had a ticket before. Where did I put the thing?*

Rose retrieved the ticket, now ringed with a coffee stain. She took it and the newspaper to the window to look at both in a better light. (Rose's Rule: Never turn on the light if you can see by daylight.) *How do you know if you're a winner? Just by the number? No, let's see . . . by the combination of numbers that match the winners. What do they say here: twenty-five thousand dollars is the jackpot? That much? Wouldn't that be something if I won! Let's see . . .* Rose compared the two rows of numbers. Mary had chosen well; Rose's ticket held all but three of the winning numerals. *I can't believe it! What do the rules say about this . . . two numbers off, ten thousand, three numbers, seven thousand five-hundred? Who do I call? Wait . . . here's the telephone number. And it says you have to go to Place of Purchase. That's easy: the 7-11 at the crossroads! Tom! I'll call Tom! He'd love to see his old granny do this! The children will never believe me. Mary, Mary, what a legacy you've left!*

"Oh, m'goodness! I'd better call Amaryllis before I call Tom. I'm supposed to be down in the Lounge for pictures in an hour."

She dialed the now-memorized number. "Frawnces? Rose McNess here. I'm running behind this morning. No, no, I feel *wonderful*. Just slower than usual. I'll be there by quarter 'til, anyway. See you! Thanks."

Rose picked up the telephone to dial the Brewster home and then replaced it quickly in the cradle.

No, I'm not even going to tell Tom . . . yet. The paper said thirty days to collect . . . and it hasn't been three weeks since the storm. There I go, counting time by the storm. There is too much excitement in this day already. I'll hide my ticket and my secret until it sinks in. I've never won anything in my life! Oh, no one is going to believe this!

Rose pulled out a deep and narrow drawer in her desk. She placed the winning ticket among a collection of string too short to save and chips of china too small to glue.

"No safer haven in this entire apartment," she confided to Max. He was always a reliable friend when it came to sharing secrets.

~~~

~~~

WYNSONG

WHISPERS

News Flash!

Mark your calendars NOW for Wynfield Farms' First

Fall Fete

NOVEMBER 19!

7 P.M. - South Lounge

This event is ably chaired by Mrs. Keynes-Livingston and promises to be THE event of the season! Imagine, an evening that will feature dramatic readings, vocal renditions of Gilbert and Sullivan, classical opera selections by a world-class star, plus a few surprises!

Plan to arrive early and get a front-row (or second, or third) seat for this event!

~~~
~~~

27

For once, Miss Moss had demonstrated salutary judgment, Rose and Frances agreed. She had refused "VV's" requests to return and take photographs during the Fete. She stood firm in her refusal, stating again that she had promised the residents that it was "private theatre." Photographs taken during a performance of any sort would be an exploitation. "An invasion of the residents' privacy." Although Miss Moss had never been to the British Isles she nonetheless had adopted a few pronunciations of the Anglophiles. "Privacy," with the short *i*, was one of her favorites.

Advance photographs had been approved. The Fete's organizers, Chairman Frances and Assistant Rose, would be photographed at ten this morning, "posing" as if seriously involved in planning the event. At 10:15, four additional participants were arriving, and so on during the morning until everyone had been "caught in the act."

"The photographs will all probably end up in the trash bin, Max, but I will do this for Mrs. Keynes-Livingston—whoops!—Frances! Saying Frawnces just does not slide off my tongue . . . Well, what shall I wear? Faithful tweed skirt and my sweater set?

Yes, that will do nicely. Enhance my *gambling grandmother image!* Frances's pearls will give class to any photo."

~~~

Albert Warrington paced the floor. His face was so drawn and wizened that he resembled a tired, puckered persimmon.

Why did I listen to Jana? Why did I promise to "show and tell?" Oh, this is not a good idea . . . not good at all. Why did I let myself be lured into this? Oh, this is not going to be a good day. I can feel it.

And thus he worried and paced, then paced and worried. At eleven in the morning he undressed, luxuriated in a hot shower, put on clean pajamas, drank a cup of warm milk and crawled back into bed with a volume of Thoreau. Thoreau always made him see things more clearly. He was instantly transported to the New England woods, tramping along with the earnest environmentalist. This had been Emily's prescription for relaxation. It had worked in the past. And it did today. Albert was asleep in ten minutes. Thoreau hit the floor with a smack. Albert Warrington missed his "photo op."

~~~

Charlie Caldwell shredded half a head of lettuce and dropped it into Caesar's bowl. He watched the comical bird toy with the greenery and then strut off to sulk on his perch.

"I wouldn't like that either, old boy," laughed the pastor. "You've had all the good stuff you're going to get today. Bedtime, Buster. Unless you eat that!"

The parrot fixed Charlie with a murderous glare before tucking his head under his wing and settling into a sulky sleep.

Tonight . . . is *going to be fun!* A *good evening! Those two ladies have worked hard putting it all together. Takes go-getters like Rose and what's-her-name to make this fly. Tonight I'm not Father Charlie. Neither priest nor pastor, just plain Charlie. Made the right decision to move to Wynfield . . . that Episcopal community would have been stuffy, not to mention boring . . . living next to preachers I've known all these years . . . none of whom I really feel close to . . . probably why Father Tim decided to stay in Mitford*

. . . he wouldn't have liked it any more than I would have . . . just wish Nancy had lived to be here with me.

Father Charlie thought fondly about his deceased wife and caught a small tear at the corner of his left eye.

I should go ahead and do what we always planned to do. Travel! Perhaps I'll join an Elderhostel trip next spring. Bet Rose would be glad to look after Caesar; she looks after everyone else!

"Caesar, no dog collar tonight! It's the new blue blazer. They'll think I'm the Captain of the H.M.S. *Pinafore* when I get up to sing! But now, on with the magazine's photographers!"

~~~

Jana Zdorek was also restless. Mille Fleur, perched nervously on her own damask-covered chair, watched her mistress's every move. Madame Zdorek had gotten up then and then sat down again at least ten times in the past half hour. The still-regal woman now anxiously checked her hair in the antique mirror, coaxing a stray wisp back into place. The deep, snow-white waves were swept up and around her handsome face, with the remaining mass twisted into one elaborate roll at the back of her head. The roll was anchored with six ivory pins of extraordinary length. Poised at the top of the roll was a tortoise-shell clasp resembling a large butterfly, with seed pearls and tiny diamonds sparkling on its wings. Madame Zdorek wore this clasp as if it were her inherited tiara.

At two in the afternoon she poured herself a glass of schnapps and nibbled on a thin piece of fruit cake. She beckoned the poodle to her side as she sat in the velour parlor chair in front of her Bechstein. Stroking Fleur's curly coat, she crooned softly in the dog's ear.

Ach! eeet will be so right, Fleur. Not to be ashamed of Maman, not now. Eet will be right. And Meester Warrington . . . ach! What surprizes he will breeng. Thees will be, ma cher, ze night to remember! Ach du Lieber. Like een Milano, n'est-ce pas? Remember, ma cher, when Maman stabbed ze monster weeth ze ivory peens?

Chuckling, she recalled a dressing-room intruder that she
~~~

had surprised and outwitted with one of her oversize hairpins. Then, Madame Zdorek and her beloved Fleur slept soundly in the plump chair for over an hour. Madame's dreams were of European opera houses and a way of life that no longer existed. But the echoes of *Encore*! and *Bravissimo*! were still hers, and very real.

~~~

Vinnie Whittington fussed with the Major's bow tie.

"There, dear. That has it! You look positively smashing. I will be the envy of every woman in the Lounge. And to think you *sing* as well!"

"My dear, are you tweaking me?" asked Major Featherstone, petting his silver mustache.

"Never. You and the doctor and rector make a wonderful combination. I told you I was never a *big* fan of Gilbert and Sullivan, but you three make it such fun. Are you ready for the big time now?"

"Eleanor Whittington, I *hit* the big time when you agreed to this living arrangement!" The Major gazed at his Southern belle with frank adoration. "Everyone may say we're crazy, when we're both confined to wheelchairs, but I've never been happier. And you, Eleanor, have you any regrets? Wait! Maybe I don't want to hear your answer on that!"

"My dear William. Look at me. I have never enjoyed life as much! And I *feel* so much better! There really is truth in that old saw 'love conquers all!' When the children get here for the wedding next month they'll think I've been to a spa! Now, how do *I* look?"

"Ah, my lovely Eleanor. You are my beautiful Butterfly!"

"Well, thank heavens you are NOT my Pinkerton! Try and leave me and I'll . . . I'll sabotage your chair!" She laughed and looked at the Major and dazzled him with her blue eyes.

The couple reached out across their wheelchairs and embraced warmly, if a bit awkwardly. The kiss they enjoyed was unhurried and heartfelt.

~~~

Lib Meecham sat in her apartment and filed her nails.

I should file my nails every week. Terrible thing for a librarian to present claws to a patron. But I'm no longer truly a librarian . . . . This job is just enough. But we have too many volumes, and Miss Moss says more are coming in this week. I've got to establish some guidelines for donors. Miss Moss takes anything that's offered. We surely don't need any more books on foreign policy . . . they don't go flying out the Library often. What did the children say: expand my horizons? Wait until I write them about my performance tonight! They won't believe it when I tell them I read Shakespeare with . . . a man!

Lib had enjoyed her practice times with Arthur Everett. He was a perfect gentleman, as her Ed had been. Arthur's laconic sagacity lightened their sessions with the Bard. So much so that Lib wondered if his scholarly demeanor was a protective armor behind which he hid his loneliness.

No, I don't think so, she thought, buffing the last fingernail. *He is a bona fide Classicist through and through. Who was it—Hesiod?—that he did his dissertation on? Now that's a good one for the crosswords. Bet he's a good teacher, too; lucky students!*

She picked up her worn volume of Shakespeare and pulled out the red leather strip marking *As You Like It*. Tonight she was "Rosalind."

"I will weary you then no longer with idle talking. Know of me then, for now I speak to some purpose, that I know you are a gentleman of good conceit."

~~~

Six o'clock. The residents had been notified of "One Seating Only, Promptly at Six." The meal was a simple buffet in the Dining Room and then everyone was invited to move directly to the South Lounge. The Fete was to start at seven.

At a quarter before seven, the South Lounge was nearly full. Many of the residents had invited outside guests to attend and there were a good number of visiting sons and daughters.

Rose and Frances Keynes-Livingston stood on either side of the broad doorway, protecting the towering arrangement in the
~~~

Chinese water jug. As they handed out programs they smiled and greeted the swelling audience, most of whom they knew. Each woman tallied the remaining empty chairs.

"What do you think, Rose?" whispered the Chairman. "More chairs?"

Rose thought that Mrs. Keynes-Livingston (Rose had given up on even *trying* to call her Frances) looked more amaryllis-like than ever. Her full mane of chestnut hair was pulled away from her face and held in a restricting bun at the back of her head. The long, thin neck that supported this head grew stalk-like out of the collar of her best gray silk shirtwaister. The ever-present strand of pearls encircled her neck like large, moist drops of dew on the emerging flower.

"What? Oh, I think we'll just make it. You and I can stand, and the late-comers can lean against the walls. I know we haven't exceeded the Fire Safety rules yet."

Just as Rose spoke these words, Romero and Ernest appeared in the hallway with the dolly loaded with additional folding chairs.

"We line theem up out here, Miss Rosa," said Romera. "It ees sell-out, your show, no?" He winked at Rose, happily enjoying the evening's excitement.

The two men rapidly dispatched their cargo and just as rapidly scooted away.

"Bravo!" cried Mrs. Keynes-Livingston. "But why didn't we get them to move this blasted vase? This isn't a good location for it, after all. It's in the way."

"Let's move it ourselves. Just to the left. We don't want Jana to think we're not appreciative." The two women carefully moved the vase without disturbing the flowers.

"Seven-five, Rose. Let's get this show started. I may lose my nerve if we don't open soon."

Miss Moss, trumped up by her unjustified sense of self-importance, stood at her place in the front row facing the audience. Her stern expression momentarily softened as, she boomed in her most mellifluous tone: "Welcome to Wynfield Farms! Welcome to Wynfield Farms! Tonight is a first for Wynfield and a treat for us all. A real celebration of talent. Without further fanfare, I am happy to present our Chairman, Mrs. Keynes-Livingston."

Her very best boom, smiled Rose. *Not once, but twice*.

A collective *gasp* rippled through the crowd. The patrician Mrs. Frances Keynes-Livingston, Hohner accordion strapped across her thin bosom, had stepped to the fore and was launching a rousing rendition of the "Pennsylvania Polka."

~~~

~~~

WYNFIELD FARMS

FALL FETE
November 19
7:00 P.M. ~~~ South Lounge

Welcome by Miss A. Elvina Moss, Resident Manager
*
Musical Welcome
Mrs. Keynes-Livingston
*
A Reading from Shakespeare—*As you Like It*
Lib Meecham
Arthur Everett
*
Musical Interlude
Mrs. Keynes-Livingston
*
Presentation
Mr. Albert Warrington
*
Selections from Gilbert and Sullivan
A Trio: The Reverend Charlie Caldwell, Major William Featherstone, Dr. Robert Lesley, accompanied by Betty Gehrmann
*
A Reading from O'Neill's *All God's Chillun Got Wings*
Henrietta and Harriet Puffenbarger
*
Musical Selections
Madame Jana Zdorek
accompanied by Betty Gehrmann
*
Musical Finale

Mrs. Keynes-Livingston and Betty Gehrmann
*

28

"Max," Rose called to her recumbent companion, "never has this bed felt so good!"

It was after eleven and Rose McNess felt the effects of the long and exhilarating day. Her back was tired, her knees were stiff and both feet hurt like the very dickens. She was ready to slip between the sheets and pull up the plump comforter.

"I'm glad Ellie didn't come in, Max, when I asked her. We would have sat up like fools talking until morning, I suspect. Bet she's as tired as I am. In fact, she didn't look as if she had her old *zip* tonight, Max. Hope she's really all right. Probably just worn out, like the rest of us! Still . . . it *would* be fun to have someone to talk with just now . . . "

Wynfield Farms' Fall Fete was now history, and in the words of the redoubtable Miss Moss, "a glorious pageant of talent has passed before us tonight."

Glorious it was, thought Rose happily. She leaned back against the pillows, removed her bifocals, and closed her eyes. *If I rest a minute I can play out the pageant like a video . . . every second, every minute . . . who needs a camcorder? Such enthusiastic applause! This old house has never witnessed such a commo-*

tion . . . And Mrs. Keynes-Livingston! If she didn't bring the crowd to its feet with that accordion. Why anyone would choose to play such a monster! Could she make those keys talk . . . especially "Lady of Spain"!

Rose snuggled further under the warmth of her comforter. She laughed aloud, causing Max to rouse himself inquiringly. *Those two Shakespeareans! They really were good: trust a librarian and a scholar. How perfect when Orlando said . . . what was it? . . . "I can live no longer by thinking"! That's when the audience howled! They certainly know Arthur! And what did Rosalind say in the end: something about kissing as many as had beards? . . . I'll have to get out my Comedies and re-read "As You Like It" . . . Hmmmm . . . the start of a new friendship between those two, I'll wager . . . And the Gilbert and Sullivan renditions were superb. Hammed it up just enough and kept it short. That was the secret of tonight's success: brevity. Old people are like children: short attention spans. Who am I fooling? I'm "old people," too! But the trio's selections were perfect, particularly that one from "Pirates." Major Featherstone literally transformed himself into Major-General Stanley, my favorite! Perhaps this will lead to a club of sorts for the fans of the D'Oyly Carte. I've had quite enough, thank you, for a while. But I don't think I'm ready to embrace Wagner as my personal favorite yet.*

"Max, are you listening? Even you, Max, would have howled at the Misses Puffenbargers! That dynamic duo!" Rose sat up straight in her bad and laughed until she shook and great tears ran down her cheeks.

"It wasn't even that funny, Max! It was just the shock of seeing them both together in public, and in costume! Probably right out of their closets if the truth be known . . . those flapper pieces never really go out of style! What an eclectic reading: O'Neill's All God's Chillun Got Wings . . . prophetic irony? Certainly dramatic, but no more so than the double-whammy they presented! I can't even remember which one was which . . . good golly, they were funny! . . . And Madame Zdorek! My protege, Max. Well, not exactly, but I was the one persuading her to participate. What a dress!"

Madame Zdorek had told the admiring clusters of friends who surrounded her after the Fete that the dress was from famed

Elsa Schiaparelli, whose *haute couture* was noted for its brilliant colors and lush fabrics. It was a dazzling, ruby-red creation, cut modestly low at the bodice to both embrace and sculpt Madame's generous bosom. From a fitted waist the heavy velveteen fell in simple folds to the floor; the back ended in a short train. The sleeves, tight and fitted, stopped just above the wrists. *Sparing us*, Rose thought, *the unflattering sight of an old woman in a sleeveless dress. Even a woman as classy as Jana!*

And classy she was. She performed as promised, chatting about the music, the composers, the opera houses where she had sung. All of which enthralled her audience who was enthralled with her. And on two occasions, clearly stirred by memories, she sang along with her voice on the recording. From her repertoire of German *Lieder* she had chosen one that showcased her still-magnificent vocal skills. Her inflections and subtle modulations in the soaring German ballad brought tears to many an eye. The rich tones flowed effortlessly. She did not attempt the high notes and displayed no evidence of strain or tension.

Clearly a star, nodded Rose. *How has she stayed in such exquisite shape? Discipline and training. And a glass of schnapps before bedtime! She is an ageless classic. Hope I didn't open Pandora's box by letting people know we have such a star among us. Who was it who said their son-in-law works for the* Washington Post? *And they were going to call him . . . Well, I won't worry about Jana; she can say "Nein!" as firmly as anyone I know.*

But if Madame Zdorek had brought the house down, it was Albert Warrington who completed the demolition with his confession. Starting with his entrance.

Poor man! Of all the people who didn't need a disaster tonight it was poor Albert! How he managed to bump into that Chinese jug after we'd moved it I'll never understand . . . but it shattered in a thousand pieces before he got through the doorway! And he is a taxidermist! I still cannot believe it! Rose shook her head in amazement at the incongruity of tonight's revelation. A shaken Albert Warrington had stepped out in front of his audience and said quietly, "I would like to tell you about my hobby."

Rose recalled the times she had watched Albert leave on his

morning walks dressed as if he were going to preside over a meeting of bankers or stockholders. Always carrying his briefcase. This very briefcase, she and all the other spellbound listeners had learned tonight, was his "tool kit." He could operate *in situ* or bring dead animals or birds back to Wynfield for further work, all with the gadgets contained within his leather case. And that rabbit nest Rose had found . . . Apparently the mother met her match with a predator and the young ones had died of exposure just prior to Albert's discovering them. He confessed to Rose after the Fete that in his haste to leave the thicket he had misplaced his covering towel and had not discovered its loss until Rose had phoned.

He started out slowly, Rose reflected. *Shattering the vase didn't help. But then—what a change! That stilted manner disappeared when he began confessing to this weird hobby. By the time his "telling and showing" was well underway, he was downright fluent in his explanations! And proud of his accomplishments. Unbelievable! It's an art form, true, but brrrr! He donates his specimens to a business firm that displays them in its offices. Said one reason he chose Wynfield Farms was because of the specimens here. And he's the one who keeps the cases sparkling clean. Who would have guessed all this about impeccable Mr. Warrington? Our tortoise has come out of his shell! He may even become quite likable! I hope so. Hope. Isn't that the one asset we all have left?*

Rose sighed. Sleep did not come.

She had managed to steer Tom aside for a few private words. He gaily agreed to become her "partner in crime." "Yes, Gan, I know exactly where that 7-11 is located; we'll tool over there in the morning. May have to wait a few days for your money. Gosh, Gan, aren't you something? Have you told Ma yet? You'd better; she won't believe me!"

Tom also knew where the Towne Garden Shop was located. Rose determined that she'd better place her order now for the seven poplars she'd decided to buy. There might be a delay in finding the full grown trees she wanted. She didn't have time to watch saplings mature! She would use her lottery winnings to fill in the gaps along the driveway. And buy benches. She intended to install two handsome teak benches with commemorative brass plaques near the lake. These would be the MARY E. GREENWAY RECTOR benches. Rose knew that she would enjoy sitting among the tranquil surroundings, remembering her friend. As would many of the other residents.

Your car, Gan? Aren't you going to use some of the money for a car? Have you thought about that?

Oh, yes, Rose had been thinking about the successor to her Nova. Lottery money most definitely would *not* go into her car fund.

She lay on her back and watched traceries of moonlight flood through the wide panes of the window in her living area. She followed the descent of the silvery fingers as they shimmered from ceiling to table, briefly spotlighting the collection of family pictures. The light moved to the wing chair and then slowly eased from her view. Still awake, she heard an occasional bird song. *What bird sings at this hour? And that faucet!* the steady drip-drip-drip of the bathroom faucet told her that she must get Romero to look at it in the morning. *Or some morning . . . no real emergency.*

"But I'll tell you what *is* an emergency, Max: these glasses! I'm calling Dr. Pierre the first thing in the morning for an appointment. The sooner the better. I am going to get contact lenses. Soft contact lenses. These bifocals have worried me long enough. Do you know I put them down in the Lounge tonight when I started handing out programs and didn't find them until after Jana sang? *There*! That decision didn't take long, did it, old boy? Just about thirty-five years of misplacing them or having them slip down the bridge of my nose!"

She breathed the heady perfume of Tom's gardenias, pungent in their fragrance. *Suffocating! Not a flower I want at my memorial service. Best make a note of that in my arrangements. But what a dear boy to think of a corsage . . . both for me and Mrs. Keynes-Livingston. Typically thoughtful, that Tom.*

Rose yawned, smiling as she did so. *I'll just rewind my mental video and play it back; much better for me than a sleeping pill.*

For the third time that evening Rose lived through Wynfield Farms' Fall Fete. She omitted nothing and concentrated this time on colors: colors of the flower arrangements in the Lounge, colors of the participants' apparel, even colors worn by various members of the audience. *There was a luscious tan ultra-suede suit. And who was the woman in the ghastly green number? Some friend of Dr. Lesley's perhaps* . . . Her mind kept wandering to the people she knew best: Lib Meecham (blue); Mrs. Keynes-Livingston (silver-gray stripes); Robert Lesley (navy blazer, tan slacks); Jana Zdorek (red). She paired each of them with the colors they had worn earlier in the evening. *That,* Rose scolded, *is a peculiar form of a mnemonic. I'm going 'round the bend*!

Even this tedious rehashing did not invite sleep. Rose plumped her pillows and lay on her back once again. Suddenly, she stiffened. Then sat upright.

I've got it! And I've been wondering why I couldn't sleep? This is it! It's not the Fete—its the after-Fete, the let-down. We've had the biggest event in weeks and now it's all over. We have nothing else to look forward to; tomorrow will come and go just like any other day. People will talk about the Fete at breakfast and at dinner and then go about their lives. No expectations, no excitement, nothing to look forward to unless . . . unless . . .

Rose snapped on the light on the bedside table. She swung both legs over the edge of the bed and felt with her feet for the soft slippers that she knew were there. She shuffled her feet into these and pulled her warm wrapper around her, tying the loose belt into an accommodating knot. She picked up her glasses and her note pad and large felt-tip pen and sat down in one of her kitchen chairs. She began to write, rapidly, boldly. The marker squeaked across the page.

Max had seen his mistress do strange things at strange hours of the night. He looked up from his cushion with sleepy eyes and then promptly resumed dreaming.

This is what has been eating me, thought Rose. *This is what has been nibbling at the corners of my brain . . . it's the unfinished business in my life. If*

Wynfield is one great big tour . . . then who leads the tour? Who else? My heart is racing already!

Rose counted the strategic spots where she would post her notices (three elevators, two bulletin boards and the Library). She printed out six copies in her most legible block print.

I can get Romero to drive us . . . or Ernest. He wouldn't be bad . . . The next thought hit Rose like a thunderbolt.

Tom! Tom would be perfect! If he doesn't get a job soon, he'd love to do it! I just know he would! And Wynfield might pay him to drive! Perhaps Kate could come along too . . .

Rose sat back in the maple chair and looked at her efforts. She grasped the fat black marker and drew two heavy lines under the headings:

ROSE'S ROAMINGS
ROSE McNESS, Number 208
"WHY THINK TRAVEL WHEN YOU CAN TRAVEL!"

"Done!" she exclaimed excitedly. She patted Max, unbelted her wrapper and kicked off her slippers and crawled back into bed. It was after three. She glanced once more at the six notices fanned out on the table and switched off the lamp.

I hope everyone will be as excited about this as I am! We'll reduce our hazards all right—by driving down the road! It takes hope to face the unknown and the unexpected, and to decide which fork of the road to take . . . and we have hope in abundance! What fun to look forward to the next curve and corner!

This, thought Rose, *is one of my better ideas. Rose's Roamings . . . a Rose and Max production . . . to keep one forever young.*

Rose turned onto her side, sighed, and welcomed deep, untroubled sleep.

~~~

~~~

Postscript

Miss Elvina Moss remained at Wynfield Farms despite her continuing ill humor and increasing whispers regarding her place on a questionable family tree.

Arthur Everett discovered the true meaning of *amor proximi* as he and Lib Meecham began an intense study of the complete works of William Shakespeare in the Wynfield Library.

Lavinia Whittington became Mrs. William Featherstone on Boxing Day in the Wynfield Chapel with family and close friends in attendance.

Albert Warrington became a popular and frequent lecturer at the local high school and at civic club luncheons.

Mrs. Keynes-Livingston collected her notes and diaries of thirty years, purchased a computer and began writing a book entitled "Lichen in the Mid-Atlantic States."

Madame Zdorek rejected all requests for concert appearances and was never heard to sing again.

Kate Alexander continued her duties at Wynfield Farms and spent many weekends exploring the surrounding mountains, usually in the company of Tom Brewster, who did shave his beard.

Rose McNess had her grandson drive her to *Mostek Imports* on Peters Creek Road in Roanoke. She purchased a rebuilt *TRIUMPH*, a '65 TR4A, British racing green with chrome wire wheels, a luggage rack on the boot, tan leather upholstery and a matching tan stripe running the length of its sporty chassis. Rose mastered the gears in two lessons and thereafter, with Max seated at her side, happily maneuvered her car in and around Wynfield Farms pursuing new destinations for *Rose's Roamings*.

~~~

~~~